BY MARY HIGGINS CLARK

My Gal Sunday
Moonlight Becomes You
Silent Night
Let Me Call You Sweetheart
The Lottery Winner
Remember Me
I'll Be Seeing You
All Around the Town
Loves Music, Loves to Dance
The Anastasia Syndrome and Other Stories
While My Pretty One Sleeps
Weep No More, My Lady
Stillwatch
A Cry in the Night
The Cradle Will Fall
A Stranger Is Watching
Where Are the Children?

Mary Higgins Clark

Pretend You Don't See Her

A NOVEL

Simon & Schuster

LP

SIMON & SCHUSTER
Rockefeller Center
1230 Avenue of the Americas
New York, NY 10020

Designed by Amy Hill

Manufactured in the United States of America

1   2   3   4   5   6   7   8   9   10

Library of Congress Cataloging-in-Publication Data
is available.

ISBN 0-684-83416-2

"Pretend You Don't See Her," words and music by Steve Allen. Copyright © 1957. Revised 1966, 1985. Meadowlane Music, Inc. ASCAP.

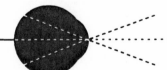

This Large Print Book carries the
Seal of Approval of N.A.V.H.

Acknowledgments

People often ask, "Where do you get your idea for a book?"

The answer in this instance is very specific. I was considering several plot possibilities with not one of them as yet triggering my imagination. Then one night I was having dinner in Rao's Bar and Grill, a legendary New York restaurant.

Toward the end of the evening, Frank Pellegrino, one of the owners and a professional singer, picked up a mike and began to sing a song Jerry Vale made popular many years ago, "Pretend You Don't See Her." As I listened to the lyrics, an idea I'd been considering crystallized: A young woman witnesses a murder and to save her life has to go into the Witness Protection Program.

Grazie, Frank!

Kudos and heartfelt thanks to my editors, Michael Korda and Chuck Adams. In my school days, I was always the one who worked best under looming deadlines. Nothing's changed. Michael and Chuck, copy supervisor Gypsy da Silva, assistants Rebecca Head and Carol Bowie, you're the best and the greatest. May your names be inscribed in the Book of Saints.

Bouquets to Lisl Cade, my publicist, and Gene Winick, my literary agent, dear and valued friends.

An author's research is immeasurably strengthened by talking to the experts. I am grateful to author and retired FBI manager Robert Ressler, who discussed the Witness Protection Program with me; attorney Alan Lippel, who clarified legal ramifications of plot points; retired detective Jack Rafferty, who answered my queries about police procedure; and Jeffrey Snyder, who actually lived as a protected witness. Thanks to all of you for sharing your knowledge and your experiences with me.

A tip of the hat to computer expert Nelson Kina of the Four Seasons Hotel in Maui, who reclaimed crucial chapters I thought I had lost.

Continuing thanks to Carol Higgins Clark, my

daughter and fellow author, who is always my splendidly on-target sounding board.

Warm wishes to good friend Jim Smith of Minneapolis, who sent me the information I needed about the city of lakes.

Deep gratitude to my cheering section, my children and grandchildren. Even the little ones were asking, "Have you finished the book yet, Mimi?"

And finally, a special award to my husband, John Conheeney, who married a writer with a deadline and, with infinite patience and good humor, survived the experience.

Bless you all. And now to quote again a fifteenth-century monk, "The book is finished. Let the writer play."

For my husband, John Conheeney
and our children

Marilyn Clark
Warren and Sharon Meier Clark
David Clark
Carol Higgins Clark
Patricia Clark Derenzo and Jerry Derenzo

John and Debbie Armbruster Conheeney
Barbara Conheeney
Patricia Conheeney
Nancy Conheeney Tarleton and David Tarleton

With love.

Later Lacey tried to find comfort in the thought that even if she had arrived seconds earlier, rather than being in time to help she would have died with Isabelle.

But it didn't happen that way. Using the key she had been given as realtor, she had entered the duplex apartment on East Seventieth Street and called Isabelle's name in the exact instant that Isabelle screamed "Don't . . . !" and a gunshot rang out.

Faced with a split-second decision to run or to hide, Lacey slammed the apartment door shut and slipped quickly into the hall closet. She had not even had time to fully close that door before a sandy-haired, well-dressed man came running down the stairs. Through the narrow opening she could see his face clearly, and it became imprinted on her mind. In fact, she had seen it before, only hours ago. The expression was now viciously cold, but clearly this was the same man to whom she had shown the apartment earlier in the day: affable Curtis Caldwell from Texas.

From her vantage point she watched as he ran past her, holding a pistol in his right hand and a leather binder under his left arm. He flung open the front door and ran out of the apartment.

The elevators and fire stairs were at the far end of the corridor. Lacey knew that Caldwell would realize immediately that whoever had come into the apartment was still there. A primal instinct made her rush out of the closet to shove the door closed behind him. He wheeled around, and for a terrible moment their eyes locked, his pale blue irises like steely ice, staring at her. He threw himself against the door but not fast enough. It slammed shut, and she snapped the dead bolt just as a key clicked in the lock.

Her pulse racing, she leaned against the door, trembling as the knob twisted, hoping there was no way Caldwell could get back in now.

She had to dial 911.

She had to get help.

Isabelle! she thought. That had to have been her cry that Lacey heard. Was she still alive?

Her hand on the banister, Lacey raced up the thickly carpeted stairs through the ivory-and-peach sitting room where in these past weeks she had sat so frequently with Isabelle and listened as the grieving mother told her over and over that she still could not believe that the death of her daughter, Heather, had been an accident.

Fearing what she would find, Lacey rushed into the bedroom. Isabelle lay crumpled across the bed, her eyes open, her bloodied hand frantically pulling at a sheaf of papers that had been under a pillow beside her. One of the pages fluttered across the room, carried by the breeze from the open window.

Lacey dropped to her knees. "Isabelle," she said. There were many other things she wanted to say—that she would call an ambulance; that it would be all right—but the words refused to pass her lips. It was too late. Lacey could see that. Isabelle was dying.

Later that scene was played out in the nightmare that came more and more frequently. The dream was always the same: She was kneeling beside Isabelle's body, listening to the dying woman's last words, as Isabelle told her about the journal, entreating her to take the pages. Then a hand would touch her shoulder, and when she looked up, there stood the killer, his cold eyes unsmiling, aiming the pistol at her forehead as he squeezed the trigger.

1

It was the week after Labor Day, and from the steady ringing of the phones in the offices of Parker and Parker, it was clear to Lacey that the summer doldrums finally were over. The Manhattan co-op market had been uncommonly slow this past month; now, finally, things would start to move again.

"It's about time," she told Rick Parker as he delivered a mug of black coffee to her desk. "I haven't had a decent sale since June. Everybody I had on the hook took off for the Hamptons or the Cape, but thank God they're all drifting back into town now. I enjoyed my month off, too, but now it's time to get back to work."

She reached for the coffee. "Thanks. It's nice to have the son and heir wait on me."

"No problem. You look great, Lacey."

Lacey tried to ignore the expression on Rick's face. She always felt as though he were undressing her with his eyes. Spoiled, handsome, and the possessor of a phony charm that he turned on at will, he made her distinctly uncomfortable. Lacey heartily wished his father hadn't moved him from the West Side office. She didn't want her job jeopardized, but lately keeping him at arm's length was becoming a balancing act.

Her phone rang, and she grabbed for it with relief. Saved by the bell, she thought. "Lacey Farrell," she said.

"Miss Farrell, this is Isabelle Waring. I met you when you sold a co-op in my building last spring."

A live one, Lacey thought. Instinctively she guessed that Mrs. Waring was putting her apartment on the market.

Lacey's mind went into its search-and-retrieve mode. She'd sold two apartments in May on East Seventieth, one an estate sale where she hadn't spoken to anyone except the building manager, the second a co-op just off Fifth Avenue. That would be the Norstrum apartment, and she vaguely remembered chatting with an attractive fiftyish redhead in the elevator, who had asked for her business card.

Crossing her fingers, she said, "The Norstrum duplex? We met on the elevator?"

Mrs. Waring sounded pleased. *"Exactly!* I'm putting my daughter's apartment on the market, and if it's convenient I'd like you to handle it for me."

"It would be very convenient, Mrs. Waring."

Lacey made an appointment with her for the following morning, hung up, and turned to Rick. "What luck! Three East Seventieth. That's a great building," she said.

"Three East Seventieth. What apartment?" he asked quickly.

"Ten B. Do you know that one by any chance?"

"Why would I know it?" he snapped. "Especially since my father, in his wisdom, kept me working the West Side for five years."

It seemed to Lacey that Rick was making a visible effort to be pleasant when he added, "From what little I heard on this end, someone met you, liked you, and wants to dump an exclusive in your lap. I always told you what my grandfather preached about this business, Lacey: You're blessed if people remember you."

"Maybe, although I'm not sure it's necessarily a blessing," Lacey said, hoping her slightly negative reaction would end their conversation. She hoped also that Rick would soon come to think of her as just another employee in the family empire.

He shrugged, then made his way to his own office, which overlooked East Sixty-second Street. Lacey's windows faced Madison Avenue. She reveled in the sight of the constant traffic, the hordes of tourists, the well-heeled Madison Avenue types drifting in and out of the designer boutiques.

"Some of us are born New Yorkers," she would explain to the sometimes apprehensive wives of executives being transferred to Manhattan. "Others come here reluctantly, and before they know it, they discover that for all its problems, it's still the best place in the world to live."

Then if questioned, she would explain: "I was raised in Manhattan, and except for being away at college, I've always lived here. It's my home, my town."

Her father, Jack Farrell, had felt that way about

the city. From the time she was little, they had explored New York City together. "We're pals, Lace," he would say. "You're like me, a city slicker. Now your mother, God love her, yearns to join the flight to the suburbs. It's to her credit that she sticks it out here, knowing I'd wither on the vine there."

Lacey had inherited not only Jack's love of this city, but his Irish coloring as well—fair skin, blue-green eyes, and dark brown hair. Her sister Kit shared their mother's English heritage— china-blue eyes, and hair the shade of winter wheat.

A musician, Jack Farrell had worked in the theater, usually in the pit orchestra, although sometimes playing in clubs and the occasional concert. Growing up, there wasn't a Broadway musical whose songs Lacey couldn't sing along with her dad. His sudden death just as she had finished college was still a shock. In fact, she wondered if she ever would get over it. Sometimes, when she was in the theater district, she still found herself expecting to run into him.

After the funeral, her mother had said with wry sadness, "Just as your dad predicted, I'm not staying in the city." A pediatric nurse, she bought a condo in New Jersey. She wanted to be near

Lacey's sister Kit and her family. Once there, she'd taken a job with a local hospital.

Fresh out of college, Lacey had found a small apartment on East End Avenue and a job at Parker and Parker Realtors. Now, eight years later, she was one of their top agents.

Humming, she pulled out the file on 3 East Seventieth and began to study it. I sold the second-floor duplex, she thought. Nice-sized rooms. High ceilings. Kitchen needed modernizing. Now to find out something about Mrs. Waring's place.

Whenever possible, Lacey liked to do her homework on a prospective listing. To that end, she'd learned that it could help tremendously to become familiar with the people who worked in the various buildings Parker and Parker handled. It was fortunate now that she was good friends with Tim Powers, the superintendent of 3 East Seventieth. She called him, listened for a good twenty minutes to the rundown of his summer, ruefully reminding herself that Tim had always been blessed with the gift of gab, and finally worked the conversation around to the Waring apartment.

According to Tim, Isabelle Waring was the mother of Heather Landi, a young singer and actress who had just begun to make her name in the theater. The daughter as well of famed restaurateur Jimmy Landi, Heather had died early last winter, killed when her car plunged down an embankment as she was driving home from a weekend of skiing in Vermont. The apartment had belonged to Heather, and now her mother was apparently selling it.

"Mrs. Waring can't believe Heather's death was an accident," Tim said.

When she finally got off the phone, Lacey sat for a long moment, remembering that she had seen Heather Landi last year in a very successful off-Broadway musical. In fact, she remembered her in particular.

She had it all, Lacey thought—beauty, stage presence, and that marvelous soprano voice. A "Ten," as Dad would have said. No *wonder* her mother is in denial.

Lacey shivered, then rose to turn down the air conditioner.

On Tuesday morning, Isabelle Waring walked through her daughter's apartment, studying it as if with the critical eye of a realtor. She was glad that she had kept Lacey Farrell's business card.

Jimmy, her ex-husband, Heather's father, had demanded she put the apartment on the market, and in fairness to him, he had given her plenty of time.

The day she met Lacey Farrell in the elevator, she had taken an instant liking to the young woman, who had reminded her of Heather.

Admittedly, Lacey didn't *look* like Heather. Heather had had short, curly, light brown hair with golden highlights, and hazel eyes. She had been small, barely five feet four, with a soft, curving body. She called herself the house midget. Lacey, on the other hand, was taller, slimmer, had blue-green eyes, and darker, longer, straighter hair, swinging down to her shoulders, but there was something in her smile and manner that brought back a very positive memory of Heather.

Isabelle looked around her. She realized that not everyone would care for the birch paneling and splashy marble foyer tiles Heather had loved, but those could easily be changed; the renovated kitchen and baths, however, were strong selling points.

After months of brief trips to New York from Cleveland, and making stabs at going through the apartment's five huge closets and the many drawers, and after repeatedly meeting with

Heather's friends, Isabelle knew it had to be over. She had to put an end to this searching for reasons and get on with her life.

The fact remained, however, that she just didn't believe Heather's death had been an accident. She knew her daughter; she simply would not have been foolish enough to start driving home from Stowe in a snowstorm, especially so late at night. The medical examiner had been satisfied, however. And Jimmy was satisfied, because Isabelle knew that if he *hadn't* been, he'd have torn up all of Manhattan looking for answers.

At the last of their infrequent lunches, he had again tried to persuade Isabelle to let it rest, and to get on with her own life. He reasoned that Heather probably couldn't sleep that night, had been worried because there was a heavy snow warning, and knew she had to be back in time for a rehearsal the next day. He simply refused to see anything suspicious or sinister in her death.

Isabelle, though, just couldn't accept it. She had told him about a troubling phone conversation she had had with their daughter just before her death. "Jimmy, Heather wasn't herself when I spoke to her on the phone. She was worried about something. Terribly worried. I could hear it in her voice."

The lunch had ended when Jimmy, in complete exasperation, had burst out, "Isabelle, get *off* it! Stop, please! This whole thing is tough enough without you going on like this, constantly re-hashing everything, putting all her friends through the third degree. Please, let our daughter rest in peace."

Remembering his words, Isabelle shook her head. Jimmy Landi had loved Heather more than anything in the world. And next to her, he loved power, she thought bitterly—it's what had ended their marriage. His famous restaurant, his invest-ments, now his Atlantic City hotel and casino. No room for me ever, Isabelle thought. Maybe if he had taken on a partner years ago, the way he has Steve Abbott now, our marriage wouldn't have failed. She realized she had been walking through rooms she wasn't really seeing, so she stopped at a window overlooking Fifth Avenue.

New York is especially beautiful in September, she mused, observing the joggers on the paths that threaded through Central Park, the nannies pushing strollers, the elderly sunning themselves on park benches. I used to take Heather's baby carriage over to the park on days like this, she remembered. It took ten years and three miscar-riages before I had her, but she was worth all the heartbreak. She was such a special baby. People were always stopping to look at her and admire her. And she knew it, of course. She loved to sit up and take everything in. She was so smart, so observant, so talented. So trusting . . .

Why did you throw it away, Heather? Isabelle asked herself once more the questions that she had agonized over since her daughter's death. *After that accident when you were a child—when you saw that car skid off the road and crash— you were always terrified of icy roads. You even talked of moving to California just to avoid winter weather. Why then would you have driven over a snowy mountain at two in the morning? You were only twenty-four years old; you had so much to live for. What happened that night? What made you take that drive? Or* who *made you?*

The buzzing of the intercom jolted Isabelle back from the smothering pangs of hopeless regret. It was the doorman announcing that Miss Farrell was here for her ten o'clock appointment.

Lacey was not prepared for Isabelle Waring's effusive, if nervous, greeting. "Good heavens, you look younger than I remembered," she said.

"How old *are* you? Thirty? My daughter would have been twenty-five next week, you know. She lived in this apartment. It was hers. Her father bought it for her. Terrible reversal, don't you think? The natural order of life is that I'd go first and someday she'd sort through *my* things."

"I have two nephews and a niece," Lacey told her. "I can't imagine anything happening to any of them, so I think I understand something of what you are going through."

Isabelle followed her, as with a practiced eye Lacey made notes on the dimensions of the rooms. The first floor consisted of a foyer, large living and dining rooms, a small library, a kitchen, and a powder room. The second floor, reached by a winding staircase, had a master suite —a sitting room, dressing room, bedroom and bath.

"It was a lot of space for a young woman," Isabelle explained. "Heather's father bought it for her, you see. He couldn't do enough for her. But it never spoiled her. In fact, when she came to New York to live after college, she wanted to rent a little apartment on the West Side. Jimmy hit the ceiling. He wanted her in a building with a doorman. He wanted her to be safe. Now he wants me to sell the apartment and keep the money. He says Heather would have wanted me to have it. He says I have to stop grieving and go on. It's just that it's still so hard to let it go, though . . . I'm trying, but I'm not sure I can . . ." Her eyes filled with tears.

Lacey asked the question she needed to have answered: "Are you sure you want to sell?"

She watched helplessly as the stoic expression on Isabelle Waring's face crumbled and her eyes filled with tears. "I wanted to find out why my daughter died. Why she rushed out of the ski lodge that night. Why she didn't wait and come back with friends the next morning, as she had planned. What changed her mind? I'm sure that somebody knows. I need a reason. I know she was terribly worried about something but wouldn't tell me what it was. I thought I might find an answer here, either in the apartment or from one of her friends. But her father wants me to stop pestering people, and I suppose he's right, that we have to go on, so yes, Lacey, I guess I want to sell."

Lacey covered the woman's hand with her own. "I think Heather would want you to," she said quietly.

That night Lacey made the twenty-five-mile drive to Wyckoff, New Jersey, where her sister Kit and her mother both lived. She hadn't seen them since early August when she had left the city for her month away in the Hamptons. Kit and her husband, Jay, had a summer home on Nantucket, and always urged Lacey to spend her vacation with them instead.

As she crossed the George Washington Bridge, Lacey braced herself for the reproaches she knew would be part of their greeting. "You only spent three days with us," her brother-in-law would be sure to remind her. "What's East Hampton got that Nantucket doesn't?"

For one thing it doesn't have *you,* Lacey thought, with a slight grin. Her brother-in-law, Jay Taylor, the highly successful owner of a large restaurant supply business, had never been one of Lacey's favorite people, but, as she reminded herself, Kit clearly is crazy about him, and between them they've produced three great kids, so who am I to criticize? If only he wasn't so damn pompous, she thought. Some of his pronouncements sounded like papal bulls.

As she turned onto Route 4, she realized how anxious she was to see the others in her family:

her mother, Kit and the kids—Todd, twelve, Andy, ten, and her special pet, shy four-year-old Bonnie. Thinking about her niece, she realized that all day she hadn't been able to shake thoughts about poor Isabelle Waring, and the things she had said. The woman's pain was so palpable. She had insisted that Lacey stay for coffee and over it had continued to talk about her daughter. "I moved to Cleveland after the divorce. That's where I was raised. Heather was five at that time. Growing up, she was always back and forth between me and her dad. It worked out fine. I remarried. Bill Waring was much older but a very nice man. He's been gone three years now. I was so in hopes Heather would meet the right man, have children, but she was determined to have a career first. Although just before she died I had gotten the sense that maybe she had met someone. I could be wrong, but I thought I could hear it in her voice." Then she had asked, her tone one of motherly concern, "What about you, Lacey? Is there someone special in your life?"

Thinking about that question, Lacey smiled wryly. Not so you'd notice it, she thought. And ever since I hit the magic number thirty, I'm very aware that my biological clock is ticking. Oh well. I love my job, I love my apartment, I love my family and friends. I have a lot of fun. So I have no right to complain. It will happen when it happens.

Her mother answered the door. "Kit's in the kitchen. Jay went to pick up the children," she explained after a warm hug. "And there's someone inside I want you to meet."

Lacey was surprised and somewhat shocked to see that a man she didn't recognize was standing near the massive fireplace in the family room, sipping a drink. Her mother blushingly introduced him as Alex Carbine, explaining that they had known each other years ago and had just met again, through Jay, who had sold him much of the equipment for a new restaurant he'd just opened in the city on West Forty-sixth Street.

Shaking his hand, Lacey assessed the man. About sixty, she thought—Mom's age. Good, solid-looking guy. And Mom looks all atwitter. What's up? As soon as she could excuse herself she went into the state-of-the-art kitchen where Kit was tossing the salad. "How long has this been going on?" she asked her sister.

Kit, her blond hair pulled back at the nape of her neck, looking, Lacey thought, for all the world like a Martha Stewart ad, grinned. "About a month. He's nice. Jay brought him by for dinner, and Mom was here. Alex is a widower. He's always been in the restaurant business, but this is the first place he's had on his own, I gather. We've been there. He's got a nice setup."

They both jumped at the sound of a door slamming at the front of the house. "Brace yourself," Kit warned. "Jay and the kids are home."

From the time Todd was five, Lacey had started taking him, and later the other children, into Manhattan to teach the city to them the way her father had taught it to her. They called the outings their Jack Farrell days—days which included anything from Broadway matinees (she had now seen *Cats* five times) to museums (the Museum of Natural History and its dinosaur bones being easily their favorite). They explored Greenwich Village, took the tram to Roosevelt Island, the ferry to Ellis Island, had lunch at the top of the World Trade Center, and skated at Rockefeller Plaza.

The boys greeted Lacey with their usual exuberance. Bonnie, shy as always, snuggled up to her. "I missed you very much," she confided. Jay told Lacey she was looking very well indeed, adding that the month in East Hampton obviously had been beneficial.

"In fact, I had a ball," Lacey said, delighted to see him wince. Jay had an aversion to slang that bordered on pretension.

At dinner, Todd, who was showing an interest in real estate and his aunt's job, asked Lacey about the market in New York.

"Picking up," she answered. "In fact I took on a promising new listing today." She told them about Isabelle Waring, then noticed that Alex Carbine showed sudden interest. "Do you know her?" Lacey asked.

"No," he said, "but I know Jimmy Landi, and I'd met their daughter, Heather. Beautiful young woman. That was a terrible tragedy. Jay, you've done business with Landi. You must have met Heather too. She was around the restaurant a lot."

Lacey watched in astonishment as her brother-in-law's face turned a dark red.

"No. Never met her," he said, his tone clipped and carrying an edge of anger. "I used to do business with Jimmy Landi. Who's ready for another slice of lamb?"

It was seven o'clock. The bar was crowded, and the dinner crowd was starting to arrive. Jimmy

Landi knew he should go downstairs and greet people but he just didn't feel like it. This had been one of the bad days, a depression brought on by a call from Isabelle, evoking the image of Heather trapped and burning to death in the overturned car that haunted him still, long after he had gotten off the phone.

The slanting light from the setting sun flickered through the tall windows of his paneled office in the brownstone on West Fifty-sixth Street, the home of Venezia, the restaurant Jimmy had opened thirty years ago.

He had taken over the space where three successive restaurants had failed. He and Isabelle, newly married, lived in what was then a rental apartment on the second floor. Now he owned the building, and Venezia was one of the most popular places to dine in Manhattan.

Jimmy sat at his massive antique Wells Fargo desk, thinking about the reasons he found it so difficult to go downstairs. It wasn't just the phone call from his ex-wife. The restaurant was decorated with murals, an idea he had copied from his competition, La Côte Basque. They were paintings of Venice, and from the beginning had included scenes in which Heather appeared. When she was two, he had the artist paint her in as a toddler whose face appeared in a window of the Doge's Palace. As a young girl she was seen being serenaded by a gondolier; when she was twenty, she'd been painted in as a young woman strolling across the Bridge of Sighs, a song sheet in her hand.

Jimmy knew that for his own peace of mind he would have to have her painted out of the murals, but just as Isabelle had not been able to let go of the idea that Heather's death must be someone else's fault, he could not let go of the constant need for his daughter's presence, the sense of her eyes watching him as he moved through the dining room, of her being with him there, every day.

He was a swarthy man of sixty-seven, whose hair was still naturally dark, and whose brooding eyes under thick unruly brows gave his face a permanently cynical expression. Of medium height, his solid, muscular body gave the impression of animal strength. He was aware that his detractors joked that the custom-tailored suits he wore were wasted on him, that try as he might, he still looked like a day laborer. He almost smiled, remembering how indignant Heather had been the first time she had heard that remark.

I told her not to worry, Jimmy thought, smiling

to himself. I told her that I could buy and sell the lot of them, and that's all that counts.

He shook his head, remembering. Now more than ever, he knew it wasn't really all that counted, but it still gave him a reason to get up in the morning. He had gotten through the last months by concentrating on the casino and hotel he was building in Atlantic City. "Donald Trump, move over," Heather had said when he'd showed her the model. "How about calling it Heather's Place, and I'll perform there, yours exclusively, Baba?"

She had picked up the affectionate nickname for father on a trip to Italy when she was ten. After that she never called him Daddy again.

Jimmy remembered his answer. "I'd give you star billing in a minute—you know that. But you better check with Steve. He's got big bucks in Atlantic City too, and I'm leaving a lot of the decisions to him. But anyway, how about forgetting this career stuff and getting married and giving me some grandchildren?"

Heather had laughed. "Oh, Baba, give me a couple of years. I'm having too much fun."

He sighed, remembering her laugh. Now there wouldn't be any grandchildren, ever, he thought

—not a girl with golden-brown hair and hazel eyes, nor a boy who might someday grow up to take over this place.

A tap at the door yanked Jimmy back to the present.

"Come in, Steve," he said.

Thank God I have Steve Abbott, he thought. Twenty-five years ago the handsome, blond Cornell dropout had knocked on the door of the restaurant before it was open. "I want to work for you, Mr. Landi," he had announced. "I can learn more from you than in any college course."

Jimmy had been both amused and annoyed. He mentally sized up the young man. Fresh, know-it-all kid, he had decided. "You want to work for me?" he had asked, then pointed to the kitchen. "Well, that's where I started."

That was a good day for me, Jimmy thought. He might have looked like a spoiled preppie, but he was an Irish kid whose mother worked as a waitress to raise him, and he had proved that he had much of the same drive. I thought then that he was a dope to give up his scholarship but I was wrong. He was born for this business.

Steve Abbott pushed open the door and turned on the nearest light as he entered the room. "Why so dark? Having a seance, Jimmy?"

Landi looked up with a wry smile, noting the compassion in the younger man's eyes. "Wool-gathering, I guess."

"The mayor just came in with a party of four."

Jimmy shoved back his chair and stood up. "No one told me he had a reservation."

"He didn't. Hizzonor couldn't resist our hot dogs, I suppose . . ." In long strides, Abbott crossed the room and put his hand on Landi's shoulder. "A rough day, I can tell."

"Yeah," Jimmy said. "Isabelle called this morning to say the realtor was in about Heather's apartment and thinks it will sell fast. Of course, every time she gets me on the phone, she has to go through it all again, how she can't believe Heather would ever get in a car to drive home on icy roads. That she doesn't believe her death was an accident. She can't let go of it. Drives me crazy."

His unfocused eyes stared past Abbott. "When I met Isabelle, she was a knockout, believe it or not. A beauty queen from Cleveland. Engaged to be married. I pulled the rock that guy had given her off her finger and tossed it out the car window." He chuckled. "I had to take out a loan to pay the other guy for his ring, but I got the girl. Isabelle married me."

Abbott knew the story and understood why Jimmy had been thinking about it. "Maybe the marriage didn't last, but you got Heather out of the deal."

"Forgive me, Steve. Sometimes I feel like a very old man, repeating myself. You've heard it all before. Isabelle never liked New York, or this life. She should never have left Cleveland."

"But she *did,* and you met her. Come on, Jimmy, the mayor's waiting."

2

In the next few weeks, Lacey brought eight potential buyers to see the apartment. Two were clearly window-shoppers, the kind whose hobby was wasting realtors' time.

"But on the other hand, you never know," she said to Rick Parker when he stopped by her desk early one evening as she was getting ready to go home. "You take someone around for a year, you want to kill yourself before you go out with her again, then what happens? The person you're ready to give up on writes a check for a million-dollar co-op."

"You have more patience than I do," Rick told her. His features, chiseled in the likeness of his aristocratic ancestors, showed disdain. "I really can't tolerate people who waste my time. RJP wants to know if you've had any real nibbles on the Waring apartment." RJP was the way Rick referred to his father.

"I don't think so. But, hey, it's still a new listing and tomorrow is another day."

"Thank you, Scarlett O'Hara. I'll pass that on to him. See you."

Lacey made a face at his retreating back. It had been one of Rick's edgy-tempered, sarcastic days. What's bugging him now, she wondered. And why, when his father is negotiating the sale of the Plaza Hotel, would he give a thought to the Waring apartment? Give me a break.

She locked her desk drawer and rubbed her forehead where a headache was threatening to start. She suddenly realized that she was very tired. She had been living in a whirl since coming back from her vacation—following up on old projects, getting new listings, catching up with friends, having Kit's kids in for a weekend . . . and devoting an awful lot of time to Isabelle Waring.

The woman had taken to calling her daily, frequently urging her to come by the apartment. "Lacey, you must join me for lunch. You do have to eat, don't you?" she would say. Or just,

"Lacey, on your way home, stop in and have a glass of wine with me, won't you? The New England settlers used to call twilight 'sober light.' It's a lonesome time of day."

Lacey stared out into the street. Long shadows were slanting across Madison Avenue, a clear indication that the days were becoming shorter. It *is* a lonesome time of day, she thought. Isabelle is such a very *sad* person. Now she's forcing herself to go through everything in the apartment and dispose of Heather's clothes and personal effects. It's quite a job. Heather apparently was a bit of a pack rat.

It's little enough to ask that I spend some time with Isabelle and listen to her, Lacey thought. I really don't mind. Actually, I like Isabelle very much. She's become a friend. But, Lacey admitted to herself, sharing Isabelle's pain brings back everything I felt when Dad died.

She stood up. I am going home and collapse, she thought. I need to.

Two hours later, at nine o'clock, Lacey, fresh from twenty minutes in the swirling Jacuzzi, was happily preparing a BLT. It had been her dad's favorite. He used to call bacon, lettuce, and tomato New York's definitive lunch-counter sandwich.

The telephone rang. She let the answering machine take it, then heard the familiar voice of Isabelle Waring. I'm not going to pick up, Lacey decided. I simply don't feel like talking to her for twenty minutes right now.

Isabelle Waring's hesitant voice began to speak in soft but intense tones. "Lacey, guess you're not home. I had to share this. I found Heather's journal in the big storage closet. There's something in it that makes me think I'm not crazy for believing her death wasn't an accident. I think I may be able to prove that someone wanted her out of the way. I won't say any more now. I'll talk to you tomorrow."

Listening, Lacey shook her head, then impulsively turned off the answering machine and the ringer on the phone. She didn't even want to know if more people tried to reach her. She wanted what was left of the night all to herself.

A quiet evening—a sandwich, a glass of wine, and a book. I've earned it, she told herself!

As soon as she got to the office in the morning, Lacey paid the price for having turned off the answering machine the night before. Her mother called, and an instant later Kit phoned; both were checking up on her, concerned that they had gotten no answer when they had called her apartment the night before. While she was trying to reassure her sister, Rick appeared in her office, looking decidedly annoyed. "Isabelle Waring has to talk to you. They put her through to me."

"Kit, I've got to go and earn a living." Lacey hung up and ran into Rick's office. "I'm sorry I couldn't get back to you last night, Isabelle," she began.

"That's all right. I shouldn't talk about all this over the phone anyhow. Are you bringing anyone in today?"

"No one is lined up so far."

As she said that, Rick slid a note across his desk to her: "Curtis Caldwell, a lawyer with Keller, Roland, and Smythe, is being transferred here next month from Texas. Wants a one-bedroom apartment between 65th and 72nd on Fifth. Can look at it today."

Lacey mouthed a thank-you to Rick and said to

Isabelle, "Maybe I *will* be bringing someone by. Keep your fingers crossed. I don't know why, but I've got a hunch this could be our sale."

"A Mr. Caldwell's waiting for you, Miss Farrell," Patrick, the doorman, told her as she alighted from a cab.

Through the ornate glass door, Lacey spotted a slender man in his mid-forties drumming his fingers on the lobby table. Thank God I'm ten minutes early, she thought.

Patrick reached past her for the door handle. "A problem you need to know about," he said with a sigh. "The air-conditioning broke down. They're here now fixing it, but it's pretty hot inside. I tell you, I'm retiring the first of the year, and it won't be a day too soon. Forty years on this job is enough."

Oh, swell, Lacey thought. No air-conditioning on one of the hottest days of the year. No wonder this guy's impatient. This does not bode well for the sale.

In the moment it took to walk across the lobby to Caldwell, her impression of the man, with his tawny skin, light sandy hair, and pale blue eyes, was uncertain. She realized that she was bracing herself to be told that he didn't like to be kept waiting.

But when she introduced herself to Curtis Caldwell, a smile brightened his face. He even joked. "Tell the truth now, Miss Farrell," he said, "how temperamental *is* the air-conditioning in this building?"

When Lacey had phoned Isabelle Waring to confirm the time of the appointment, the older woman, sounding distracted, had told her she would be busy in the library, so Lacey should just let herself in with her realtor's key.

Lacey had the key in hand when she and Caldwell stepped off the elevator. She opened the door, called out, "It's me, Isabelle," and went to the library, Caldwell behind her.

Isabelle was at the desk in the small room, her back to the door. An open leather loose-leaf binder lay to one side; some of its pages were spread across the desk. Isabelle did not look up or turn her head at Lacey's greeting. Instead, in a muffled voice, she said, "Just forget I'm here, please."

As Lacey showed Caldwell around, she briefly explained that the apartment was being sold because it had belonged to Isabelle Waring's daughter, who had died last winter in an accident.

Caldwell did not seem interested in the history of the apartment. He clearly liked it, and he did not show any resistance to the six-hundred-thousand-dollar asking price. When he had inspected the second floor thoroughly, he looked out the window of the sitting room and turned to Lacey. "You say it will be available next month?"

"Absolutely," Lacey told him. This is it, she thought. He's going to make a bid.

"I don't haggle, Miss Farrell. I'm willing to pay the asking price, provided I absolutely can move in the first of the month."

"Suppose we talk to Mrs. Waring," Lacey said, trying not to show her astonishment at the offer. But, she reminded herself, just as I told Rick yesterday, this is the way it happens.

Isabelle Waring did not answer Lacey's knocks at the library door. Lacey turned to the prospective buyer. "Mr. Caldwell, if you don't mind waiting for me just a moment in the living room, I'll have a little talk with Mrs. Waring and be right out."

"Of course."

Lacey opened the door and looked in. Isabelle Waring was still sitting at the desk, but her head was bowed now, her forehead actually touching the pages she had been reading. Her shoulders were shaking. "Go away," she murmured. "I can't deal with this now."

She was grasping an ornate green pen in her right hand. She slapped it against the desk. "Go away."

"Isabelle," Lacey said gently, "this is very important. We have an offer on the apartment, but there's a proviso I have to go over with you first."

"Forget it! I'm not going to sell. I need more time here." Isabelle Waring's voice rose to a high-pitched wail. "I'm sorry, Lacey, but I just don't want to talk now. Come back later."

Lacey checked her watch. It was nearly four o'clock. "I'll come back at seven," she said, anxious to avoid a scene and concerned that the older woman was on the verge of hysterical tears.

She closed the door and turned. Curtis Caldwell was standing in the foyer between the library and the living room.

"She doesn't want to sell the apartment?" His tone was shocked. "I was given to understand that—"

Lacey interrupted him. "Why don't we go downstairs?" she said, her voice low.

They sat in the lobby for a few minutes. "I'm sure it will be all right," she told him. "I'll come back and talk to her this evening. This has been a painful experience for her, but she'll be fine. Give me a number where I can call you later."

"I'm staying at the Waldorf Towers, in the Keller, Roland, and Smythe company apartment."

They stood to go. "Don't worry. This will work out fine," she promised. "You'll see."

His smile was affable, confident. "I'm sure it will," he said. "I leave it in your hands, Miss Farrell."

He left the apartment building and walked from Seventieth Street to the Essex House on Central Park South, and went immediately to the public phones. "You were right," he said when he had reached his party. "She's found the journal. It's in the leather binder the way you described it. She's also apparently changed her mind about selling the apartment, although the real estate woman is going back there tonight to try to talk some sense into her."

He listened.

"I'll take care of it," he said, and hung up. Then Sandy Savarano, the man who called himself Curtis Caldwell, went into the bar and ordered a scotch.

3

Her fingers crossed, Lacey phoned Isabelle Waring at six o'clock. She was relieved to find that the woman now was calm.

"Come over, Lacey," she said, "and we'll talk about it. But even if it means sacrificing the sale, I can't leave the apartment yet. There's something in Heather's journal that I think could prove to be very significant."

"I'll be there at seven," Lacey told her.

"Please. I want to show what I've found to you too. You'll see what I mean. Just let yourself in. I'll be upstairs in the sitting room."

Rick Parker, who was passing by Lacey's office, saw the troubled expression on her face and came in and sat down. "Problem?"

"A big one." She told him of Isabelle Waring's erratic behavior and about the possibility of losing the potential sale.

"Can you talk her out of changing her mind?" Rick asked quickly.

Lacey saw the concern on his face, concern that she was fairly certain wasn't for her or for Isabelle Waring. Parker and Parker would lose a hefty commission if Caldwell's offer was refused, she thought. That's what's bothering him.

She got up and reached for her jacket. The afternoon had been warm, but the forecast was for a sharp drop in temperature that evening. "We'll see what happens," she said.

"You're leaving already? I thought you said you were meeting her at seven."

"I'll walk over there, I think. Probably stop for a cup of coffee along the way. Marshal my arguments. See you, Rick."

She was still twenty minutes early but decided to go up anyway. Patrick, the doorman, was busy with a delivery, but smiled when he saw her. He waved her to the self-service elevator.

As she opened the door and called Isabelle's

name, she heard the scream and the shot. For a split second she froze, then sheer instinct made her slam the door and step into the closet before Caldwell came rushing down the stairs and out into the corridor, a pistol in one hand, a leather binder under his arm.

Afterwards she wondered if she imagined that somewhere in her brain she heard her father's voice saying, "Close the door, Lacey! Lock him out!" Was it his protective spirit that gave her the strength to force the door closed as Caldwell pushed against it, and then to bolt it?

She leaned against the door, hearing the lock click as he tried to get back into the apartment, remembering the look of the stalking predator in his pale blue eyes in that instant in which they had stared at each other.

Isabelle!

Dial 911 . . . Get help!

She had stumbled up the winding staircase, then through the ivory-and-peach sitting room and into the bedroom, where Isabelle was lying across the bed. There was so much blood, spreading now to the floor.

Isabelle was moving, pulling at a sheaf of papers that were under a pillow. The blood was on them too.

Lacey wanted to tell Isabelle that she would get help . . . that it would be all right, but Isabelle began to try to speak: "Lacey . . . give Heather's . . . journal . . . to her father." She seemed to be gasping for air. "Only to him . . . Swear that . . . only . . . to him. You . . . read it . . . Show . . . him . . . where . . ." Her voice trailed off. She drew in a shuddering breath, as though trying to stave off death. Her eyes were becoming unfocused. Lacey knelt next to her. With the last of her strength, Isabelle squeezed Lacey's hand. "Swear . . . please . . . man . . . !"

"I do, Isabelle, I do," Lacey said, her voice breaking with a sob.

Suddenly the pressure on her hand was gone. She knew that Isabelle was dead.

"You all right, Lacey?"

"I guess so." She was in the library of Isabelle's apartment, seated in a leather chair facing the desk where Isabelle had been seated just a few hours ago, reading the contents of the leather loose-leaf binder.

Curtis Caldwell had been carrying that binder. When he heard me he must have grabbed it, not realizing that Isabelle had taken pages out of it. Lacey hadn't seen it that closely, but it looked heavy, she thought, and fairly cumbersome.

The pages she had picked up in Isabelle's room were in Lacey's briefcase now. Isabelle had made her swear to give them only to Heather's father. She had wanted her to show him something that was in them. But show him what? she wondered. And shouldn't she tell the police about them?

"Lacey, drink some coffee. You need it."

Rick was crouching beside her, holding a steaming cup out to her. He had already explained to the detectives that he had no reason to question a phone call from a man claiming to be an attorney with Keller, Roland, and Smythe, an attorney transferring to New York from Texas. "We do a lot of business with the firm," Rick had explained. "I saw no reason to call and confirm."

"And you're sure this Caldwell guy is the one you saw running out of here, Ms. Farrell?"

The older of the two detectives was about fifty and heavyset. But he's light on his feet, Lacey thought, her mind wandering. He's like that actor who was Dad's friend, the one who played the father in the revival of *My Fair Lady*. He sang

"Get Me to the Church on Time." What *was* his name?

"Ms. Farrell?" An edge of impatience had crept into the detective's voice.

Lacey looked back up at him. Detective Ed Sloane, that was this man's name, she thought. But she still couldn't remember the name of the actor. What had Sloane asked her? Oh, yes. Was Curtis Caldwell the man she'd seen running down the stairs from Isabelle's bedroom?

"I'm absolutely sure it was the same man," she said. "He was carrying a pistol and the leather binder."

Mentally she gave herself a hard slap. She hadn't meant to talk about the journal. She had to think all this through before talking about it.

"The leather binder?" Detective Sloane's tone became sharp. "What leather binder? That's the first you've mentioned it."

Lacey sighed. "I really don't know. It was open on Isabelle's desk this afternoon. It's one of those leather binders that zips closed. Isabelle was reading the pages in it when we were in here earlier." She should tell them about the pages that *weren't* inside the leather binder when Caldwell took it. Why wasn't she telling them? she thought. Because she'd sworn to Isabelle that she would give them to Heather's father. Isabelle had struggled to stay alive until she had heard Lacey's promise. She couldn't go back on her word . . .

Suddenly Lacey felt her legs begin to shake. She tried to hold them still by pressing her hands on her knees, but they still wouldn't stop trembling.

"I think we'd better get a doctor for you, Ms. Farrell," Sloane said.

"I just want to go home," Lacey whispered. "Please let me go home."

She knew Rick was saying something to the detective in a low voice, something she couldn't hear, didn't really *want* to hear. She rubbed her hands together. Her fingers were sticky. She looked down, then gasped. She hadn't realized that her hands were sticky with Isabelle's blood.

"Mr. Parker is going to take you home, Ms. Farrell," Detective Sloane was saying. "We'll talk to you more tomorrow. When you've rested." His voice was very loud, Lacey thought. Or was it? No. It was just that she was hearing Isabelle scream *Don't . . . !*

Was Isabelle's body still crumpled on the bed? she wondered.

Lacey felt hands under her arms, urging her to stand. "Come on, Lacey," Rick was saying.

Obediently she got up, allowed herself to be guided through the door, then down the foyer. Curtis Caldwell had stood in the foyer that afternoon. He had heard what Isabelle said to her about not selling the apartment.

"He didn't wait in the living room," she said.

"Who didn't?" Rick asked.

Lacey didn't answer. Suddenly she remembered her briefcase. That's where the pages from the journal were.

She remembered the feel of the pages in her hand, crumpled, blood soaked. That's where the blood came from. Detective Sloane had asked her if she had touched Isabelle.

She had told him that she had held Isabelle's hand as she died.

He must have noticed the blood on her fingers. There must be blood on her briefcase too. Lacey had a sudden moment of total clarity. If she asked Rick to get it for her from the closet, he would notice the blood on the handle. She had to get it herself. And keep them from seeing it until she could wipe it clean.

There were so many people milling around.

Flashes of light. They were taking pictures. Looking for fingerprints, dusting powder on tables. Isabelle wouldn't have liked that, Lacey thought. She was so neat.

Lacey paused at the staircase and looked up toward the second floor. Was Isabelle still lying there? she wondered. Had they covered her body?

Rick's arm was firmly around her. "Come on, Lacey," he said, urging her toward the door.

They were passing the closet where she had put her briefcase.

I can't ask him to get it for me, Lacey reminded herself. Breaking away, she opened the closet door and grabbed her briefcase in her left hand.

"I'll carry it," Rick told her.

Deliberately she sagged against him, weighing down his arm with her right hand, making him support her, tightening her grip on the handle of her briefcase.

"Lacey, I'll get you home," Rick promised.

She felt as though everyone's eyes were staring at her, staring at the bloody briefcase. Was this the way a thief felt? she wondered. *Go back. Give them the journal; it's not yours to take,* a voice inside her insisted.

Isabelle's blood was on those pages. *It's not mine to give, either,* she thought hopelessly.

When they reached the lobby, a young police officer came up to them. "I'll drive you, Miss Farrell. Detective Sloane wants to make sure you get home okay."

Lacey's apartment was on East End Avenue at Seventy-ninth Street. When they arrived there, Rick wanted to come upstairs with her, but she demurred. "I just want to go to bed," she said, and kept shaking her head at his protests that she shouldn't be alone.

"Then I'll call you first thing in the morning," he promised.

She lived on the eighth floor and was alone in the elevator as it made what seemed to be an interminably long ascent before stopping. The corridor reminded her of the one outside Isabelle's front door, and Lacey looked around fearfully as she ran down it.

Once inside her apartment, the first thing she did was to shove the briefcase under the couch. The living room windows overlooked the East River. For long minutes Lacey stood at one of the windows, watching the lights as they flickered across the water. Finally, even though she was shivering, she opened the window and gulped in the fresh, cool night air. The sense of unreality that had overwhelmed her for the past several hours was beginning to dissipate, but in its place was an aching awareness of being as tired as she had ever felt in her life. Turning, she looked at the clock.

Ten-thirty. Only a little over twenty-four hours ago, she had refused to pick up the phone and talk to Isabelle. Now Isabelle would never call her again . . .

Lacey froze. The door! Had she double-locked the door? She ran to check it.

Yes, she had, but now she threw the dead bolt and wedged a chair under the handle. She realized suddenly that she was shaking again. I'm afraid, she thought, and my hands are sticky—sticky with Isabelle Waring's blood.

Her bathroom was large for a New York apartment. Two years ago, when she had modernized the whole space, she had added the wide, deep Jacuzzi. She had never been as happy she had gone to the expense as she was tonight, she thought, as steaming water clouded the mirror.

She stripped, dropping her clothes on the floor. Stepping into the tub, she sighed with relief as she sank into the warmth, then held her hands under the faucet, scrubbing them deliberately. Finally she pushed the button that sent the water swirling around her body.

It was only later, when she was snugly wrapped in a terry-cloth robe, that Lacey allowed herself to think about the bloodied pages in her briefcase.

Not now, she thought, not now.

Still unable to shake the chilling sensation that had haunted her all evening, she remembered there was a bottle of scotch in the liquor cabinet. She got it out, poured a little into a cup, filled the cup with water, and microwaved it. Dad used to say there was nothing like a hot toddy to help shake off a chill, she thought. Only his version was elaborate, with cloves and sugar and a cinnamon stick.

Even without the trimmings, however, it did the trick. As she sipped the drink in bed, she felt a calmness begin to settle over her and fell asleep as soon as she turned off the light.

And almost immediately awakened with a shriek. *She was opening the door to Isabelle Waring's apartment; she was bending over the dead woman's body; Curtis Caldwell was aiming the pistol at her head.* The image was vivid and immediate.

It took her several moments to realize that the

shrill sound was the ringing of the telephone. Still shaking, she picked up the receiver. It was Jay, her brother-in-law. "We just got back from dinner and heard on the news that Isabelle Waring was shot," he said. "They reported that there was a witness, a young woman who could identify the killer. Lacey, it wasn't you, I hope."

The concern in Jay's voice was comforting. "Yes, it was me," she told him.

For a moment there was silence. Then he said quietly, "It's never good to be a witness."

"Well, I certainly never wanted to be one!" she said angrily.

"Kit wants to talk to you," Jay said.

"I *can't* talk now," Lacey said, knowing full well that Kit, loving and concerned, would ask questions that would force her to tell it all again —all about going to the apartment, hearing the scream, seeing Isabelle's killer.

"Jay, I just can't talk now!" she pleaded. "Kit will understand."

She hung up the phone and lay in the darkness, calming herself, willing herself to go back to sleep, realizing that her ears were straining to hear another scream, followed by the sound of footsteps racing toward her.

Caldwell's footsteps.

Her last thought as she drifted off to sleep was of something Jay had said in his call. He said it was never good to be a witness. Why did he say that? she wondered.

When he had left Lacey in the lobby of her apartment building, Rick Parker had taken a taxi directly to his place on Central Park West and Sixty-seventh Street. He knew what would be awaiting him there, and he dreaded it. By now, Isabelle Waring's death would be all over the news. There had been reporters outside her building when they had come out, and chances were that he had been caught on-camera getting into the police car with Lacey. And if so, then his father would have seen it, since he always watched the ten-o'clock news. Rick checked his watch: it was now quarter of eleven.

As he had expected, when he entered his dark apartment he could see that the light on his telephone answering machine was flashing. He pressed the PLAY button. There was one message; it was from his father: "No matter what time it is, call me when you get in!"

Rick's palms were so wet that he had to dry

them on his handkerchief before picking up the phone to return the call. His father answered on the first ring.

"Before you ask," Rick said, his voice ragged and unnaturally high pitched, "I had no choice. I had to go over there because Lacey had told the police that I'd been the one who'd given her Caldwell's number, so they sent for me."

Rick listened for a minute to his father's angry voice, then he finally managed to break in to respond: "Dad, I've told you not to worry. It's all fine. Nobody knows that I was involved with Heather Landi."

4

Sandy Savarano, the man known to Lacey as Curtis Caldwell, had raced from Isabelle Waring's apartment and down the fire stairs to the basement and out through the delivery entrance. It was risky, but sometimes you had to take risks.

Quick strides took him to Madison Avenue, the leather binder tucked under his arm. He took a taxi to the small hotel on Twenty-ninth Street where he was staying. Once in his room, he tossed the binder on the bed and promptly poured a generous amount of scotch into a water glass. Half of it he bolted down; the rest he would sip. It was a ritual he followed after a job like this.

Carrying the scotch, he picked up the binder

and settled in the hotel room's one upholstered chair. Up until the last-minute glitch the job had been easy enough. He had gotten back into the building undetected when the doorman was at the curb, helping an old woman into a cab. He had let himself into the apartment with the key he had taken off the table in the foyer when Lacey Farrell was in the library with the Waring woman.

He had found Isabelle in the master bedroom, propped up on the bed, her eyes closed. The leather binder had been on the night table beside the bed. When she realized he was there, she had jumped up and tried to run, but he had blocked the door.

She hadn't started screaming. No, she'd been too scared. That was what he liked most: the naked fear in her eyes, the knowledge that there would be no escape, the awareness that she was going to die. He savored that moment. He always liked to take his pistol out slowly, keeping eye contact with his victim while he pointed it, taking careful aim. The chemistry between him and his target in that split second before his finger squeezed the trigger thrilled him.

He pictured Isabelle as she started shrinking away from him, returning to the bed, her back to the headboard, her lips struggling to form words. Then finally the single scream: *"Don't!"*—mingling suddenly with the sound of someone calling her from downstairs—just as he shot her.

Savarano drummed his fingers angrily on the leather binder. The Farrell woman had come in at that precise second. Except for her, everything would have been perfect. He had been a fool, he told himself, letting her lock him out, forcing him to run away. But he *did* get the journal, and he did kill the Waring woman, and that was the job he was hired to do. And if Farrell became a problem he would kill her too, somehow . . . He would do what he had to; it was all part of the job.

Carefully Savarano unzipped the leather binder and looked inside. The pages were all neatly clamped in place, but when he thumbed through them he found they were all blank.

Unbelieving, he stared down at the pages. He started turning them rapidly, looking for handwriting. They were blank, all of them—none had been used. The actual journal pages must still be in the apartment, he realized. What should he do? He had to think this through.

It was too late to get the pages now. The cops

would be swarming all over the apartment. He'd have to find another way to get them.

But it wasn't too late to make sure that Lacey Farrell never got the chance to ID him in court. That was a chore he might actually enjoy.

5

Sometime near dawn Lacey fell into a heavy, dream-filled sleep in which shadows moved slowly down long corridors and terrified screams came relentlessly from behind locked doors.

It was a relief to wake up at quarter of seven even though she dreaded what she knew the day would bring. Detective Sloane had said he would want her to go to headquarters and work with an artist to come up with a composite sketch of Curtis Caldwell.

But as she sat wrapped in her robe, sipping coffee and looking down at the barges slowly making their way up the East River, she knew there was something she had to decide about first: the journal.

What am I going to do about it? Lacey asked herself. Isabelle thought there was something in it that proved Heather's death was not an accident. Curtis Caldwell stole the leather binder after he killed Isabelle.

Did he kill her because he was afraid of what Isabelle had found in that journal? Did he steal what he thought was the journal to make sure no one else could read it?

She turned and looked. Her briefcase was still there, under the couch; the briefcase in which she had hidden the bloodstained pages.

I have to turn them over to the police, she thought. But I believe I know a way I can do it and still keep my promise to Isabelle.

At two o'clock, Lacey was in a small office in the police station, sitting across a conference table from Detective Ed Sloane and his assistant, Detective Nick Mars. Detective Sloane seemed to be a little short of breath, as though he had been hurrying. Or maybe he's just been smoking too much, Lacey decided. There was an open pack of cigarettes poking out of his breast pocket.

Nick Mars was another story. He reminded her

of a college freshman football player she had had a crush on when she was eighteen. Mars was still in his twenties, baby faced with full cheeks, innocent blue eyes, and an easy smile, and he was nice. In fact, she was sure that he was being set up as the good guy in the good guy/bad guy scenario interrogators play. Sloane would bluster and occasionally rage; Nick Mars would soothe, his manner always calm, solicitous.

Lacey had been at the station for almost three hours, plenty of time to figure out the scenario they had worked up for her benefit. As she was trying to describe Curtis Caldwell's face to the police artist, Sloane was clearly annoyed that she wasn't being more specific.

"He didn't have any scars or birthmarks or tattoos," she had explained to the artist. "At least none that I could see. All I can tell you is that he had a thin face, pale blue eyes, tanned skin, and sandy hair. There was nothing distinguishing about his features. They were in proportion— except for his lips, maybe. They were a little thin."

But when she saw the artist's sketch, she had said, hesitantly, "It isn't really the way he looked."

"Then how *did* he look?" Sloane had snapped.

"Take it easy, Ed. Lacey's had a pretty rough time." Nick Mars had given her a reassuring smile.

After the artist had failed to come up with a sketch she felt resembled the man she had seen, Lacey had been shown endless mug shots. However, none of them resembled the man she knew as Curtis Caldwell, another fact that clearly upset Sloane.

Now Sloane finally pulled out a cigarette and lit up, a clear sign of exasperation. "Okay, Ms. Farrell," he said brusquely, "we need to go over your story."

"Lacey, how about a cup of coffee?" Mars asked.

"Yes, thank you." She smiled gratefully at him, then warned herself again: Watch out. Remember —good guy/bad guy. It was clear Detective Sloane had something new on his agenda.

"Ms. Farrell, I'd just like to review a few things about this crime. You were pretty upset when you dialed 911 last night."

Lacey raised her eyebrows. "With good reason," she said, nodding.

"Absolutely. And I'd say you were virtually in shock when we talked with you after we got there."

"I guess I was." In truth, most of what had happened last evening was a haze to her.

"I didn't escort you to the door when you left, but I understand you had the presence of mind to remember that you'd left your briefcase in the hall closet next to the door of the Waring apartment."

"I remembered it as I passed the closet, yes."

"Do you remember that the photographers were taking pictures at that time?"

She thought back. The film of powder on the furniture. The flashes of light.

"Yes, I do," she replied.

"Would you look at this picture then, please?" Sloane slid an eight-by-ten photograph across the desk. "Actually," he explained, "what you see is an enlargement of a section of a routine shot taken in the foyer." He nodded to the younger man. "Detective Mars picked up this little detail."

Lacey stared at the picture. It showed her in profile, gripping her briefcase, holding it away from Rick Parker as he reached for it.

"So you not only remembered to get your briefcase, but you insisted on carrying it yourself."

"Well, in good part that's my nature. And with

my coworkers I feel it's especially important to be self-reliant," Lacey explained, her voice low and calm. "In truth, though, I probably was acting on automatic pilot. I really don't remember what was in my head."

"No, I think you do," Detective Sloane said. "In fact, I think you were acting very deliberately. You see, Ms. Farrell, there were traces of blood in that closet—Isabelle Waring's blood. Now how would it have gotten there, do you suppose?"

Heather's journal, Lacey thought. The blood-stained loose-leaf pages. A couple of them had fallen on the carpet in the closet as she was jamming them into the briefcase. And of course her hands had been bloody. But she couldn't tell this to the detective—not yet, anyway. She still needed time to study the pages. She looked at her hands, resting in her lap. I should say something, she thought. But what?

Sloane leaned across the desk, his manner more aggressive, even accusatory. "Ms. Farrell, I don't know what your game is, or what you're not telling us, but clearly this was no ordinary murder. The man who called himself Curtis Caldwell didn't rob that apartment or kill Isabelle Waring at random. The whole crime was carefully planned and executed. Your appearance on the scene was the only thing that probably did not go according to plan." He paused, then continued, his voice filled with irritation. "You told us he was carrying Mrs. Waring's leather binder. Describe it to me again."

"The description won't change," Lacey said. "It was the size of a standard loose-leaf binder and had a zipper around it so that when it was closed nothing would fall out."

"Ms. Farrell, have you ever seen this before?" Sloane shoved a sheet of paper across the table.

Lacey looked at it. It was a loose-leaf page covered with writing. "I can't be sure," she said.

"Read it, please."

She skimmed it. It was dated three years earlier. It began, *Baba came to see the show again. Took all of us back to the restaurant for dinner* . . .

Heather's journal, she thought. I must have missed this page. How many more did I miss? she wondered suddenly.

"Have you ever seen this before?" Sloane asked her again.

"Yesterday afternoon when I brought the man I know as Curtis Caldwell to see the apartment, Isabelle was in the library, seated at the desk. The leather binder was open, and she was reading loose-leaf pages that she'd taken out of it. I can't be positive that this is one of them, but it probably is."

At least that much is true, she thought. Suddenly she regretted not taking time this morning to make copies of the journal before going to the station.

That was what she had decided to do—give the original to the police, a copy to Jimmy Landi, and keep a copy for herself. Isabelle's intention was that Jimmy read the journal; she clearly had felt that he might see something significant in it. He should be able to read a copy as well as the original, as could she, since, for whatever reason, Isabelle had made her promise to read the pages too.

"We found that page in the bedroom, under the chaise," Sloane told her. "Maybe there were other loose pages. Do you think that's possible?" He didn't wait for her to answer. "Let's get back to the smear of Isabelle Waring's blood we found in the downstairs closet. Do you have any idea how that got there?"

"I had Isabelle's blood on my hands," Lacey said. "You know that."

"Oh, yes, I know that, but your hands weren't dripping with blood when you grabbed that briefcase of yours as you were leaving last night. So what happened? Did you put something in that briefcase before we got there, something you took from Isabelle Waring's bedroom? I think so. Why don't you tell us what it was? Were there perhaps more pages like the one you just read scattered around her room? Is that a good guess?"

"Take it easy, Eddie. Give Lacey a chance to answer," Mars urged him.

"Lacey can have all the time she wants, Nick," Sloane snapped. "But the truth is going to be the same. She took something from that room; I'm sure of it. And don't you wonder why an innocent bystander would take something like that from the victim's home? Can you guess why?" he asked Lacey.

She wanted desperately to tell them she had the journal, and why she had it. But if I do, she thought, they'll demand I turn it over immediately. They won't let me make a copy for Heather's father. And I certainly can't tell them I'm making a copy for myself; they're reacting as though I had something to do with Isabelle's death, she thought. *I'll give the original to them tomorrow.*

She stood up. "No, I can't. Are you finished with me, Detective Sloane?"

"For today I am, Ms. Farrell, yes. But please

keep in mind that being an accessory after the fact in a murder investigation carries serious penalties. *Criminal* penalties," he added, putting a touch of menace into the words. "And one other thing: if you did take any of those pages, I have to wonder just how 'innocent' a bystander you were. After all, you did happen to be responsible for bringing the killer into Isabelle Waring's home."

Lacey left without responding. She had to get to the office, but first she was going to go home to get Heather Landi's journal. She would stay at her desk this evening until everyone else had left and make the copies she needed. Tomorrow she would turn over the original to Sloane. I'll try to make him understand why I took it, she thought nervously.

She started to hail a cab, then decided to walk home. The midafternoon sun felt good. She still had the sensation of being chilled to the bone. As she crossed Second Avenue, she sensed someone close behind her and spun around quickly to meet the puzzled eyes of an elderly man.

"Sorry," she mumbled as she darted to the curb.

I expected to see Curtis Caldwell, Lacey thought, upset to realize she was trembling. If the journal was what he was after, then he didn't get it. Would he come back for it? He knows I saw him and can identify him as a murderer. Until the police caught Caldwell—if they caught him— she was in danger, she was certain of that. She tried to force the thought out of her mind.

The lobby of her building felt like a sanctuary, but when Lacey got off at her floor, the long corridor seemed frightening and, key in hand, she hurried to the apartment and quickly dashed inside.

I'll never carry this briefcase again, she vowed as she retrieved it from under the couch and carried it into the bedroom and set it on her desk, carefully avoiding touching the bloody handle.

Gingerly she removed the journal pages from the briefcase, wincing at the sight of the ones stained with blood. Finally she put them all in a manila envelope and fished around in her closet for a tote bag.

Ten minutes later, that bag firmly under her arm, she stepped out onto the street. As she nervously hailed a cab she tried to convince herself that whoever Caldwell was, and for whatever reason he had killed Isabelle, he must surely be miles away by now, on the run.

6

Sandy Savarano, alias Curtis Caldwell, was taking no chances of being recognized as he used a pay phone down the block from Lacey Farrell's apartment building. He wore a gray wig over his sandy hair, there was a graying stubble covering his cheeks and chin, and his lawyer's suit had been replaced by a shapeless sweater worn over faded jeans. "When Farrell left the police station she walked home and went inside," he said as he glanced down the street. "I'm not going to hang around. There's a squad car parked across from her building. It may be there to keep an eye on her."

He had started walking west, then changed his mind and turned back. He decided to watch the police car for a while as a test of his theory that the policemen had been assigned to guard Lacey Farrell. He didn't have to wait long. He watched from half a block away as the familiar figure of a young woman in a black suit, carrying a tote bag, emerged from the building and hailed a cab. As it sped away, he looked to see what the cops in the squad car would do. A moment later a car ran the red light at the corner, and the flashing lights on the roof of the squad car went on as it leaped from the curb.

Good, he thought. That's one less thing to get in my way.

7

After they returned to the restaurant from making arrangements for Isabelle's cremation, Jimmy Landi and Steve Abbott went directly to Jimmy's office. Steve poured liberal amounts of scotch into tumblers and placed one of them on Landi's desk, commenting, "I think we both need this."

Landi reached for the glass. "I know I do. This has been an awful day."

Isabelle would be cremated when her body was released and her ashes taken to Gate of Heaven Cemetery in Westchester to be placed in the family mausoleum.

"My parents, my child, my ex-wife will be together up there," he said, looking up at Abbott. "It doesn't make sense, does it, Steve? Some guy claims he's looking to buy an apartment, then comes back and kills Isabelle, a defenseless woman. It's not like she was flashing expensive jewelry. She didn't have any. She never even cared for that stuff."

His face contorted in a mixture of anger and anguish. "I *told* her she had to get rid of the apartment! Her going on and on about Heather's death, worrying that it wasn't an accident! She was driving herself crazy over it—and me too—and being in that apartment just made it worse. Besides, she needed the money. That Waring guy she married didn't leave her a dime. I just wanted her to get on with her life. And then she gets killed!" His eyes glistened with tears. "Well, she's with Heather now. Maybe that's where she wanted to be. I don't know."

Abbott, in an obvious effort to change the subject, cleared his throat and said, "Jimmy, Cynthia is coming over around ten for dinner. How about joining us?"

Landi shook his head. "No, but thanks, I appreciate it. You've been wet-nursing me for almost a year, Steve, ever since Heather died, but it can't go on. I'll be okay. Stop worrying about me and pay attention to your girlfriend. Are you going to marry her?"

"I'm not rushing into anything," Abbott said, smiling. "Two divorces are enough."

"You're right. That's why I stayed single all these years. And you're young still. You've got a long way to go."

"Not so long. Don't forget I turned forty-five last spring."

"Yeah? Well, I turn sixty-eight next month," Jimmy said with a grunt. "But don't go counting me out yet. *I've* still got a long way to go before I cash in my chips. *And don't you forget it!*"

Then he winked at Abbott. Both men smiled. Abbott swallowed the last of his scotch and stood. "You bet you have. And I'm counting on it. When we open our place in Atlantic City, the rest of them might as well close their doors. Right?"

Abbott noticed Jimmy Landi glancing at his watch and said, "Well, I'd better get downstairs and do some glad-handing."

Shortly after Abbott had left, the receptionist buzzed Jimmy. "Mr. Landi, a Miss Farrell wants to talk to you. She says to tell you she's the realtor who was working with Mrs. Waring."

"Put her on," he snapped.

Back in the office, Lacey had responded to Rick Parker's questions about her interview with

Detective Sloane with noncommittal answers. "He showed me pictures. Nobody looked anything like Caldwell."

Once again she declined Rick's offer of dinner. "I want to catch up on some paperwork," she said with a wan smile.

And it's true, she thought.

She waited until everyone in the domestic real estate division left before carrying the tote bag to the copier, where she made two copies of Heather's journal, one for Heather's father, one for herself. Then she placed a call to Landi's restaurant.

The conversation was brief: Jimmy Landi would be waiting for her.

Pretheater was a busy taxi time, but she was in luck: a cab was just discharging a passenger right in front of her office building. Lacey raced across the sidewalk and jumped in the taxi just before someone else tried to claim it. She gave the address of Venezia on West Fifty-sixth Street, leaned back and closed her eyes. Only then did she relax her grip on the tote bag, though she still held it securely under her arm. Why was she so uneasy? she wondered. And why did she have the sensation of being watched?

At the restaurant she could see that the dining

room was full and the bar jammed. As soon as she gave her name, the receptionist signaled the maitre d'.

"Mr. Landi is waiting for you upstairs, Ms. Farrell," he told her.

On the phone she had said simply that Isabelle had found Heather's journal and wanted him to have it.

But when she was in his office, sitting opposite the brooding, solid-looking man, Lacey felt as though she were firing at a wounded target. Even so, she felt she had to be straightforward in telling him Isabelle Waring's dying words.

"I promised to give the journal to you," she said. "And I promised to read it myself. I don't know why Isabelle wanted me to read it. Her exact words were 'Show . . . him . . . where.' She wanted me to show you something in it. I suspect that for some reason she thought I'd find what it was that apparently confirmed her suspicion that your daughter's death was not a simple accident. I'm trying to obey her wishes." She opened her tote bag and took out the set of pages she had brought with her.

Landi glanced at them, then turned away.

Lacey was sure that the sight of his daughter's

handwriting was starkly painful to the man, but his only comment was a testy, "These aren't the originals."

"I don't have the original pages with me. I'm giving them to the police in the morning."

His face flushed with sudden anger. "That's not what Isabelle asked you to do."

Lacey stood up. "Mr. Landi, I don't have a choice. Surely you understand that it's going to take a lot of explaining to the police to make them understand why I removed evidence from a murder scene. I'm certain that eventually the original pages will be returned to you, but for now, I'm afraid you'll have to make do with a copy." As will I, she said to herself as she left.

He did not even look up as she walked out.

When Lacey arrived at her apartment, she turned on the entrance light and had taken several steps inside before the chaos in front of her registered. Drawers had been spilled, closets ransacked, furniture cushions had been tossed on the floor. Even the refrigerator had been emptied and left open. Appalled and terrified, she stared at the mess, then stumbled through the debris to call the superintendent; while he dialed 911, she put in a call to Detective Sloane.

He arrived shortly after the local precinct cops. "You know what they were looking for, don't you," Sloane said matter-of-factly.

"Yes, I do," Lacey told him. "Heather Landi's journal. But it's not here. It's in my office. I hope whoever did this hasn't gone there."

In the squad car on the way to her office, Detective Sloane read Lacey her rights. "I was keeping the promise I made to a dying woman," she protested. "She asked me to read the journal and then give it to Heather Landi's father, and that's what I've done. I took him a copy this evening."

When they got to her office, Sloane did not leave her side as she unlocked the cabinet and reached for the manila envelope in which she had placed the original pages of the journal.

He opened the clasp, pulled out a few of the sheets, studied them, then looked at her. "You're sure you're giving me everything?"

"This is everything that was with Isabelle Waring when she died," Lacey said, hoping he wouldn't press her. While it was the truth, it wasn't the whole truth: The copy of the journal pages that she had made for herself was locked in her desk.

"We'd better go down to headquarters, Ms. Farrell. We need to talk about this whole thing a bit more, I believe."

"My apartment," she protested. "Please. I have to clean it up." I sound ridiculous, she thought. Someone may have killed Isabelle because of Heather's journal, and I might have been killed if I'd been home tonight, and all I can think of is the mess there. She realized that her head was aching. It was after ten o'clock and she hadn't had anything to eat for hours.

"Your apartment can wait to be cleaned," Sloane told her brusquely. "We need to go over all this now."

But when they reached the precinct station, he did have Detective Nick Mars send out for a sandwich and coffee for her. Then he began. "All right, let's take this from the top again, Ms. Farrell," he said.

The same questions over and over, Lacey thought, shaking her head. Had she ever met Heather Landi? Wasn't it odd that on the basis of a chance meeting in an elevator months earlier,

Isabelle Waring had called her to offer an exclusive on the apartment? How often had she seen Waring in the last weeks? For lunches? dinners? end-of-the-day visits?

"She called early evening 'sober light,' " Lacey heard herself saying, searching her mind to try to find anything she could tell them that they might not have heard before. "She said that was what the Pilgrims called it; she said she found it a very lonely time."

"And she had no old friends to call?"

"I only know that she called me. Maybe she thought that because I was a single woman in Manhattan, I might be able to help her get some insight into her daughter's life," Lacey said. "And death," she added as an afterthought. She could visualize Isabelle's sad face, the high cheekbones and wide-set eyes hinting at the beauty she must have been as a young woman. "I think it was almost the way one might talk to a cabdriver or a bartender. You find a sympathetic ear, knowing that you don't have to worry about that person reminding you of what you said when you get over the difficult time."

Do I make sense? she wondered.

Sloane's demeanor didn't give any indication

of his reaction. Instead he said, "Let's talk about how Curtis Caldwell got back into the Waring apartment. There was no sign of forced entry. Isabelle Waring clearly didn't let him in, then go back and prop herself up on the bed with him there. Did you give him a key?"

"No, of course not," Lacey protested. "But wait a minute! Isabelle always left a key in a bowl on the table in the foyer. She told me she did it so that if she ran downstairs for her mail she didn't have to bother with her key ring. Caldwell could have seen it there and taken it. But what about my apartment?" she protested. "How did someone get in there? I have a doorman."

"And an active garage in the building and a delivery entrance. These so-called secured buildings are a joke, Ms. Farrell. You're in the realty business. You know that."

Lacey thought of Curtis Caldwell, pistol in hand, rushing to find her, wanting to kill her. "Not a very good joke." She realized she was fighting tears. "Please, I want to go home," she said.

For a moment she thought that they might keep her there longer, but then Sloane got up. "Okay. You can go now, Ms. Farrell, but I must warn you that formal charges may be pending against you for removing and concealing evidence from a crime scene."

I should have talked to a lawyer, Lacey thought. How could I have been such a fool?

Ramon Garcia, the building superintendent, and his wife, Sonya, were in the process of straightening up Lacey's apartment when she arrived. "We couldn't let you come back to this mess," Sonya told her, running a dust cloth over the top of the bureau in the bedroom. "We put things back in the drawers for you, not your way, I'm sure, but at least things are not still on the floor."

"I don't know how to thank you," Lacey said. The apartment had been full of police when she left, and she was dreading what she would find when she returned.

Ramon had just completed replacing the lock. "This was taken apart by an expert," he said. "And he had the right tools. How come he didn't pick up your jewelry box?"

That was the first thing the police had told her to check. Her several gold bracelets, her diamond stud earrings, and her grandmother's pearls were there, undisturbed.

"I guess that wasn't what he was after," Lacey said. To her own ears her voice sounded low and tired.

Sonya looked at her sharply. "I'll come back tomorrow morning. Don't worry. When you get home from work everything will be shipshape."

Lacey walked with them to the door. "Does the dead bolt still work?" she asked Ramon.

He tried it. "No one's gonna get in while that's on, at least without a battering ram. You're safe."

She closed and locked the door behind them. Then she looked around her apartment and shuddered. What have I gotten myself into? she wondered.

8

Mascara and a light lip liner were usually all the cosmetics Lacey wore, but in the morning light, when she saw the shadows under her eyes and noted the pallor of her skin, she added blush and eye shadow and fished in the drawer for lipstick. They did little, however, to brighten her outlook. Even wearing a favorite brown-and-gold jacket didn't help dispel a sense of gloom. A final check in the mirror told her she still looked limp and weary.

At the door of the office she paused, took a deep breath, and straightened her shoulders. An incongruous memory hit her. When she was twelve and suddenly taller than the boys in her class, she had started to slump when she walked.

But Dad told me height was delight, she thought, and he made a game of the two of us walking around with books on our heads. He said walking tall made you look confident to other people.

And I *do* need that confidence, she said to herself a few minutes later, when she was summoned to Richard Parker Sr.'s office.

Rick was in with his father. The elder Parker was obviously angry. Lacey glanced at Rick. No sympathy there, she thought. It really *is* Parker and Parker today.

Richard Parker Sr. did not mince words. "Lacey, according to security, you came in here last night with a detective. What was that all about?"

She told him as simply as she could, explaining that she had decided she had to turn the journal over to the police, but first she needed to make a copy for Heather's father.

"You kept concealed evidence in this office?" the older Parker asked, raising an eyebrow.

"I intended to give it to Detective Sloane today," she said. She told them about her apartment having been burglarized. "I was only trying to do what Isabelle Waring asked me to do," she said. "Now it seems I may have committed an indictable offense."

"You don't have to know much law to know that," Rick interjected. "Lacey, that was really a dumb thing to do."

"I wasn't thinking straight," she said. "Look, I'm sorry about this, but—"

"I'm sorry about it too," Parker Sr. told her. "Have you any appointments today?"

"Two this afternoon."

"Liz or Andrew can handle them for you. Rick, see to it. Lacey, you plan on working the phones for the immediate future."

Lacey's sense of lethargy disappeared. "That's not fair," she said, suddenly angry.

"Nor is it fair to drag this firm into a murder investigation, Ms. Farrell."

"I'm sorry, Lacey," Rick told her.

But you're Daddy's boy on this one, she thought, fighting down the urge to say more.

As soon as she got to her desk, one of the new secretaries, Grace MacMahon, came over with a cup of coffee and handed it to her. "Enjoy."

Lacey looked up to thank her, then strained to hear as Grace tried to tell her something without being overheard. "I got in early today. There was a detective here talking with Mr. Parker. I couldn't tell what he was saying, but I did hear that it had something to do with you."

Sloane was fond of saying that good detective work began with a hunch. After twenty-five years on the force, he had ample proof, for many of his hunches had turned out to be correct. That was why he expounded his theories to Nick Mars as they studied the loose-leaf pages that comprised Heather Landi's journal.

"I say that Lacey Farrell still isn't coming clean with us," he said angrily. "She's more involved in this thing than she's letting on. We know she took the journal out of the apartment; we know she made a copy of it to give to Jimmy Landi."

He pointed to the bloodstained pages. "And I'll tell you something else, Nick. I doubt we'd have seen these if I hadn't scared her yesterday by telling her that we'd found traces of Isabelle Waring's blood on the floor of the closet, right where she'd left her briefcase."

"And have you thought of this, Eddie?" Mars asked. "Those pages aren't numbered. So how do we know that Farrell hasn't destroyed the ones she didn't want us to see? It's called editing. I agree with you. Farrell's fingerprints aren't just all over these pages. They're all over the whole case."

An hour later, Detective Sloane received a call from Matt Reilly, a specialist in the Latent Print Unit housed in room 506. Matt had run a fingerprint that had been lifted from the outer door of Lacey's apartment through SAFIS, the Statewide Automated Fingerprint Identification System. He reported it was a match with the fingerprint of Sandy Savarano, a low-level mobster who had been a suspect in a dozen drug-related murders.

"Sandy Savarano!" Sloane exclaimed. "That's crazy, Matt. Savarano's boat blew up with him in it two years ago. We covered his funeral in Woodlawn Cemetery."

"We covered someone's funeral," Reilly told him dryly. "Dead men don't break into apartments."

For the rest of the day, Lacey watched helplessly as clients she had developed were assigned to other agents. It galled her to pull out the tickler files, make follow-up calls regarding potential sales, and then have to turn the information over to others. It was the way she had started out when she was a rookie, but that was eight years ago.

She was also made uncomfortable by the feeling of being watched. Rick was constantly in and out of the sales area where her cubicle was located, and she sensed that he was keeping close tabs on her.

Several times when she went to get a new file, she caught him looking at her. He seemed to be watching her all the time. She had a hunch that by the end of the day, she would be told to stay away from the office until the investigation was concluded, so if she was going to take the copy of Heather's journal with her, she would have to get it out of her desk when Rick wasn't looking.

She finally got her chance to retrieve the pages at ten minutes of five, when Rick was called into his father's office. She had barely managed to slip the manila envelope into her briefcase when Richard Parker Sr. summoned her to his office and told her she was being suspended.

9

"Not too hungry, I hope, Alex?" Jay Taylor asked as he checked his watch again. "Lacey isn't usually this late."

It was obvious that he was irritated.

Mona Farrell jumped to her daughter's defense. "The traffic is always terrible this time of day, and Lacey might have gotten delayed before she even left."

Kit shot her husband a warning glance. "I think with what Lacey has been through, nobody should be upset that she's a little late. My God, she came within a hair of being killed two days ago, then had her apartment burglarized last night. She certainly doesn't need to be hassled anymore, Jay."

"I agree," Alex Carbine said heartily. "She's had a rough couple of days."

Mona Farrell looked at Carbine with a grateful smile. She was never totally at ease with her frequently pompous son-in-law. It didn't take much to make him testy, and he usually had little patience with anyone, but she had noticed that he was deferential to Alex.

This evening they were having cocktails in the living room, while the boys were watching television in the den. Bonnie was with the grown-ups, however, having begged to stay up past her bedtime to see Lacey. She was standing at the window, watching for her.

It's eight-fifteen, Mona thought. Lacey was due here at seven-thirty. This really isn't like her. What can be keeping her?

The full impact of everything that was happening hit Lacey when she arrived home at five-thirty and realized that for practical purposes she was out of a job. Parker Sr. had promised that she would continue to receive her base salary—"For a short time to come, at least," he had said.

He's going to fire me, she realized. He's going

to use the excuse that I jeopardized the firm by copying and concealing evidence there. I've worked for him for eight years. I'm one of his best agents. Why would he even *want* to get rid of me? His own son gave me Curtis Caldwell's name and told me to set up an appointment. And I bet he's not planning to give me any of the severance due after so many years of employment. He'll say the firing's for cause. Can he get away with that? It looks like I'm about to be in trouble on several fronts, she thought, shaking her head at the sudden bad fortune that had come her way. I need to talk to a lawyer, but who?

A name came to her mind. Jack Regan!

He and his wife, Margaret, a couple in their mid-fifties, lived on the fifteenth floor of her building. She had chatted with them at a cocktail party last Christmas and remembered hearing people ask him about a criminal case he had just won.

She decided to call right away, but then found that their phone number wasn't listed.

The worst thing that can happen is that they'll slam the door in my face, Lacey decided, as she took the elevator to the fifteenth floor. Ringing their bell, she realized that she was glancing nervously around in the corridor.

Their surprise at seeing her gave way to a genu-

inely warm welcome. They were having a predin-
ner sherry and insisted she join them. They had
heard about the burglary.

"That's part of the reason that I'm here," she
began.

Lacey left an hour later, having retained Regan
to represent her in the likely event that she was
facing indictment for holding on to the journal
pages.

"The least of the charges would be obstructing
governmental administration," Regan had told
her. "But if they believe you had an ulterior motive for taking the journal, it could get a lot more
serious than that."

"My only motive was to keep a promise to a
dying woman," Lacey protested.

Regan smiled, but his eyes were serious. "You
don't have to convince *me,* Lacey, but it wasn't
the smartest thing to do."

She kept her car in the garage in the basement
of her building, a luxury that, if everything went
as she feared, she probably could no longer afford. It was one of several unpleasant realizations
she had had to face that day.

The rush hour was over, but even so there was a lot of traffic. I'll be an hour late, Lacey thought as she inched her car across the George Washington Bridge, where a blocked lane was creating havoc. Jay must be in a wonderful mood, she thought, smiling ruefully but genuinely worried about keeping her family waiting.

As she drove along Route 4 she debated how much she would tell them about what was going on. Everything, I guess, she finally decided. If Mom or Kit call me at the office and I'm not there, they'll have to know why.

Jack Regan is a good lawyer, she assured herself as she turned onto Route 17. He'll straighten this out.

She glanced in her rearview mirror. Was that car following her? she wondered, as she exited onto Sheridan Avenue. Stop it, she warned herself. You're getting paranoid.

Kit and Jay lived on a quiet street in a section of pricey homes. Lacey pulled up to the curb in front of their house, got out of the car, and started up the walk.

"She's here," Bonnie called out joyously, "Lacey's here!" She ran for the door.

"About time," Jay grunted.

"Thank God," Mona Farrell murmured. She knew that despite Alex Carbine's presence, Jay was about to explode with irritation.

Bonnie tugged at the door and opened it. As she raised her arms for Lacey's hug, there was the sound of shots, and bullets whistled past them. A flash of pain coursed through her head, and Lacey threw herself forward, her body covering Bonnie's. It sounded as though the screams were coming from inside the house, but at that moment Lacey's whole mind seemed to be screaming.

In the sudden quiet that followed the shots, she quickly ran a mental check of the situation. The pain she felt was real, but she realized with a stab of anguish that the gush of blood against her neck was coming from the small body of her niece.

10

In the waiting room on the pediatrics floor of Hackensack Medical Center, a doctor smiled reassuringly at Lacey. "Bonnie had a close call, but she'll make it. And she's very insistent, Ms. Farrell, that she wants to see you."

Lacey was with Alex Carbine. After Bonnie was wheeled out of the operating room, Mona, Kit, and Jay had followed her crib to her room. Lacey had not gone with them.

My fault, my fault—it was all she could think. She was only vaguely aware of the headache caused by the bullet that had creased her skull. In fact, her whole mind and body seemed numb, floating in a kind of unreality, not yet fully comprehending the horror of all that was happening.

The doctor, understanding her concern and aware that she was blaming herself, said, "Ms. Farrell, trust me, it will take a while for that arm and shoulder to mend, but eventually she'll be as good as new. Children heal fast. And they forget fast too."

As good as new, Lacey thought bitterly, staring straight ahead. She was rushing to open the door for me—that's all she was doing. Bonnie was just waiting for me. And it almost cost her her life. Can anything ever be "good as new" again?

"Lacey, go on in and see Bonnie," Alex Carbine urged.

Lacey turned to look at him, remembering with gratitude how Alex had dialed 911 while her mother tried to stem the blood that was spurting from Bonnie's shoulder.

In her niece's room, Lacey found Jay and Kit sitting on either side of the crib. Her mother was at the foot, now icy calm, her trained nurse's eyes observant.

Bonnie's shoulder and upper arm were heavily bandaged. In a sleepy voice she was protesting, "I'm not a baby. I don't want to be in a crib." Then she spotted Lacey and her face brightened. "Lacey!"

Lacey tried to smile. "Snazzy-looking bandage, girlfriend. Where do I sign it?"

Bonnie smiled back at her. "Did you get hurt too?"

Lacey bent over the crib. Bonnie's arm was resting on a pillow.

As she died, Isabelle Waring's arm had been reaching under a pillow, pulling out the bloodied pages. It's because I was there two days ago that Bonnie is here tonight, Lacey thought. *We could be planning her funeral right now.*

"She really is going to be all right, Lacey," Kit said softly.

"Didn't you have any sense that you were being followed?" Jay asked.

"For God's sake, Jay, are you crazy?" Kit snapped. "Of course she didn't."

Bonnie is hurt and they're at each other's throats because of me, Lacey thought. I can't let this happen.

Bonnie's eyelids were drooping. Lacey leaned down and kissed her cheek.

"Come back tomorrow, please," Bonnie begged.

"I have some stuff to do first, but I'll be back real soon," Lacey promised her.

Her lips lingered for a moment on Bonnie's

cheek. I'll never expose you to danger again, she vowed.

Back in the waiting area, Lacey found detectives from the Bergen County prosecutor's office waiting for her. "We've been contacted by New York," they told her.

"Detective Sloane?" she asked.

"No. The U.S. Attorney's office, Miss Farrell. We've been asked to see that you get home safely."

11

Gary Baldwin, United States Attorney for the Southern District of the state, generally wore a benign expression that seemed incongruous to anyone who had ever seen him in action at a trial. Rimless glasses enhanced the scholarly look of his thin face. Of medium height and slender build, and soft-spoken in his demeanor, he neverthe-less could annihilate a witness during cross-examination and accomplish it without even raising his voice. Forty-three years old, he was known to have national political ambitions and clearly would like to crown his career in the U.S. Attorney's office with a major, headline-grabbing case.

That case might have just landed in his lap. It

certainly had all the proper ingredients: A young woman happens on a murder scene in an apartment on Manhattan's expensive Upper East Side, the victim the ex-wife of a prominent restaurateur. Most important, the woman has seen the assailant and can identify him.

Baldwin knew that if Sandy Savarano had come out of hiding to do this job, it *had* to be tied to drugs. Thought to be dead for the past two years, Savarano had made a career of being an enforcer who eliminated anyone who got in the way of the drug cartel he worked for. He was about as ruthless as they get.

But when the police had shown Lacey Farrell the mug shots they had of Savarano, she had not recognized him. Either her memory was faulty, or Savarano had had enough plastic surgery to successfully disguise his identity. Chances are it's the latter, Baldwin thought, and if so, then it means that Lacey Farrell is just about the only person who can actually identify him.

Gary Baldwin's dream was to arrest and prosecute Savarano, or better yet, get him to plea-bargain and give evidence against the real bosses.

But the call he had just received from Detective Eddie Sloane had infuriated him. The journal that seemed to be a key part of this case had been stolen from the precinct. "I was keeping it in my cubby in the squad room—locked, of course— while Nick Mars and I read it to see if there was anything useful in it," Sloane explained. "It disappeared sometime last night. We're turning the station house upside down to find out who lifted it."

Then Sloane had added, "Jimmy Landi has the copy Farrell gave him. I'm on my way to get it from him."

"Make sure you get it before that disappears too," Baldwin said.

He slammed the phone down. Lacey Farrell was due in his office, and he had a lot of questions for her.

Lacey knew that she was being naïve in hoping that turning over Heather Landi's journal to the police would end her involvement in the case. When she finally got home from New Jersey the night before, it was almost dawn, but still she was unable to sleep, alternating between self-recrimination that she had put Bonnie in mortal danger, and a sense of bewilderment at the way that her whole life seemed to be falling apart. She felt like a pariah, knowing that because she could identify the man she knew as Curtis Caldwell, not only was she in danger, but anyone close to her was as well.

I can't go to visit Mom or Kit or the kids, she thought. I can't have them visit me. I'm afraid to go out on the street. How long is this going to last? And what will make it end?

Jack Regan had joined her in the waiting room outside the U.S. Attorney's office. He gave her a reassuring smile when a secretary said, "You can go in now."

It was Baldwin's habit to keep people waiting once inside his office while he ostensibly completed making notes in a folder. Under lowered eyelids, he studied Lacey Farrell and her lawyer as they took seats. Farrell looked like a woman under severe stress, he decided. Not surprising given the fact that only last night, in a spray of gunfire, a bullet had grazed her skull and another had seriously injured a four-year-old child. It was a miracle that no one had been killed in the shooting, Baldwin added to himself as he finally acknowledged their presence.

He did not mince words. "Ms. Farrell," he said, "I am very sorry for the problems you've been having, but the fact is you seriously impaired a major criminal investigation by removing evidence from a crime scene. For all we know, you may have destroyed some of that evidence. What you did turn over is now missing, which is a stunning sign of its significance."

"I did *not* destroy—" Lacey began in heated protest, just as Jack Regan snapped, "You have no right to accuse my client—"

They were interrupted by Baldwin, who held up his hand for silence. Ignoring Regan, his voice icy, he said, "Ms. Farrell, we have only your word for that. But you have my word for this: The man you know as Curtis Caldwell is a ruthless killer. We need your testimony to help convict him, and we intend to make sure that nothing happens to prevent that."

He paused and stared at her. "Ms. Farrell, it is within my power to hold you as a material witness. I promise you it won't be pleasant. It would mean that you'd be kept under twenty-four-hour guard in a special facility."

"How long a time are you talking about?" Lacey demanded.

"We don't know, Ms. Farrell. It would be however long it takes to apprehend and, with your help, convict the murderer. I do know that until Isabelle Waring's killer is arrested, your life isn't worth a plugged nickel, and until now we've never had a case against this man where we thought we'd be able to prosecute him successfully."

"Would I be safe after I testify against him?" Lacey asked. As she sat facing the U.S. Attorney, she had a sudden sense of being in a car that was hurtling down a steep hill, out of control, about to crash.

"No, you wouldn't be," Jack Regan said firmly.

"On the contrary," Baldwin told them. "He's claustrophobic. He will do anything to avoid going to prison. Now that we can link him to a murder, he may well be persuaded to turn state's evidence once we've got him, in which case we would not even bring him to trial. But until that happens we must keep you safe, Ms. Farrell."

He paused. "Have you ever heard of the witness protection program?"

12

In the quiet of his locked office, he studied Heather's journal again. It was in there, all right. But he had taken care of the problem. The cops were following up all the names they had. Good luck to them. They were on a wild-goose chase.

Finally he turned the pages over. The blood on them had dried a long time ago, probably just minutes after it had been shed. Even so, his hands felt sticky. He wiped them with his handkerchief, dampened by water from the always-present pitcher. Then he sat completely still, the only movement the opening and closing of his fingers, a sure sign of his agitation.

Lacey Farrell had not been seen for three months. They were either holding her as a material witness, or she had disappeared into the witness protection program. She supposedly had made one copy of the journal, for Jimmy Landi, but what would have stopped her from making another copy for herself?

Nothing.

Wherever she was, she would have figured out that if the journal was worth killing for, it had to have something of value in it. Isabelle had talked her head off to Farrell. God knows what she had said.

Sandy Savarano was back in hiding. He had seemed to be the perfect one to send to retrieve the journal and to take care of Isabelle Waring, but he had been careless. Stupidly careless. Twice. He had let Farrell see him at Waring's apartment at the time of the murder, and now she could identify him. (And if the Feds catch him, he told himself, she will.) Then he had left a fingerprint at Farrell's apartment that tied him to the burglary. Sandy would give everything up in a minute rather than go to prison, he reflected.

Farrell had to be tracked down, and Savarano sent to eliminate her.

Then, just maybe, he would be safe at last . . .

13

The name on the bell at the small apartment building on Hennepin Avenue in Minneapolis was "Alice Carroll." To the neighbors, she was an attractive young woman in her late twenties who didn't have a job and kept pretty much to herself.

Lacey knew that was the way they described her. And they're right about keeping to myself, she thought. After three months, the sensation of sleepwalking was ending and an intense sense of isolation setting in.

I didn't have a choice, she reminded herself, when at night she lay awake remembering how she had been told to pack suitcases with heavy clothing but bring neither family pictures, nor items with her name or initials.

Kit and her mother had come to help her pack and to say good-bye. We all thought of it as temporary, a kind of forced vacation.

At the last minute her mother had tried to come with her. "You can't go off alone, Lacey," she had argued. "Kit and Jay have each other and the children."

"You'd be lost without the kids," Lacey had reminded her, "so don't even think that way, Mom."

"Lacey, Jay is going to keep paying the maintenance on your apartment," Kit had promised.

Her knee-jerk response—"I can handle it for a while"—had been an empty boast. She had realized immediately that once she moved and took on her new identity, she could have no involvement with anyone or any part of her life in New York. Even a maintenance check signed with an assumed name could be traced.

It had happened quickly and efficiently. Two uniformed cops had taken her out in a squad car as though she were going to the precinct for questioning. Her bags were brought down to the garage, where an unmarked van was parked. Then she was transferred to an armored van that took her to what they called "a safe site" and orientation center in the Washington, D.C., area.

Alice in Wonderland, Lacey would think as she passed the time in that enclosure, watching her identity disappear. In those weeks she worked with an instructor to create a new background for herself. All the things she had been were gone. They existed in her memory, of course, but after a time she began to question even that reality. Now there were only weekly phone calls from safe hookups, letters mailed through safe channels—otherwise there was no contact. None. Nothing. Only the overwhelming loneliness.

Her only reality became her new identity. Her instructor had walked her to a mirror. "Look in there, Lacey. You see that young woman? Everything you think you know about her isn't so. Just forget her. Forget all about her. It'll be rough for a while—you'll feel like you are playing some kind of game, pretending. There's an old Jerry Vale song that says it all. I can't sing, but I do know the lyrics; they go like this:

Pretend you don't see her at all . . . it's too late for running . . . look somewhere above her . . . pretend you don't see her at all . . .

That was when Lacey had chosen her new name, Alice Carroll, after Alice in *Alice's Adventures in Wonderland* and *Through the Looking Glass,* by Lewis Carroll.

It fit her situation perfectly.

14

The racket from the renovation going on in the apartment next to the one that had belonged to Heather Landi assaulted the ears of Rick Parker as soon as he stepped off the elevator in the building at Fifth Avenue and Seventieth Street. Who the hell was the contractor, he wondered, fuming with irritation. A demolition expert?

Outside, the sky was heavy with snow clouds. Flurries were predicted by evening. But even the vague, gray light coming through the windows revealed the general look of neglect that permeated the foyer and living room of Heather Landi's apartment.

Rick sniffed. The air was stale, dry, and dusty.

He turned on the light and saw that a thick layer of powdery dust covered the tabletops, bookshelves, and cabinets.

He swore silently. Damn superintendent, he thought. It was his job to see to it that a contractor thoroughly sealed off the premises he was renovating.

He yanked the intercom off the hook and shouted to the doorman, "Tell the good-for-nothing super to get up here. Now."

Tim Powers, large and by nature amiable, had been superintendent of 3 East Seventieth for fifteen years. He knew full well that in the landlord-tenant world, it was the super who was always caught in the middle, but as he would tell his wife philosophically at the end of a bad day, "If you can't stand the heat, then get the hell out of the kitchen." He had learned to sympathize with irate co-op dwellers when they complained that the elevator was too slow, the sink was dripping, the toilet running, or the heat uneven.

But standing in the doorway as he listened to Rick Parker's tirade, Tim decided that in all these years of putting up with angry complaints, he had never experienced the near manic fury that was being hurled at him now.

He knew better than to tell Rick where to get off. He might be a young jerk riding on his papa's coattails, but that didn't make him any the less a Parker, and the Parkers owned one of the biggest real estate/building management companies in Manhattan.

Rick's voice grew louder and his anger more pronounced. Finally, when he stopped for breath, Tim seized the opportunity to say, "Let's get the right person in here to hear this." He went back into the hall and pounded on the door of the next apartment, shouting, "Charley, get out here."

The door was yanked open, and the sounds of hammering and banging grew louder. Charley Quinn, a grizzled-faced man dressed in jeans and a sweatshirt, and carrying a roll of blueprints, came out into the corridor. "I'm busy, Tim," he said.

"Not busy enough," Powers said. "I've talked to you before about sealing up that job when you start ripping the walls out. Mr. Parker, maybe you'll explain why you're so upset."

"Now that the police have finally released this apartment," Rick shouted, "we are responsible for selling it for the owner. But will you tell me how the hell we can bring anyone in here with all the mess you're causing? The answer is, we can't."

He shoved Tim aside, stalked out into the hall, and rang for the elevator. When the door closed behind him, the superintendent and the contractor looked at each other.

"He's on something," Powers said flatly. "What a jerk."

"He may be a jerk," Quinn said quietly, "but he looks to me like the kind of guy who could go off the deep end." He sighed. "Offer to get a cleaning service in here, Tim. We'll pay for it."

Rick Parker knew better than to go directly to the office. He didn't want to run into his father. *I shouldn't have blown my stack like that,* he told himself. He was still shaking with anger.

January was a lousy month in New York, he thought. As he turned in to Central Park and walked rapidly along a jogging path, a runner brushed into him. "Watch out!" Rick snapped.

The jogger didn't break pace. "Cool it, man," he yelled back over his shoulder.

Cool it! Sure, Rick thought. The old man's finally letting me handle some sales again, and that nosy detective has to show up this morning of all times.

Detective Sloane had come by, asking the same questions, going over the same territory. "When you got that call from the man who identified himself as Curtis Caldwell, did it ever occur to you to check with the law firm he claimed was his employer?" he had asked for the umpteenth time.

Rick jammed his hands in his pockets, remembering how lame his response had sounded. "We do a lot of business with Keller, Roland, and Smythe," he had said. "Our firm manages their building. There was no reason not to take the call on faith."

"Have you any idea how the caller would have *known* his background wouldn't be checked? I understand that Parker and Parker has a standing policy of screening all applicants, of being sure that the people you take to look at upscale apartments are on the level."

Rick remembered the dread he had experienced when, without knocking, his father had joined them.

"I have told you before and I'll tell you again,

I have no idea how that caller knew enough to use the law firm's name," Rick had said.

Now he kicked at a ball of crusted, dirty snow that was lying in his path. Were the police getting suspicious of the fact that he had been the one to set up the meeting? Were they starting to suspect that there never had been a phone call?

I should have figured out a better story, he thought, kicking savagely at the frozen earth. But it was too late now. He was stuck with it, so he *had* to make it stick.

15

The key word in this program is "security," Lacey thought as she started a letter to her mother. What do you write about? she asked herself. Not about the weather. If I were to mention that it's ten degrees below zero and there's been a record twenty-six-inch snowfall in one day, it would be a dead giveaway that I'm in Minnesota. That's the sort of information they warn you about.

I can't write about a job because I don't have one yet. I *can* say that my fake birth certificate and my fake social security card just came through, so now I can *look* for a job. I suppose I can tell them that now I have a driver's license, at least, and my advisor, a deputy U.S. marshal, took me to buy a secondhand car.

The program pays for it. Isn't that great? But of course I can't say that the marshal's name is George Svenson, and I certainly won't let Mom and Kit know that I bought a three-year-old maroon Bronco.

Instead she wrote:

My advisor is a good guy. He's got three teen-aged daughters.

No, take that last part out, she thought. Too specific.

My advisor is a good guy. Very patient. He went with me to buy furniture for the studio.

Too specific. Make that *apartment.*

But you know me. I didn't want a lot of matched stuff, so he humored me and we went to some garage sales and house sales and I found some really nice secondhand furniture that at least has character. But I sure miss my own digs, and do tell Jay that I'm really grateful to him for keeping up the maintenance on the place for me.

That was safe enough, Lacey thought, and I really am grateful to Jay. But I *will* pay him back every nickel, she vowed to herself.

She was allowed to call home once a week on a secure telephone hookup. The last call she had made, she could hear Jay in the background, hurrying Kit. Well, it *was* a pain in the neck to have to sit and wait for a call at a specific time; she couldn't deny that. And no one could call her back.

It sounds as though the holidays were fun for the kids, and I'm so happy that Bonnie's arm is getting stronger. Sounds like the boys' skiing trip was a blast. Tell them I'm nutty enough to try snowboarding with them when I get back.

Take care of yourself, Mom. Sounds as though you and Alex are having fun. So what if he talks your ear off once in a while? I think he's a nice guy, and I'll never forget how helpful he was that awful night while Bonnie was in surgery.

Love you all. Keep praying that they find and arrest Isabelle Waring's murderer and he plea-bargains and I get off the hook.

Lacey signed her name, folded the letter and put it in an envelope. Deputy Marshal Svenson would mail it for her through the secure mail-forwarding channel. Writing to her mother and Kit or speaking to them on the phone took away something of the sense of isolation. But when the letter was finished or the phone call completed, the letdown that followed was rough.

Come on, she warned herself, knock off the self-pity. It won't do any good and, thank God, the holidays are over. "Now *they* were a genuine problem," she said aloud, realizing suddenly that she was getting in the habit of talking to herself.

To try to break up Christmas Day she had gone to the last Mass at St. Olaf's, the church named for the warrior king of Norway, then ate at the Northstar Hotel.

At Mass when the choir sang *"Adeste Fidelis"* tears had sprung to her eyes as she thought of the last Christmas her father was alive. They had gone to midnight Mass together at St. Malachy's in Manhattan's theater district. Her mother had always said that Jack Farrell could have made it big if he had chosen to try for a career as a singer rather than as a musician. He really did have a good voice. Lacey remembered how that night she had stopped singing herself, just to listen to the clarity of tone and warmth of feeling he put into the carol.

When it was over, he had whispered, "Ah, Lace, there's something grand about the Latin, isn't there?"

At her solitary meal, her tears had welled up again as she thought about her mother and Kit and Jay and the children. She and her mother always went to Kit's house on Christmas, arriving with the presents for the kids that "Santa had dropped off" at their houses.

At ten, Andy, like Todd at that age, was still a believer. At four, Bonnie was already savvy. Lacey had sent gifts to everyone through secure channels this year, but that didn't hold a candle to *being* there, of course.

As she had tried to pretend she was enjoying the food she had ordered at the Northstar, she found herself thinking of Kit's festive holiday table with the Waterford chandelier sparkling, its lights reflected off the Venetian glassware.

Knock it off! Lacey warned herself as she dropped the envelope into a drawer, where it would await Deputy Marshal Svenson's pickup.

For lack of something else to do, she reached into the bottom drawer of her desk and pulled out the copy she had made of Heather Landi's journal.

What could Isabelle possibly have wanted me to see in it? she asked herself for the hundredth time. She had read it so often she felt as though she could quote it word for word.

Some of the entries were in a close sequence, daily and sometimes several times a day. Others were spaced a week, a month, or as much as six weeks apart. In all, the journal spanned the four years Heather had spent in New York. She wrote in detail about looking for an apartment, about her father insisting she live in a safe building on the East Side. Heather clearly had preferred Manhattan's West Side; as she put it, "It isn't stuffy and has life."

She wrote about singing lessons, about auditioning and getting her first part in a New York production—an Equity showcase revival of *The Boy Friend*. That entry had made Lacey smile. Heather had ended it by writing "Julie Andrews, move over. Heather Landi is on her way."

She wrote in detail about the plays she had attended, and her analysis of them and of the actors' performances was thoughtful and mature. She wrote interestingly as well about some of the more glamorous parties she attended, many of them apparently through her father's connections. But some of the gushing about her boyfriends was surprisingly *im*mature. Lacey got the clear impression that Heather had been pretty much held down by both her mother and father until, after two years of college, she opted to come to New York and try for a career in the theater.

It was obvious that she had been close to both parents. All the references to them were warm and loving, even though several times she had complained about the need to please her father.

There *was* one entry that had intrigued Lacey from the first time she read it:

Dad exploded at one of the waiters today. I have never seen him that angry before. The poor waiter was almost crying. I see what Mom meant when she warned me about his temper and said that I should rethink my decision to tell him that I wouldn't live on the East Side when I moved to New York. He'd kill me if he ever found out how right he was about that. God, I was stupid!

What had happened to make Heather write that? Lacey wondered. It can't be too important. Whatever it was, it took place four years before she died and that's the only reference to it.

It was clear from the last few entries that Heather was deeply troubled about something. She wrote several times about being caught "between a rock and a hard place. I don't know what to do." Unlike the others, those last entries were on unlined paper.

There was nothing specific in those entries, but obviously they had triggered Isabelle Waring's suspicions.

But it could have had to do with a job decision,

or a boyfriend, or anything, Lacey thought hopelessly, as she put the pages back in the drawer. God knows *I'm* between a rock and a hard place right now.

That's because someone wants to kill you, a voice inside her head whispered.

Lacey slammed the drawer shut. Stop it! she told herself fiercely.

A cup of tea might help, she decided. She made it, then sipped it slowly, hoping to dispel the heavy sense of fear-filled isolation that was again threatening to overwhelm her.

Feeling restless, she turned on the radio. Usually she flipped the dial to a music station, but it was set on the AM band, and a voice was saying, "Hi, I'm Tom Lynch, your host for the next four hours on WCIV."

Tom Lynch!

Lacey was shocked out of her homesickness. She had made a list of all the names mentioned in Heather Landi's journal, and one of them was Tom Lynch, an out-of-town broadcaster on whom it seemed Heather had once had a mild crush.

Was it the same person? And, if so, was it possible Lacey could learn something about Heather from him?

It was worth pursuing, she decided.

16

Tom Lynch was a hearty Midwesterner. Raised in North Dakota, he was one of the breed of stalwarts who thought twenty degrees was a bracing temperature, and believed that only sissies complained about the cold.

"But today they've got a point," he said with a smile to Marge Peterson, the receptionist at Minneapolis radio station WCIV.

Marge looked at him with maternal affection. He certainly brightened her day, and since he had taken over the station's afternoon talk show, he apparently had been having the same effect on many other people in the Minneapolis–St. Paul area. She could tell from the steadily increasing volume of fan mail that crossed her desk that the popular thirty-year-old anchorman was headed for big-time broadcasting. His mixture of news, interviews, commentary, and irreverent humor at- . tracted a wide age range of listeners. And wait until they get a look at him, she thought as she looked up at his bright hazel eyes, his slightly rumpled medium brown hair, his warm smile, and his attractively uneven features. He's a natural for television.

Marge was happy at his success—and therefore the station's—but realized that it was a double-edged sword. She knew that several other stations had tried to hire him away, but he had announced his strategy was to build WCIV into the number-one station in the listening area before considering moving on. And now it's happening, she thought with a sigh, and soon we'll be losing him.

"Marge, anything wrong?" Tom asked, his expression solicitous. "You look worried."

She laughed and shook her head. "Nothing wrong at all. You're off to the gym?"

As Lynch was signing off that afternoon, he had told his listeners that since even a penguin couldn't jog outside in this weather, he would be heading off to the Twin Cities Gym later on, and he hoped to see some of them there. Twin Cities was one of his sponsors.

"You bet. See you later."

"How did you hear about us, Miss Carroll?" Ruth Wilcox asked as Lacey filled out the membership form for the Twin Cities Gym.

"On the Tom Lynch program," Lacey said. The woman was studying her, and she felt the need to elaborate. "I've been thinking of joining a gym for some time, and since I can try this one out a few times before deciding . . ." She let her voice trail off. "It's also convenient to my apartment," she finished lamely.

At least this will give me some practice in trying to get a job, she told herself fiercely. The prospect of filling out the form had frightened her, since it was the first time she had actually used her new identity. It was all very well to practice it with her advisor, Deputy Marshal George Svenson, but quite another to actually try to live it.

On the drive to the gym she had mentally reviewed the details: She was Alice Carroll, from Hartford, Connecticut, a graduate of Caldwell

College, a safe alma mater because the school
was now closed. She had worked as a secretary
in a doctor's office in Hartford. The doctor retired
at the same time that she broke up with her boyfriend, so it just seemed like the right time to
make a move. She had chosen Minneapolis because she visited there once as a teenager and
loved it. She was an only child. Her father was
dead, and her mother had remarried and was living in London.

None of which matters at the moment, she
thought as she reached into her purse for her new
social security card. She would have to be careful; she had automatically started to write her real
number but caught herself. Her address: One East
End Avenue, New York, NY 10021 flashed into
her mind. *No,* 520 Hennepin Avenue, Minneapolis, MN 55403. Her bank: Chase; *no,* First State.
Her job? She put a dash through that space. Rela-
tive or friend to notify in case of accident: Svenson had provided her with a phony name, address,
and telephone number to use in that situation.
Any call that was made to the number would go
to him.

She got to the questions on medical history.
Any problems? Well, yes, she thought. A slight
scar where a bullet creased my skull. Shoulders

that always feel tense because I always have the feeling that someone is looking for me, and that someday when I'm out walking, I'll hear footsteps behind me, and I'll turn and . . .

"Stuck on a question?" Wilcox asked brightly. "Maybe I can help."

Instantly struck with paranoia, Lacey was sure she detected a skeptical look appear in the other woman's eyes. She can *sense* that there's something phony about me, she thought. Lacey managed a smile. "No, not stuck at all." She signed "Alice Carroll" to the form and pushed it across the desk.

Wilcox studied it. "Purr-fect." The pattern on her sweater was kittens playing with a spool of yarn. "Now let me show you around."

The place was attractive and well equipped with a good supply of exercise paraphernalia, a long jogging track, airy rooms for aerobics classes, a large pool, steam and sauna facilities, and an attractive juice bar.

"It gets fairly crowded early in the morning and right after work," Wilcox told her. "Oh, look, there he is," she said, interrupting herself. She called out to a broad-shouldered man who was headed away from them and toward the men's locker room: "Tom, come here a minute."

He stopped and turned, and Ms. Wilcox vigorously waved her arm, gesturing for him to come over.

A moment later she was introducing them. "Tom Lynch, this is Alice Carroll. Alice is joining us because she heard you talk about us on your radio program," Ms. Wilcox told him.

He smiled easily. "I'm glad I'm so persuasive. Nice to meet you, Alice." With a quick nod, and another bright smile, he left them.

"Isn't he a doll?" Wilcox asked. "If I didn't have a boyfriend I really like . . . well, never mind that. The trouble is, the single women sometimes come on too strong to him, keep trying to talk to him. But when he's here, he's here to exercise."

Helpful hints, Lacey thought. "So am I," she said crisply, hoping she sounded convincing.

17

Mona Farrell sat alone at a table in the popular new restaurant, Alex's Place. It was eleven o'clock, and the dining room and bar were still crowded with after-theater patrons. The pianist was playing "Unchained Melody," and Mona felt a sharp sense of loss. That song had been one of Jack's favorites.

The lyrics drifted through her mind. *And time can do so much . . .*

Mona realized that lately she seemed always to be on the verge of tears. Oh, Lacey, she thought, where *are* you?

"Well, I guess I can take some time to sit with a pretty woman."

Mona looked up, startled back into reality, and watched as Alex Carbine's smile faded.

"You crying, Mona?" he asked anxiously.

"No. I'm fine."

He sat across from her. "You're not fine. Anything special, or just the way things are?"

She attempted a smile. "This morning I was watching CNN, and they showed that minor earthquake in Los Angeles. It wasn't *that* minor. A young woman lost control of her car, and it flipped over. She was slim and had dark hair. They showed her being placed on a stretcher." Mona's voice quivered. "And for an awful moment I thought it was Lacey. She could be there, you know. She could be anywhere."

"But it wasn't Lacey," Alex said reassuringly.

"No, of course not, but I'm at the point that whenever I hear about a fire or flood or an earthquake, I worry that Lacey might be there and be caught in it."

She tried to smile. "Even Kit is getting sick of listening to me. The other day there was an avalanche on Snowbird Mountain, and some skiers were caught in it. Fortunately they were all rescued, but I kept listening for the names. Lacey loves to ski, and it would be just like her to go out in a heavy storm."

She reached for her wineglass. "Alex, I shouldn't be dumping all of this on you."

Carbine reached for her hand. "Yes, you should, Mona. When you talk to Lacey, maybe you should tell her what this whole thing is doing to you. I mean, maybe if you just had some idea of where she is, it would be easier to cope."

"No, I can't do that. I have to try *not* to let her know. It would be that much harder for her. I'm lucky. I've got Kit and her family. And you. Lacey's all alone."

"Tell her," Alex Carbine said firmly. "And then keep what she tells you to yourself."

He patted her hand.

18

"When you create someone like the mythical boyfriend, have a real person in mind," Deputy Marshal George Svenson had warned Lacey. "Be able to visualize that guy and the way he talks so that if you have to answer questions about him, it will be easier to be consistent. And remember, develop the trick of answering questions by asking questions of your own."

Lacey had decided that Rick Parker was the mythical boyfriend she had broken up with. She could imagine breaking up with him more easily than having him as a boyfriend, but thinking of him at least did make consistency easier.

She began going to the gym daily, always in the late afternoon. The exercise felt good, and it gave her a chance to focus her thoughts as well. Now that she had the social security card she was anxious to get a job, but Deputy Marshal Svenson told her the protection program would not provide false references.

"How am I supposed to get a job without a reference?" she had asked.

"We suggest you volunteer to work without pay for a couple of weeks, then see if you're hired."

"*I* wouldn't hire someone without references," she had protested.

It was obvious, though, that she would just have to try. Except for the gym, she was without any human contact. Being alone so much, the time was passing too slowly, and Lacey could feel depression settling over her like a heavy blanket. She had even come to dread the weekly talk with her mother. It always ended the same way, with her mother in tears, and Lacey ready to scream with frustration.

In the first few days after she started going to the gym, she had managed to make something of a friend of Ruth Wilcox. It was to her that she first tried out the story of what had happened to bring her to Minneapolis: her mother had remarried and moved to London; the doctor she worked for retired; and she had ditched her boyfriend. "He had a quick temper and could be very sarcastic," she explained, thinking of Rick.

"I know the type," Wilcox assured her. "But let me tell you something. Tom Lynch has been asking me about you. I think he likes you."

Lacey had been careful not to seem too interested in Lynch, but she had been laying the groundwork for a planned encounter. She timed her jogging to be finished just as he was starting. She signed up for an aerobics class that looked out on the jogging track and chose a spot where he would see her as he ran by. Sometimes on his way out he stopped in the juice bar for a vitamin shake or a coffee. She began to go into the shop a few minutes before he finished his run and to sit at a table for two.

The second week, her plan worked. When he entered the bar, she was alone at the small table and all the other tables were taken. As he looked around, their eyes met. Keeping her fingers crossed, she pointed casually to the empty chair.

Lynch hesitated, then came over.

She had combed Heather's journal and copied down any mention of him. The first time he appeared had been about a year and a half ago, when Heather had met him after one of the performances of her show.

> The nicest guy came out with us to Barrymore's for a hamburger. Tom Lynch, tall, really attractive, about thirty, I'd guess. He has his own radio program in St. Louis but says he is moving to Minneapolis soon. Kate is his cousin, that's why he came to the show tonight. He said that the hardest thing about being out of New York was not being able to go to the theater regularly. I talked to him a lot. He said he was going to be in town for a few days. I hoped he'd ask me out, but no such luck.

An entry four months later read:

> Tom Lynch was in town over the weekend. A bunch of us went skiing at Stowe. He's really good. And nice. He's the kind of guy Baba would love to see me with. But he isn't giving me or any of the girls a second look,

and anyhow it wouldn't make any difference now.

Three weeks later Heather had died in the accident—if it *was* an accident. When she copied the references to him, Lacey had wondered if either Isabelle or the police had ever spoken to Lynch about Heather. And what had Heather meant by writing "anyhow it wouldn't make any difference now"?

Did she mean that Tom Lynch had a serious girlfriend? Or did it mean that Heather was involved with someone herself?

All these thoughts raced through Lacey's head as Lynch settled down across the table from her.

"It's Alice Carroll, isn't it," he asked in a tone that was more affirmation than question.

"Yes, and you're Tom Lynch."

"So they tell me. I understand you've just moved to Minneapolis."

"That's right." She hoped her smile did not look forced.

He's going to ask questions, she thought nervously. This could be my first real test. She picked up the spoon and stirred her coffee, then realized that very few people felt the need to stir black coffee.

Svenson had told her to answer questions with questions. "Are you a native, Tom?"

She knew he wasn't, but it seemed like a natural thing to ask.

"No. I was born in Fargo, North Dakota. Not that far from here. Did you see the movie, *Fargo*?"

"I loved it," she said, smiling.

"And after seeing it, you still moved here? It was practically banned in these parts. Folks thought it made us look like a bunch of hicks."

Even to her own ears it sounded lame when she tried to explain the move to Minneapolis: "My mother and I visited friends here when I was sixteen. I loved everything about the city."

"It wasn't in weather like this, I trust."

"No, it was in August."

"During the black fly season?"

He was teasing. She knew it. But when you're lying, everything takes on a different slant. Next he asked her where she worked.

"I'm just settling in," she replied, thinking that at least that was an honest statement. "Now it's time to look for a job."

"What kind?"

"Oh, I worked in billing in a doctor's office,"

she replied, then added hastily, "but I'm going to try something different this time around."

"I don't blame you. My brother's a doctor, and those insurance forms keep three secretaries busy. What kind of doctor did you work for?"

"A pediatrician." Thank God, after listening to Mom all these years, I can sound as though I know what I'm talking about there, Lacey thought. But why on earth did I mention the billing department? I don't know one insurance form from another.

Anxious to change the drift of the conversation, she said, "I was listening to you today. I liked your interview with the director of last week's revival of *Chicago.* I saw the show in New York before I moved here and loved it."

"My cousin Kate is in the chorus of the road company of *The King and I* that's in town now," Lynch said.

Lacey saw the speculative look in his eyes. He's trying to decide whether to ask me to go with him to see it. Let him, she prayed. His cousin Kate had worked with Heather; she was the one who introduced them.

"It's opening tomorrow night," he said. "I have two tickets. Would you like to go?"

19

In the three months that followed Isabelle's death, Jimmy Landi felt detached. It was as if whatever part of his brain controlled his emotions had been anesthetized. All his energy, all his thinking were channeled into the new casino-hotel he was building in Atlantic City. Situated between Trump Castle and Harrah's Marina, it was carefully designed to outshine them both, a magnificent gleaming white showcase with rounded turrets and a golden roof.

And as he stood in the lobby of this new building and watched the final preparations being made for the opening a week away, he thought to himself, I've done it! I've actually done it! Carpets were being laid, paintings and draperies were being hung, cases and cases of liquor disappeared into the bar.

It was important to outshine everyone else on the strip, to show them up, to be different in a special way. The street kid who had grown up on Manhattan's West Side, who had dropped out of school at thirteen and gone to work as a dishwasher at The Stork Club, was on top now, and he was going to rub another success in everyone's face.

Jimmy remembered those old days, how when the kitchen door swung open, he would try to sneak a glance at the celebrities in the club's dining room. In those days they all had glamour, not just the stars but everyone who came there. They'd never dream of showing up looking as if they had slept in their clothes.

The columnists were there every night, and they had their own tables. Walter Winchell. Jimmy Van Horne. Dorothy Kilgallen. Kilgallen! Boy, did they all kowtow to her. Her column in the *Journal-American* was a must-read; everybody wanted her on his side.

I studied them, Jimmy thought, as he stood in the lobby, workmen milling around him. And I learned everything I needed to know about this business in the kitchen. If a chef didn't show up,

I could take over. He had worked his way up, becoming first a busboy, then a waiter, then maitre d'. By the time Jimmy Landi was in his thirties, he was ready to have his own place.

He learned how to deal with celebrities, how to flatter them without surrendering his own dignity, how to glad-hand them, but make them glad to get his nod of recognition and approval. I also learned how to treat my help, he thought—tough, but fair. Nobody who deliberately pulled anything on me got a second chance. Ever.

He watched with approval as a foreman sharply reprimanded a carpet layer who had placed a tool on the mahogany reservations desk.

Looking through wide, clear-glass doors, he could see gaming tables being set up in the casino. He walked into the massive space. Off to the right, glittering rows of slot machines seemed to be begging to be tried. Soon, he thought. Another week and they'll be lined up to use them, God willing.

He felt a hand on his shoulder. "Place looks okay, doesn't it, Jimmy?"

"You've done a good job, Steve. We'll open on time, and we'll be ready."

Steve Abbott laughed. *"Good* job? I've done a

great job. But you're the one with vision. I'm just the enforcer, the one who rides herd on everyone. But I wanted it done on time too. I wasn't going to have painters slopping around on opening night. It'll be ready." He turned back to Landi. "Cynthia and I are on our way back to New York. What about you?"

"No. I want to hang around here for a while. But when you get back to the city, would you make a call for me?"

"Sure."

"You know the guy who touches up the murals?"

"Gus Sebastiani?"

"That's right. The artist. Get him in as fast as possible and tell him to paint Heather out of all the pictures."

"Jimmy, are you sure?" Steve Abbott searched his partner's face. "You may regret doing that, you know."

"I won't regret it. It's time." Abruptly he turned away. "You better get going."

Landi waited a few minutes, then walked over to the elevator and pushed the top button.

Before he left he wanted to stop in again at the piano bar.

It was an intimate corner room with rounded windows overlooking the ocean. The walls were painted a deep, warm blue, with silver bars of music from popular songs randomly scattered against drifting clouds. Jimmy had personally selected the songs. They all had been among Heather's favorites.

She wanted me to call this whole operation Heather's Place, he thought. She was kidding. With a glimmer of a smile, Jimmy corrected himself. She was half kidding.

This *is* Heather's place, he thought as he looked around. Her name will be on the doors, her music is on these walls. She'll be part of it all, just the way she wanted, but not like in the restaurant where I have to look at her picture all the time.

He had to put it all behind him.

Restlessly he walked to a window. Far below, just above the horizon, the half-moon was glistening on churning waves.

Heather.

Isabelle.

Both gone. For some reason, Landi had found himself thinking more and more about Isabelle. As she was dying, she'd made that young real estate woman promise to give him Heather's journal. What was her name? Tracey? No. Lacey. Lacey Farrell. He was glad to have it, but what was so important in it? Right after he got it, the cops had asked to take his copy to compare it with the original.

He had given it to them, although reluctantly. He had read it the night Lacey Farrell gave it to him. Still he was mystified. What did Isabelle think he would find in it? He had gotten drunk before he tried to read it. It hurt too much to see her handwriting, to read her descriptions of things they did together. Of course, she also wrote about how worried she was about *him.*

"Baba," Jimmy thought.

The only time she ever called me "Dad" was when she thought I was sore at her.

Isabelle had seen a conspiracy in everything, then ironically ended up a random victim of a con man who cased the apartment by pretending to be a potential buyer, then came back to burglarize it.

It was one of the oldest games in the world, and Isabelle had been an unsuspecting victim. She simply had been in the wrong place at the wrong time.

Or *had* she? Jimmy Landi wondered, unable to shake the worrisome residue of doubt. Was there even the faintest chance that she had been right, that Heather's death *hadn't* been an accident? Three days before Isabelle died, a columnist in the *Post* had written that Heather Landi's mother, Isabelle Waring, a former beauty queen, "may be on the right track in suspecting the young singer's death wasn't accidental."

The columnist had been questioned by police and admitted she had met Isabelle casually and had gotten an earful of her theories about her daughter's death. As for the mention in the column, she had completely fabricated the suggestion that Isabelle Waring had proof.

Was Isabelle's death related to that item? Jimmy Landi wondered. Did someone panic?

These were questions that Jimmy had avoided. If Isabelle had been murdered to silence her, it meant that someone had deliberately caused Heather to burn to death in her car at the bottom of that ravine.

Last week the cops had released the apartment, and he had phoned the real estate people, instructing them to put it back on the market. He needed closure. He would hire a private detective to see if there was anything the cops had missed. And he would talk to Lacey Farrell.

The sound of hammering finally penetrated his consciousness. He looked around him. It was time to go. With heavy steps he walked across the room and entered the corridor. He pulled the heavy mahogany doors closed, then stood back to look at them. An artist had designed the gold letters that were to be fastened on the doors. They should be ready in a day or two.

"Heather's Place," they would read, for Baba's girl, Jimmy thought. If I find that someone deliberately hurt you, baby, I'll kill him myself. I promise you *that*.

20

It was time to call home, an event that Lacey both longed for and dreaded. This time the location for the secure phone call was a room in a motel. "Never the same place," she said when George Svenson opened the door in response to her knock.

"No," he agreed. Then he added, "The line's ready. I'll put the call through for you. Now, remember everything I told you, Alice."

He always called her Alice.

"I remember every word." Chanting, she recited the list: "Even to name a supermarket could give away my location. If I talk about the gym, don't dare refer to it as the Twin Cities Gym. Stay away from the weather. Since I don't have a job, that's a safe subject. Stretch it out."

She bit her lower lip. "I'm sorry, George," she said contritely. "It's just that I get an attack of nerves before these calls."

She saw a flicker of sympathy and understanding in his craggy face.

"I'll make the connection, then take a walk," he told her. "About half an hour."

"That's fine."

He nodded and picked up the receiver. Lacey felt her palms get moist. A moment later she heard the door click behind him as she said, "Hi, Mom. How's everyone?"

Today had been more difficult than usual. Kit and Jay were not home. "They had to go to some cocktail reception," her mother explained. "Kit sends her love. The boys are fine. They're both on the hockey team at school. You should see how they can skate, Lacey. My heart's in my mouth when I watch them."

I taught them, Lacey thought. I bought ice skates for them when they barely had started to walk.

"Bonnie's a worry, though," her mother added. "Still so pale. Kit takes her to the therapist three times a week, and I work out with her weekends. But she misses you. So much. She has an idea that you're hiding because someone may try to kill you.''

Where did she get that idea? Lacey wondered. Dear God, who put that notion in her head?

Her mother answered the unasked question: ''I think she overheard Jay talking to Kit. I know he irritates you sometimes, but in fairness, Lace, he's been very good, paying for your apartment and keeping up your insurance. I also learned from Alex that Jay has a big order to sell restaurant supplies to the casino-hotel that Jimmy Landi is opening in Atlantic City, and apparently he has been worried that if Landi knew he was related to you, the order might get canceled. Alex said that Jimmy felt terrible about what happened to his ex-wife, and Jay was afraid that he'd start to blame you somehow for her death. You know, for bringing that man in to see the apartment without checking on him first.''

Maybe it's too bad I wasn't killed along with Isabelle, Lacey thought bitterly.

Trying to sound cheerful, she told her mother that she was going to a gym regularly and really enjoying it. ''I'm okay, really I am,'' she said. ''And this won't go on too long, I promise. From what they tell me, when the man I can identify is arrested, he'll be persuaded to turn state's evidence rather than go to prison. As soon as they make a deal with him, I'll be off the hook. Whoever he fingers will be after him, not me. We just have to keep praying that it happens soon. Right, Mom?"

She was horrified to hear deep sobs coming from the other end of the connection. "Lacey, I can't live like this," Mona Farrell wailed. "Every time I hear about a young woman anywhere who's been in an accident, I'm sure it's you. You've got to tell me where you are. You've got to."

"Mom!"

"Lacey, please!"

"If I tell you, it's strictly between us. You can't repeat it. You can't even tell Kit."

"Yes, darling."

"Mom, they'd withdraw the protection, they'd throw me out of the program if they knew I told you."

"I have to know."

Lacey was looking out the window. She saw the ample frame of George Svenson approaching the steps. "Mom," she whispered. "I'm in Minneapolis."

The door was opening. "Mom, have to go. Talk to you next week. Kiss everybody for me. Love you. Bye."

"Everything okay at home?" Svenson asked.

"I guess so," Lacey said, as a sickening feeling came over her that she had just made a terrible mistake.

21

Landi's restaurant on West Fifty-sixth Street was filled with a sparkling after-theater crowd, and Steve Abbott was acting as host, going from table to table, greeting and welcoming the diners. Former New York Mayor Ed Koch was there. "That new TV show you're on is fabulous, Ed," Steve said, touching Koch's shoulder.

Koch beamed. "How many people get paid that kind of money for being a judge in small-claims court?"

"You're worth every penny."

He stopped at a table presided over by Calla Robbins, the legendary musical-comedy performer who had been coaxed out of retirement to star in a new Broadway show. "Calla, the word is that you're marvelous."

"Actually, the word is that not since Rex Harrison in *My Fair Lady* has anyone faked a song with such flair. But the public seems to like it, so what's wrong with that?"

Abbott's eyes crinkled as he bent down and kissed her cheek. "Absolutely nothing." He signaled to the captain hovering nearby. "You know the brandy Ms. Robbins enjoys."

"There go the profits," Calla Robbins said, laughing. "Thanks, Steve. You know how to treat a lady."

"I try." He smiled.

"I hear the new casino will knock everyone dead," chimed in Robbins's escort, a prominent businessman.

"You heard right," Steve agreed. "It's an amazing place."

"The word is that Jimmy is planning to get you to run it," the man added.

"The word is this," Steve said decisively. "Jimmy's principal owner. Jimmy's the boss. That's the way it is, and that's the way it's going to be. And don't you forget it. He sure doesn't let *me* forget it."

From the corner of his eye he saw Jimmy enter the restaurant. He waved him over.

Jimmy joined them, his face wreathed in a big smile for Calla.

"Who is boss in Atlantic City, Jimmy?" she asked. "Steve says you are."

"Steve has it right," Jimmy said, smiling. "That's why we get along so good."

As Jimmy and Steve moved away from Robbins's table, Landi asked, "Did you set up a dinner with that Farrell woman for me?"

Abbott shrugged. "Can't reach her, Jimmy. She's left her job, and her home phone is disconnected. I guess she's off on some kind of vacation."

Jimmy's face darkened. "She can't have gone too far. She's a witness. She can identify Isabelle's killer when they find him. That detective who took my copy of Heather's journal has to know where she is."

"Want me to talk to him?"

"No, I'll do it. Well, look who's here."

The formidable figure of Richard J. Parker was coming through the restaurant doors.

"It's his wife's birthday," Steve explained. "They have a reservation for three. That's why R. J.'s wife is with him for a change."

And that punk son of his completes the happy

family, Jimmy thought, as he hurried across to the foyer to welcome them with a warm smile.

The elder Parker regularly brought his real estate clients there for dinner, which was the only reason Jimmy hadn't banned his son, Rick Parker, from the restaurant ages ago. Last month he had gotten drunk and noisy at the bar and had had to be escorted to a cab. A few times when he had come in for dinner, it was obvious to Jimmy that Rick was high on drugs.

R. J. Parker returned Jimmy Landi's hearty handshake. "What more festive place to bring Priscilla than Landi's, right, Jimmy?"

Priscilla Parker gave Landi a timid smile, then looked anxiously at her husband for approval.

Jimmy knew that R. J. not only cheated on his wife, but that he bullied her unmercifully as well.

Rick Parker nodded nonchalantly. "Hi, Jimmy," he said with a slight smirk.

The aristocrat condescending to greet the peasant innkeeper, Jimmy thought. Well, without his father's clout that jerk couldn't get a job cleaning toilets.

Smiling broadly, Jimmy personally escorted them to their table.

As Priscilla Parker sat down, she looked around. "This is such a pretty room, Jimmy," she said. "But there's something different. What is it? Oh, I see," she said, "the paintings of Heather are gone."

"I thought it was time to remove them," Jimmy said gruffly.

He turned abruptly and left, so he did not see R. J. Parker's angry glance at his son, nor the way Rick Parker stared at the mural of the Bridge of Sighs, from which the painting of Heather as a young woman was now missing.

It was just as well.

22

It had been nearly four months since Lacey had had a reason to get dressed up. And I didn't bring dress-up clothes, she thought, as she looked in the closet for something that would be appropriate for a festive evening out.

I didn't bring many of my things because I thought that by now Caldwell, or whatever his real name is, would have been caught and made a deal to turn state's evidence, and I'd be out of the loop and back to real life.

That's the kind of thinking that gets me in trouble, she reminded herself as she reached for the long black wool skirt and evening sweater she had bought at an end-of-season closeout sale at

Saks Fifth Avenue last spring, neither of which she'd had a chance to wear in New York.

"You look okay, Alice," she said aloud when she studied herself in the mirror a few minutes later. Even on sale the skirt and sweater had been an extravagance. But it was worth it, she decided. The effect of understated elegance gave a lift to her spirits.

And I certainly *need* a lift, Lacey thought as she fished in her jewelry box for earrings and her grandmother's pearls.

Promptly at six-thirty, Tom Lynch called on the intercom from the lobby. She was waiting with the apartment door open when he stepped out of the elevator and walked down the hall.

The obvious admiration in his face as he approached was flattering. "Alice, you look lovely," he said.

"Thanks. You're pretty fancy yourself. Come—"

She never finished saying come in. The door to the elevator was opening again. Had someone followed Tom up? Grabbing his arm, she propelled him into the apartment and bolted the door.

"Alice, is anything wrong?"

She tried to laugh, but knew the effort sounded

false and shrill. "I'm so foolish," she stammered. "There was a . . . a deliveryman who rang the bell a couple of hours ago. He honestly was on the wrong floor, but my apartment was burglarized last year . . . in Hartford," she added hastily. "Then the elevator door opened again behind you . . . and . . . and I guess I'm just still jumpy," she finished lamely.

There was no deliveryman, she thought. *And my apartment was burglarized, but it wasn't in Hartford. I'm not just jumpy. I'm terrified that whenever an elevator door opens I'll see Caldwell standing there.*

"I can understand why you'd be nervous," Tom said, his tone serious. "I went to Amherst and used to visit friends in Hartford occasionally. Where did you live, Alice?"

"On Lakewood Drive." Lacey conjured up the pictures of a large apartment complex she had studied as part of her preparation in the safe site, praying that Tom Lynch wouldn't say his friends lived there too.

"Don't know it," he said, slowly shaking his head. Then, as he looked around the room, he added, "I like what you've done here."

The apartment *had* taken on a mellow, comfortable look, she had to admit. Lacey had painted the walls a soft ivory and then painstakingly ragged them to give them texture. The rug she had picked up at a garage sale was a machine-made copy of a Chelsea carpet, and it was old enough to have acquired a soft patina. The dark blue velvet couch and matching love seat were well worn, but still handsome and comfortable. The coffee table, which had cost her twenty dollars, had a scarred leather top and Regency legs. It was a duplicate of the one she had grown up with, and it gave her a sense of comfort. The shelves next to the television were filled with books and knick-knacks, all things she had bought at garage sales.

Lacey started to comment on how much she enjoyed shopping at garage sales, but stopped herself. Most people wouldn't be completely furnishing an apartment with garage-sale items. No, she thought, most people who relocate move their furniture as well. She settled for thanking Tom for his compliment and was glad when he suggested they get started.

He's different tonight, she thought as an hour later they sat companionably sipping wine and eating pizza. In the gym he had been cordial but reserved whenever they passed each other, and she assumed it had been a last-minute impulse that made him invite her to go with him to the opening tonight.

But now, being with him had taken on the feeling of an enjoyable and interesting date. For the first time since the night Isabelle died, Lacey realized, she was actually *enjoying* herself. Tom Lynch responded freely to the questions she asked him. "I was raised in North Dakota," he said. "I told you that. But I never lived there again after I went to college. When I graduated, I moved to New York, fully expecting to set the broadcast industry on fire. It didn't happen, of course, and a very wise man told me that the best way to make it was to start out in a smaller broadcast area, make a name for yourself there, then gradually work your way up to larger markets. So in the last nine years I've been in Des Moines, Seattle, St. Louis, and now here."

"Always radio?" Lacey asked.

Lynch smiled. "The eternal question. Why not go for television? I wanted to do my own thing, develop a program format, have the chance to see what works and what doesn't work. I know I've learned a lot, and recently I've had some inquiries from a good cable station in New York, but I think it's too soon to make that kind of move."

"Larry King went from radio to television," Lacey said. "He certainly made the transition fine."

"Hey, that's me, the next Larry King." They had shared one small pizza. Lynch eyed the last piece then started to put it on her plate.

"You take it," Lacey protested.

"I don't really want—"

"You're salivating for it."

They laughed together and a few minutes later when they left the restaurant and crossed the street to the theater, he put his hand under her elbow.

"You have to be careful," he said. "There are patches of black ice everywhere around here."

If only you knew, Lacey thought. My life is a sheet of black ice.

It was the third time she had seen a producton of *The King and I.* The last time had been when she was a freshman in college. That had been on Broadway, and her father had been in the orchestra pit. Wish you were playing in this one tonight, Jack Farrell, she thought. As the overture began, she felt tears welling in her eyes and forced them back.

"You okay, Alice?" Tom asked quietly.

"I'm fine." How did Tom sense that she was distressed? she wondered. Maybe he's psychic, she thought. I hope not.

Tom's cousin, Kate Knowles, was playing the role of Tuptim, the slave girl who tries to escape from the king's palace. She was a good actress with an exceptional voice. About my age, Lacey thought, maybe a little younger. She praised her enthusiastically to Tom during intermission, then asked, "Will she be riding with us to the party?"

"No. She's going over with the cast. She'll meet us there."

I'll be lucky to get any time with her, Lacey worried.

Kate and the other leads in the play were not the only "stars" at the party, Lacey realized. Tom Lynch was constantly surrounded by people. She slipped away from him to trade her wine for a

Perrier, but then did not rejoin him when she saw he was with an attractive young woman from the cast. Obviously impressed by him, she was talking animatedly.

I don't blame her, Lacey thought. He's good-looking, he's smart, and he's nice. Heather Landi apparently had been attracted to him, although the second time she wrote about him in her journal there was the suggestion that one of them was involved with someone else.

Sipping the Perrier, she walked over to a window. The party was in a mansion in Wayzata, a decidedly upscale suburb twenty minutes from downtown Minneapolis. The well-lighted property bordered on Lake Minnetonka, and standing at the window, Lacey could see that beyond the snow-covered lawn the lake was frozen solid.

She realized that the real estate agent in her was absorbing the details of the place—the fabulous location, the fine appointments in the eighty-year-old house. There were details in the design and construction you just don't come by anymore—at any price—in new homes, she thought as she turned to study the living room, where nearly one hundred people were gathered without even making the room seem crowded.

For a moment she thought longingly of her office in New York, of getting new listings, matching buyer to property, the thrill of closing a sale. I want to go home, she thought.

Wendell Woods, the host of the party, came over to her. "It's Miss Carroll, isn't it?"

He was an imposing man of about sixty with steel gray hair.

He's going to ask me where I'm from, Lacey thought.

He did, and she hoped she sounded credible when she gave the well-rehearsed version of her background in Hartford. "And now I'm settled in and ready to start job hunting," she told him.

"What kind of job?" he asked.

"Well, I don't want to go back to work in a doctor's office," she said. "I've always had an idea I'd like to try my hand at real estate."

"That's mostly commission income, you know. Plus you'd have to learn the area," he said.

"I understand that, Mr. Woods," Lacey said. Then she smiled. "I'm a quick study."

He's going to put me in touch with someone, she thought. I *know* he is.

Woods took out a pen and his own business card. "Give me your phone number," he said.

"I'm going to pass it on to one of my depositors. Millicent Royce has a small agency in Edina; her assistant just left to have a baby. Maybe you two can get together."

Lacey gladly gave the number to him. *I'm being recommended by the president of a bank and I'm supposedly new to the real estate field,* she thought. *If Millicent Royce is interested in meeting me, she may not bother to check references.*

When Woods turned to speak to another guest, Lacey glanced about the room. Seeing that Kate Knowles was momentarily alone, she quickly made her way to her. "You were wonderful," she said. "I've seen three different productions of *The King and I,* and your interpretation of Tuptim was great."

"I see you two have gotten together."

Tom Lynch had joined them. "Alice, I'm sorry," he apologized. "I got waylaid. I didn't mean to leave you on your own so long."

"Don't worry, it worked out fine," she told him. *You don't know how fine,* she thought.

"Tom, I wanted a chance to visit with you," his cousin said. "I've had enough of this party. Let's take off and have a cup of coffee somewhere." Kate Knowles smiled at Lacey. "Your friend was just telling me how good I was. I want to hear more."

Lacey glanced at her watch. It was one-thirty. Not wanting to stay up all night, she suggested having coffee at her place. On the drive back into Minneapolis, she insisted that Kate sit in the front seat with Tom. She was sure they wouldn't stay long in the apartment, and at least they were getting some of the family gossip out of the way.

How can I bring up Heather Landi's name without seeming too abrupt? she wondered, reminding herself that Kate was only in town for a week.

"I made these cookies this morning," Lacey said as she set a plate on the coffee table. "Try them at your own risk. I haven't baked since high school."

After she poured the coffee, she tried to steer the conversation around so that she could introduce Heather's name. In her journal, Heather had written about meeting Tom Lynch after a performance. But if I say that I saw the show, chances are I would have remembered if I'd seen Kate in it, Lacey thought. She said, "I went down to New York about a year and a half ago and saw a revival of *The Boy Friend.* I read in your bio in the program tonight that you were in it, but I'm sure I'd remember if I'd seen you."

"You must have gone the week I was out with the flu," Kate said. "Those were the only performances I missed."

Lacey tried to sound offhand. "I do remember that there was a young actress with a really fine voice in the lead. I'm trying to think of her name."

"Heather Landi," Kate Knowles said promptly, turning to her cousin. "Tom, you remember her. She had a crush on you. Heather was killed in a car accident," she said, shaking her head. "It was such a damn shame."

"What happened?" Lacey asked.

"Oh, she was driving home from a ski lodge in Stowe and went off the road. Her mother, poor thing, couldn't accept it. She came around to the theater, talking to all of us, searching for some reason behind the accident. She said that Heather had been upset about something shortly before that weekend and wanted to know if we had any idea what it was about."

"Did you?" Tom asked.

Kate Knowles shrugged. "I told her that I had noticed that Heather was terribly quiet the last week before she died, and I agreed that she *was* worried about something. I suggested that Heather may not have been concentrating on driving when she went into the skid."

It's a dead end, Lacey thought. Kate doesn't know anything I don't already know.

Kate Knowles put down her coffee cup. "That was great, Alice, but it's very late, and I've got to be on my way." She stood, then turned back to Lacey. "It's funny that Heather Landi's name should come up; I'd just been thinking about her. A letter her mother had written to me, asking that I try again to remember anything I could that might give her a reason for Heather's behavior that weekend, finally caught up with me. It had been forwarded to two other cities before reaching me here." She paused, then shook her head. "There is one thing I might write her about, although it's probably not significant. A guy I've dated some—Bill Merrill, you met him, Tom— knew Heather too. Her name came up, and he mentioned that he had seen her the afternoon before she died, in the après-ski bar at the lodge. Bill had gone there with a bunch of guys, including a jerk named Rick Parker who's in real estate in New York and apparently had pulled something on Heather when she first came to the city. Bill said that when Heather spotted Parker she practically ran out of the lodge. It's probably nothing, but Heather's mom is so anxious for any information about that weekend that she'd surely want to know. I think I'll write her first thing tomorrow."

The sound of Lacey's coffee cup shattering on the floor broke the trancelike state she had entered when she heard Kate's mention of Isabelle's letter and then of Rick Parker's name. Quickly covering her confusion, and refusing their help, she busied herself with cleaning up the mess while calling out her good nights to Kate and Tom as they headed for the door.

Alone in the kitchen, Lacey pressed her back against the wall, willing herself to be calm, resisting the urge to call out to Kate not to bother with the letter to Isabelle Waring, since it was too late for it to matter to her.

23

After nearly four months of investigation, U.S. Attorney Gary Baldwin was no nearer to locating Sandy Savarano than he had been when he had still believed Savarano was buried in Woodlawn Cemetery.

His staff had painstakingly studied Heather Landi's journal, and had tracked down the people named in it. It was a process that Isabelle Waring also had attempted, Baldwin thought, as he once again studied the police artist's rendering of Sandy Savarano's face as drawn from Lacey Farrell's description of him.

The artist had attached a note to the drawing: "Witness does not appear to have a good eye for noticing the kind of detail that would make the suspect identifiable."

They had tried talking to the doorman in the building where the murder took place, but he remembered virtually nothing of the killer. He said he saw too many people come and go there, and besides, he was about to retire.

So that leaves me with only Lacey Farrell to personally finger Savarano, Baldwin thought bitterly. If anything happens to her, there's no case. Sure, we got his fingerprint off Farrell's door after her apartment was burglarized, but we can't even prove he went inside. Farrell's the only one who can tie him to Isabelle Waring's murder. Without her to ID him, forget it, he told himself.

The only useful information his undercover agents had been able to glean about the killer was that before his staged death, Savarano's claustrophobia apparently had become acute. One agent was told: "Sandy had nightmares about cell doors clanging closed behind him."

So what had brought him out of retirement? Baldwin wondered. Big bucks? A favor he had to repay? Maybe both. And throw in the thrill of the hunt, of course. Savarano was a vicious predator.

Part of it could have been simple boredom. Retirement might have been too tame for him.

Baldwin knew Savarano's rap sheet by heart. "Forty-two years old, a suspect in a dozen murders, but hasn't seen the inside of a prison since he was a kid in reform school! A smart guy, as well as a born killer.

If I were Savarano, Baldwin thought, my one purpose in life right now would be to find Lacey Farrell and make sure she never gets the chance to finger me.

He shook his head, and his forehead creased with concern. The witness protection program wasn't foolproof; he knew that. People got careless. When they called home, they usually said something on the phone that gave away their hiding place, or they started writing letters. One mobster who was put in the program after cooperating with the government was dumb enough to send a birthday card to an old girlfriend. He was shot to death a week later.

Gary Baldwin had an uneasy feeling about Lacey Farrell. Her profile made her sound like someone who could find it difficult to be alone for a long stretch of time. Plus she seemed to be exceptionally trusting, a trait that could get her in real trouble. He shook his head. Well, there was nothing he could do about it except to send word to her through channels not to let her guard down, even for a minute.

24

Mona Farrell drove into Manhattan for what had become her standing Saturday dinner date with Alex Carbine. She always looked forward to the evening with him, even though he left the table frequently to greet his regular customers and the occasional celebrities who came to his restaurant.

"It's fun," she assured him. "And I really don't mind. Don't forget I was married to a musician. You don't know how many Broadway shows I sat through alone because Jack was in the orchestra pit!"

Jack would have liked Alex, Mona thought as she exited the George Washington Bridge and turned south onto the West Side Highway. Jack had been quick-witted and great fun, and quite gregarious. Alex was a much quieter man, but in him it was an attractive quality.

Mona smiled as she thought of the flowers that Alex had sent her earlier. The card read simply, "May they brighten your day. Yours, Alex."

He knew that the weekly phone call from Lacey tore her heart out. He understood how painful the whole experience was for her, and the flowers were Alex's way of saying it.

She had confided to him that Lacey had told her where she was living. "But I haven't even told Kit," she explained. "Kit would be hurt if she thought I didn't trust her."

It's funny, Mona thought, as the traffic on the West Side Highway slowed to a crawl because of a blocked right lane, things have always gone smoothly for Kit, but not for Lacey. Kit met Jay when she was at Boston College and he was in graduate school at Tufts. They fell in love, married, and now had three wonderful kids and a lovely home. Jay might be pontifical and occasionally pompous, but he certainly was a good husband and father. Just the other day, he had surprised Kit with an expensive gold-leaf necklace she had admired in the window of Groom's Jewelry in Ridgewood.

Kit said that Jay had told her business suddenly

had become very good again. I'm glad, Mona thought. She had been worried for a while that things were not going well. Certainly in the fall it was obvious that he had a lot on his mind.

Lacey *deserves* happiness, Mona told herself. Now's the time for her to meet the right person and get married and start a family, and I'm sure she's ready. Instead she's alone in a strange city and she has to stay there and pretend to be someone else because her life is in danger.

She reached the parking lot on West Forty-sixth Street at seven-thirty. Alex didn't expect her at the restaurant until eight, which meant she would have time to do something that had occurred to her earlier.

A newsstand in Times Square carried out-of-town newspapers—she would see if they had any from Minneapolis. It would make her feel closer to Lacey if she became familiar with the city, and there would be some comfort in just knowing that Lacey could be reading the paper as well.

The night was cold but clear, and she enjoyed the five-block walk to Times Square. How often we were here when Jack was alive, she thought.

We'd get together with friends after a show. Kit was never as interested in the theater as Lacey. She was like Jack—in love with Broadway. She must be missing it terribly.

At the newsstand she found a copy of the *Minneapolis Star Tribune*. Lacey may have read this same edition this morning, she thought. Even touching the paper made Lacey seem closer.

"Would you like a bag, lady?"

"Oh, yes, please." Mona fished in her purse for her wallet as the vendor folded the paper and put it in a plastic bag.

When Mona reached the restaurant, there was a line at the checkroom. Seeing that Alex was already at their table, she hurried over to him. "Sorry, I guess I'm late," she said.

He got up and kissed her cheek. "You're not late, but your face is cold. Did you walk from New Jersey?"

"No. I was early and decided to pick up a newspaper."

Carlos, their usual waiter, was hovering nearby. "Mrs. Farrell, let me take your coat. Do you want to check your package?"

"Why not keep that?" Alex suggested. He took the bag from her and put it on the empty chair at their table.

It was, as always, a pleasant evening. By the time they were sipping espresso, Alex Carbine's hand was covering hers.

"Not too busy a night for you," Mona said teasingly. "You've only been up and down about ten times."

"I thought that might be why you bought a newspaper."

"Not at all, although I did glance at the head-lines." Mona reached for her purse. "My turn to get up. I'll be right back."

Alex saw her to her car at eleven-thirty. At one o'clock the restaurant closed and the staff went home.

At ten of twelve a phone call was made. The message was simple. "Tell Sandy it looks like she's in Minneapolis."

25

What had happened between Heather Landi and Rick Parker?

Lacey was stunned to learn they had known each other. After Tom Lynch and Kate Knowles had left Friday night, she had been unable to sleep and had sat up for hours, trying to make sense of it all. Over the weekend her mind had constantly replayed the night of Isabelle Waring's death. What had Rick been thinking as he sat there, listening to her being quizzed about how well she had known Isabelle, and if she had ever known Heather? Why hadn't he *said* something?

According to what Kate had been told, on the last day of her life, Heather had been visibly upset when she saw Rick at the skiing lodge in Stowe.

Kate had referred to Rick as a "jerk who's in real estate in New York" and had said that he "had pulled something on Heather when she came to the city."

Lacey remembered that, in her journal, Heather alluded to an unpleasant incident that happened when she was looking for an apartment on the West Side. Could that have involved Rick? Lacey wondered.

Before being transferred to Madison Avenue, Rick had spent five years in the West Side office of Parker and Parker. He changed offices about three years ago.

Which means, Lacey thought, that he was working the West Side at precisely the time Heather Landi came to New York and was apartment hunting. Did she go to Parker and Parker and meet Rick? And if she did, what had happened between them?

Lacey shook her head in anger. Could Rick be involved in *all* of this mess? she wondered. Am I stuck here because of him?

Rick was the one who gave me Curtis Caldwell's name as a potential buyer for Isabelle's apartment, she reminded herself. It was because of *him* that I brought Caldwell there. If Rick had known Caldwell somehow, then maybe the police would be able to track Caldwell down through Rick. And if they arrest Caldwell, then I'll be able to go home.

Lacey stood up and began to pace the room excitedly. This could be part of what Isabelle had seen in the journal. She had to get this information to Gary Baldwin at the U.S. Attorney's office.

Lacey's fingers itched to pick up the phone and call him, but direct contact was absolutely forbidden. She would have to leave a message for George Svenson to call her, then either write or talk to Baldwin through secure channels.

I have to talk to Kate again, Lacey thought. I have to find out more about Bill Merrill, the boyfriend who had mentioned Heather's reaction to Rick Parker, and I have to find out where he lives. Baldwin will want to talk to him, I'm sure. He can place Rick Parker in Stowe only hours before Heather died.

Kate had mentioned that the cast was staying at the Radisson Plaza Hotel for the week. Lacey glanced at her watch. It was ten-thirty. Even if Kate was a late sleeper, like most show-business people, she probably would be awake by now.

A still slightly sleepy voice answered the phone, but when she realized who was calling,

Kate livened up and seemed pleased enough at Lacey's suggestion that they get together for lunch the next day. "Maybe we should try to get Tom to join us, Kate," she suggested. "You know how nice he is. He'll take us to a good restaurant and pay the tab to boot." Then laughing, she added, "Forget it. I just realized, his program goes on at noon."

Just as well, Lacey thought. No doubt Tom would pick up on the fact that she was pumping Kate for informaton. But he *is* nice, she thought, remembering how concerned he had been that he wasn't paying her enough attention at the party.

She arranged to meet Kate at the Radisson at twelve-thirty the next day. As she replaced the receiver, she felt a sudden surge of hope. It's almost like seeing the first ray of sunshine after a long, terrible storm, she decided, as she walked to the window and pulled back the curtain to look out.

It was a perfect Midwestern winter's day. The outdoor temperature was only twenty-eight degrees, but the sun was shining warmly in a cloudless sky. There appeared to be no wind, and Lacey could see that the sidewalks were clear of snow.

Until today, she had been too nervous to go for a real run, afraid that she would look over her shoulder and see Caldwell behind her, his pale, icy eyes fixed on her. But suddenly, feeling as though there was the possibility of some sort of breakthrough in the case, she decided that she had to *try,* at least, to resume some kind of normal life.

When she had packed to move, Lacey had brought her cold-weather jogging clothes: a warm-up suit, jacket, mittens, hat, scarf. She quickly put them on and headed to the door. Just as she was turning the knob, the phone rang. Her first instinct was to let it go, but then she decided to pick it up.

"Ms. Carroll, you don't know me," a crisp voice told her. "I'm Millicent Royce. I hear you may be looking for a job in the real estate field. Wendell Woods talked to me about you this morning."

"I *am* looking, or rather, just about to start looking," Lacey said hopefully.

"Wendell was quite impressed with you and suggested we should meet. The office is in Edina."

Edina was fifteen minutes away. "I know where that is."

"Good. Take down the address. Are you free this afternoon by any chance?"

When Lacey left the apartment and jogged down the street, it was with the sense that her luck might be changing at last. If Millicent Royce *did* hire her, it would mean she would have something to do to fill her days until she could go home.

After all, she thought wryly, as Ms. Royce just told me, real estate can be a very *exciting* career. I bet she doesn't know the half of it!

Tom Lynch's four-hour program was a mixture of news, interviews, and offbeat humor. It was broadcast each weekday from noon till four o'clock, and his guests ran the spectrum from political figures, authors, and visiting celebrities to local VIPs.

He spent most mornings before the show in his office at the station, roaming the Internet in search of items of interest, or poring over newspapers and periodicals from all over the country, looking for unusual subjects to discuss.

On the Monday morning following the opening of *The King and I,* he was not comfortable with the fact that he had been thinking about Alice

Carroll all weekend. Several times he had been tempted to call her, but he always replaced the receiver before the connection was made.

He reminded himself that he would almost certainly see her at the gym during the week; he could just suggest casually that they go out for dinner or to a movie. Phoning and planning a date might potentially take on undue significance, and then it would be uncomfortable if he didn't ask her out again, or if she refused, and they still kept running into each other.

He knew his concern on that subject was a standing joke with his friends. As one of them had told him recently, "Tom, you're a nice guy, but if you don't call some girl again, trust me, she'll get through the day."

Remembering that conversation, Tom silently acknowledged that if he had a few dates with Alice Carroll and then didn't call her again, she clearly would get through the day very well without him.

There was something so quietly contained about her, he thought, as he watched the clock and realized he was an hour away from air time. She didn't talk much about herself, and something in her told him that she didn't invite questions. That first afternoon, when they had coffee together in the gym, she hadn't seemed happy when he teased her about moving to Minneapolis. Then Friday evening he had sensed that when the overture to *The King and I* began, she had been close to tears.

Some girls have a fit if their date doesn't give them full attention at a party. But it hadn't bothered Alice a bit that he had left her on her own when people came up to talk to him.

The clothes she had worn to the opening were expensive. A blind man could see that.

He had overheard her tell Kate that she had seen *The King and I* three times. And she had talked knowledgeably with Kate about the revival of *The Boy Friend*.

Expensive outfits. Trips in and out of New York from Hartford to go to the theater. These generally weren't the kinds of things one was able to do on the salary of a clerk in a doctor's office.

Tom shrugged and reached for the phone. It was no use. His questions were a sign of his interest in her, and the fact was, he couldn't stop thinking of her. He was going to call Alice and ask her if she wanted to have dinner tonight. He wanted to see her. He reached for the phone, dialed, and waited. After four rings the answering machine clicked on. Her voice, low and pleasing, said: "You've reached 555-1247. Please leave a message and I'll get back to you."

Tom hesitated, then hung up, deciding to call back later. He felt more uncomfortable than ever over the fact that he was so intensely disappointed at not having reached her.

26

On Monday morning Sandy Savarano took Northwest flight 1703 from La Guardia Airport in New York to Minneapolis–St. Paul International Airport in Minneapolis.

He rode first class, as he had on the flight from Costa Rica, where he now lived. He was known to his neighbors there as Charles Austin, a well-to-do U.S. businessman who had sold his company two years ago at age forty and retired to the tropical good life.

His twenty-four-year-old wife had driven him to the airport in Costa Rica and made him promise not to stay away too long. "You're supposed to be retired now," she had said, pouting lovingly as she kissed him good-bye.

"That doesn't mean that I turn down found money," he had said.

It was the same answer he had given her about the several other jobs he had undertaken since he staged his death two years ago.

"Lovely day to fly."

The voice was that of a young woman in her late twenties who was seated next to him. In a way, she reminded him very slightly of Lacey Farrell. But then, Farrell was on his mind, since she was the reason he was on his way to Minneapolis now. The only person in the world who can finger me for a murder, he thought. She doesn't deserve to live. And she won't for long.

"Yes, it is," he agreed shortly.

He saw the look of interest in the young woman's eyes and was amused. Women actually found him attractive. Dr. Ivan Yenkel, a Russian immigrant who had given him this new face two years ago, had been a genius, no doubt about it. His remolded nose was thinner; the bump caused by the break he had suffered in reform school was gone. The heavy chin was sculpted, his ears smaller and flat against his head. Formerly heavy eyebrows were thinned and spaced farther apart. Yenkel had fixed his drooping eyelids and removed the circles under his eyes.

His dark brown hair was now the color of sand, a whimsy he had chosen in honor of his nickname, Sandy. Pale blue contact lenses completed the transformation.

"You look fabulous, Sandy," Yenkel had boasted when the last bandage came off. "No one would ever recognize you."

"No one ever will."

Sandy always got a thrill, remembering the look of astonishment in Yenkel's eyes as he died.

I don't intend to go through it again, Sandy thought, as with a dismissive smile to his seatmate he pointedly picked up a magazine and opened it.

Pretending to read, he reviewed his game plan. He had a two-week reservation at the Radisson Plaza Hotel under the name James Burgess. If he hadn't found Farrell by then, he would move to another hotel. No use arousing curiosity by staying too long.

He had been supplied with some suggestions as to where he might find her. She regularly used a health club in New York. It made sense to assume she would do the same thing in Minneapolis, so he would make the rounds of health clubs there. People didn't change their habits.

She was a theater buff. Well, the Orpheum in

Minneapolis had touring shows virtually every week, and the Tyrone Guthrie Theater would be another place to look.

Her only job had been in real estate. If she was working, the odds were she would be in a real estate agency.

Savarano had located and eliminated two other witnesses who had been in the witness protection program. He knew the government did not give false references—most of the people in the program began jobs in small outfits where they had gotten to know someone and had been hired on faith.

The flight attendant was making her announcement: "We are beginning our descent into the Twin Cities . . . place your seats in the upright position . . . fasten your seat belts . . ."

Sandy Savarano began to anticipate the look he would see in Lacey Farrell's eyes when he shot her.

27

Royce Realty was located at Fiftieth Street and France Avenue South in Edina. Before leaving the apartment, Lacey studied the map, trying to determine the best way to drive there. Her mother had once remarked that it was a wonder how Lacey could have such good practical sense and such a lousy sense of direction. She surely was right about the last part, Lacey thought, shaking her head. New York had been a snap—she and the client would hail a cab, and it took them wherever they wanted. A sprawling city like Minneapolis, though, with so many scattered residential areas, was another matter. How will I ever take people around to see properties if I get lost every five minutes? she wondered.

Following the map carefully, however, she got to the office having made only one wrong turn. She parked her car, then stood for a moment in front of the entrance to Royce Realty, looking in through the wide glass door.

She could see that the agency office was small, but attractive. The reception room had oak-paneled walls that were covered with pictures of houses, a cheerful red-and-blue checked carpet, a standard desk, and comfortable-looking leather chairs. There was a short corridor leading off the reception area to an office. Through the open door she could see a woman working at a desk.

Here goes nothing, she thought, taking a deep breath. If I get through this scene successfully, I'll be ready to make my Broadway debut soon. That is, of course, if I ever get back to New York. As she opened the door to the agency, chimes signaled her arrival. The woman looked up, then came out to meet her.

"I'm Millicent Royce," she said as she extended her hand, "and you must be Alice Carroll."

Lacey liked her immediately. She was a handsome woman of about seventy whose ample girth was clothed in a well-tailored brown knit suit, and whose clear unlined complexion was devoid of makeup. Her shiny gray-white hair was swept back into a bun, a hairstyle that reminded Lacey of her grandmother.

Her smile was welcoming, but as Lacey sat down she could see that Millicent Royce's keen blue eyes were studying her intently. She was glad she had decided to wear the maroon jacket and gray slacks. They were conservative, but attractive—no-nonsense, but with style. Besides, she had always believed the outfit brought her luck on sales calls. Now maybe it would help her get a job.

Millicent Royce waved her to a chair and sat down opposite her. "It's turning out to be a terribly busy day," she said apologetically, "so I don't have much time. Tell me about yourself, Alice."

Lacey felt as though she were in an interrogation room with a spotlight shining on her. Millicent Royce's eyes did not leave Lacey's face as she answered. "Let's see. I just turned thirty. I'm healthy. My life has changed a lot in the last year."

God knows that's true, Lacey thought.

"I'm from Hartford, Connecticut, and after finishing college I worked for eight years for a doctor who retired."

"What kind of work?" Mrs. Royce asked.

"Receptionist, general office, some billing, submitting the medical forms."

"Then you're experienced with a computer?"

"Yes, I am." She watched as the older woman's eyes glanced at the computer on the reception room desk. There was a stack of papers beside it.

"This job entails answering the phones, keeping listings up to date, preparing flyers of new listings, calling potential buyers when a new listing comes in, helping with an open house. No actual selling. That's my job. But I've got to ask: What makes you think you'd like real estate?"

Because I love matching people to places, Lacey thought. *I love guessing right and seeing someone's eyes light up when I take that person into a house or apartment and know that it's exactly what he or she wants. I love the wheeling and dealing that goes into settling on a price.*

Dismissing these thoughts, she said instead, "I know I don't want to work in a doctor's office anymore, and I've always been intrigued by the idea of your business."

"I see. Well, let me call your retired doctor and talk to him, and if he vouches for you—as I'm sure he will—then I say, let's give it a try. Do you have his phone number?"

"No. He changed it and made it unlisted. He was adamant about not wanting to be contacted by his former patients."

Lacey could tell from the slight frown on Millicent Royce's face that this obviously sharp lady was finding her answers too evasive.

She remembered what George Svenson had told her: "Offer to work free for a couple of weeks, or even a month."

"I have a suggestion," Lacey said. "Don't pay me anything for a month. After that, if you're happy with me, you'll hire me. Or if you feel I have no aptitude for the work, you'll tell me to forget it."

She met Millicent Royce's steady gaze without flinching. "You won't regret it," she said quietly.

Mrs. Royce shrugged her shoulders. "In Minnesota, the Land of Lakes, that's known as an offer I can't refuse."

28

"Why wasn't Mr. Landi informed about this earlier?" Steve Abbott asked quietly.

It was Monday afternoon. Abbott had insisted on accompanying Jimmy to a meeting with Detectives Sloane and Mars in the 19th Precinct station house.

"I want to know what's going on!" Jimmy had said to him that morning, the anger in his voice reflected in his face. "Something's up. The cops have to know where Lacey Farrell is. She can't have just disappeared. She's a witness to a murder!"

"Did you call them?" Steve had asked.

"You bet I did. But I ask about her and they just tell me to have Parker and Parker assign another agent to handle the sale of the apartment. That's not what I called about. Do they think that's what's bugging me, that this is about money? That's nuts! I told them I was coming to see them, and *I wanted answers."*

Abbott knew that painting Heather out of the restaurant murals had if anything increased Jimmy Landi's anger and depression. "I'm going with you," he had insisted.

When they had arrived, Detectives Sloane and Mars brought them into the interrogation room off the squad room. They had admitted reluctantly that Lacey Farrell had been placed in the federal witness protection program because an attempt had been made on her life.

"I asked why Mr. Landi hadn't been informed earlier about what happened to Ms. Farrell," Abbott repeated. "I want an answer."

Sloane reached for a cigarette. "Mr. Abbott, I have assured Mr. Landi that the investigation is continuing, and it is. We're not going to rest until we find and prosecute Isabelle Waring's murderer."

"You gave me a cock-and-bull story about some guy whose racket is getting into expensive apartments as a potential buyer and then coming back to burglarize them," Jimmy said, his anger exploding once again. "At that point you told me you thought Isabelle's death was just a matter of having been at the wrong place at the wrong time. Now you're telling me that the Farrell woman is in the witness protection program, *and* you're admitting that Heather's journal was stolen from under your noses right here in this station. Don't play games with me. This was no random killing, and you've known it from day one."

Eddie Sloane saw the anger and disgust that flared in Jimmy Landi's eyes. I don't blame him, the detective thought. His ex-wife is dead; we lose something intended for him that may be crucial evidence; the woman who brought the killer into his ex-wife's apartment has disappeared. I sympathize because I know how *I'd* feel.

For both detectives it had been a lousy four months since that October evening when the 911 call from 3 East Seventieth had been received in the station house. As the case developed, Eddie was grateful that the district attorney had gone toe to toe with U.S. Attorney Baldwin's office. The DA had been adamant that the NYPD was not signing off on this one.

"A murder occurred in the 19th Precinct," he had told Baldwin, "and like it or not, we're in it for the duration. We'll share information with you, of course, but you've got to share it with us. When Savarano is collared, we'll cooperate in a plea bargain if you can cut a deal with him. But we'll cooperate only, and I repeat *only,* if you don't try to upstage us. We have a very real interest in this case, and we intend to be involved."

"It wasn't a cock-and-bull story, Mr. Landi," Nick Mars said heatedly. "We want to find Mrs. Waring's killer just as much as you do. But if Ms. Farrell hadn't taken that journal from Isabelle Waring's apartment, apparently with the idea of giving it to you, we might be a lot further along in this investigation."

"But I believe that it was after it arrived here that this journal was stolen," Steve Abbott said, his voice dangerously quiet. "And are you now suggesting that Ms. Farrell may have tampered with the journal?"

"We don't think she did, but we can't be sure," Sloane admitted.

"Be honest with us, Detective. You can't be sure of very much except that you botched this investigation," Abbott snapped, his anger now evident. "Come on, Jimmy. I think it's time we hire our own investigator. With the police in charge, I don't think we'll ever find out what's going on."

"That's what I should have done the minute I

got the call about Isabelle!" Jimmy Landi said, getting to his feet. "I want the copy of my daughter's journal I gave you before you lose that one too."

"We ran off extras," Sloane said calmly. "Nick, get the set Mr. Landi gave us."

"Right away, Eddie."

While they waited, Sloane said, "Mr. Landi, you told us very specifically that you read the journal before you gave it to us."

Jimmy Landi's eyes darkened. "I did."

"You told us that you read the journal *carefully*. Thinking back, would you say that's true?"

"What's carefully?" Jimmy asked rather irritably. "I looked through it."

"Look, Mr. Landi," Sloane said, "I can only imagine how difficult all this is for you, but I'm going to ask you to read it carefully now. We've gone through it as thoroughly as we know how, and except for a couple of ambiguous references in the early pages about something involving an incident that happened on the West Side, we can't find anything even *potentially* helpful. But the fact is that Mrs. Waring told Lacey Farrell that she'd found something in those pages that might help prove your daughter's death was not an accident—"

"Isabelle would have found something suspicious in the Baltimore catechism," Jimmy said, shaking his head.

They sat in silence until Nick Mars returned to the interrogation room with a manila envelope which he held out to Landi.

Jimmy yanked it from him and opened the envelope. Pulling out the contents, he glanced through them, then stopped at the last page. He read it, then glared at Mars. "What are you trying to pull now?" he asked.

Sloane had the sickening feeling that he was about to hear something he didn't want to know.

"I can tell you right now that there were more pages than this," Landi said. "The last couple of pages in the set I gave you weren't written on lined paper. I remember because they were all messed up. The originals of those pages must have had bloodstains . . . I couldn't stand the sight of them. So where are they? Did you lose those too?"

29

Upon arrival at the Minneapolis–St. Paul airport, Sandy Savarano went directly from the plane to the baggage area where he picked up his heavy black suitcase. Then he found a men's room and locked himself in a stall. There, he placed the suitcase across the toilet and opened it.

He took out a hand mirror and a zippered case containing a gray wig, thick gray eyebrows, and round glasses with a tortoiseshell frame.

He removed his contact lenses, revealing his charcoal brown eyes, then with deft movements placed the wig on his head, combed it so that it covered part of his forehead, pasted on the eyebrows, and put on the glasses.

With a cosmetic pencil he added age spots to

his forehead and the backs of his hands. Reaching into the sides of the suitcase he took out orthopedic oxfords and exchanged them for the Gucci loafers he had been wearing.

Finally he unpacked a bulky tweed overcoat with heavily padded shoulders, placing in the bag the Burberry he had worn getting off the plane.

The man who left the stall looked twenty years older and totally different from the man who had entered it.

Sandy next went to the car rental desk where a car had been reserved for him in the name of James Burgess of Philadelphia. He opened his wallet and took out a driver's license and a credit card. The license was a clever fake; the credit card was legitimate, an account having been set up for him using the Burgess name.

Cold, bracing air greeted him as he exited the terminal and joined a group of people waiting at the curb for the jitney to take them to the car rental area. While he waited he studied the map the clerk had marked for him and began to memorize the routes that led in and out of the city and to estimate the length of time each should require. He liked to plan everything out carefully. No surprises—that was his motto. Which made the unexpected arrival of that Farrell woman at Isabelle Waring's apartment all the more irritating. He had been surprised and had made a mistake by letting her get away.

He knew that his attention to detail was the main reason he was still a free man, while so many of his fellow graduates of reform school were off serving long prison terms. The very thought made him shiver.

The clanging of a cell door . . . Waking up and knowing that he was trapped there, that it would never be any different . . . Feeling the walls and ceiling close in on him, squeezing him, suffocating him . . .

Underneath the strands of hair he had so carefully combed over his forehead, Sandy could feel beads of sweat forming. It won't happen to me, he promised himself. I'd rather die first.

The jitney was approaching. Impatiently, he raised his arm to be sure the vehicle stopped. He was anxious to get started, anxious to begin the task of finding Lacey Farrell. As long as she was alive, she remained a constant threat to his freedom.

As the jitney stopped to admit him, he felt something slam against the back of his legs. He spun around and found himself facing the young woman who had been his seatmate on the plane. Her suitcase had toppled over against him.

Their eyes met, and he took a deep breath. They were standing only inches apart, yet there was no trace of recognition in her expression. Her smile was apologetic. "I'm so sorry," she said.

The jitney door was opening. Savarano got on, knowing that this clumsy woman had just confirmed that with his disguise he would be able to get close to Farrell without fear of recognition. This time she would have no chance to escape him. That was a mistake he would not repeat.

30

When Millicent Royce agreed to try her out on a volunteer basis, Lacey suggested that she spend the rest of the afternoon familiarizing herself with the files in the computer and going through the mail that was stacked on the reception desk.

After four months away from an office, it was pure pleasure to be at a desk, going through listings, familiarizing herself with the price range of homes in the area covered by the agency.

At three o'clock, Mrs. Royce took a potential buyer to see a condominium and asked Lacey to cover the phone.

The first call was a near disaster. She answered, "Royce Realty, Lace—"

She slammed down the receiver and stared at

the phone. She had been about to give her real name.

A moment later the phone began to ring again.

She had to pick it up. It was probably the same person. What could she say?

The voice on the other end sounded slightly irritated. "I guess we got cut off," Lacey said lamely.

For the next hour the phone continued to ring, and Lacey carefully managed each call. It was only later, when she was jotting down the message that the dentist's office called to confirm Millicent Royce's appointment for the following week, that she realized being back in her own milieu could be a trap. As a precaution she went through all the messages she had taken. A woman had phoned to say that her husband was being transferred to Minneapolis and that a friend had suggested that she call the Royce agency to help her find a house.

Lacey had asked the usual real estate broker questions: price range? how many bedrooms? any limits on the age of a house? was school district a factor? would purchase be contingent on sale of present home? She had even put the answers in real estate shorthand: "min. 4BR/3b./fpl/cen air/."

I was proud of myself, she thought as she copied the woman's name and phone number on a different sheet of paper, careful to disguise her working knowledge of the business. At the end she added the message, "good potential prospect due to immediate relocation." Maybe even that sounded too knowledgeable, she thought, but let it stand when she looked up to see that Millicent Royce was on her way in.

Mrs. Royce looked tired and was obviously pleased to get the messages and to see how efficiently Lacey had separated the mail for her. It was nearly five o'clock. "I *will* see you in the morning, Alice?" There was a hopeful note in her voice.

"Absolutely," Lacey told her. "But I do have a lunch date I can't break."

As she drove back into the city, Lacey felt a letdown setting in. As usual, she had no plans for the evening, and the thought of going back to the apartment and preparing another solitary meal was suddenly repugnant to her.

I'll go to the gym and work out for a while, she decided. At least between that exercise and the run this morning, I may be tired enough to sleep.

When she got to the gym, Ruth Wilcox beckoned her over. "Guess what?" she said, her tone conspiratorial. "Tom Lynch was really disappointed when you didn't show up this afternoon. He even came over and asked if you'd been here earlier. Alice, I think he likes you."

If he does, he likes someone who doesn't really exist, Lacey thought with a trace of bitterness. She stayed in the gym for only a half hour, then drove home. The answering machine was blinking. Tom had phoned at four-thirty. "Thought I might see you at the gym, Alice. I enjoyed Friday night. If you pick this up by seven and feel like having dinner tonight, give me a call. My number is—"

Lacey pushed the STOP button on the machine and erased the message without waiting to hear Tom's phone number. It was easier to do that than to spend another evening lying to someone who in different circumstances she would have enjoyed dating.

She fixed herself a BLT on toast for dinner. Comfort food, she thought.

Then she remembered—this was what I was eating the night before Isabelle Waring died. Isabelle phoned, and I didn't pick up. I was tired and didn't want to talk to her.

Lacey remembered that in the message she had left on the answering machine, Isabelle said she had found Heather's journal and declared that something in it made her think she might have proof that Heather's death hadn't been an accident.

But the next morning, when she phoned me at the office, she wouldn't talk about it, Lacey recalled. Then she stayed in the library reading the journal when I brought Curtis Caldwell in. And a few hours later she was dead.

Mental images suddenly threatened to close her throat as she finished the last bite of the sandwich: Isabelle in the library, weeping as she read Heather's journal. Isabelle with her last breath begging Lacey to give that journal to Heather's father.

What is it that's been bothering me? Lacey asked herself. It was something about the library that last afternoon, something I noticed when I spoke to Isabelle in there. What *was* it? She mentally revisited that afternoon, struggling to make the elusive image come into focus.

Finally she gave up. She simply couldn't remember.

Let it go for now, Lacey told herself. Later I'll try to put my mind in the search-and-retrieve mode. After all, the mind *is* a computer, isn't it?

That night in her dreams she had vague visions of Isabelle holding a green pen and weeping as she read Heather's journal in the last hours of her life.

31

After checking into the Radisson Plaza Hotel, half a block from the Nicollet Mall, Sandy Savarano spent the rest of his first day in Minneapolis poring over the phone book and making a list of the health clubs and gyms in the metropolitan area.

He made a second list of all the real estate agencies, putting in a separate column the ones whose ads indicated they were geared to commercial sales. He knew that Lacey Farrell would have to try to find a job without benefit of references, and the odds were those agencies would be unwilling to hire anyone without some kind of background check. He would start calling the others tomorrow.

His plan was simple. He would just say that he was conducting an informal survey for the National Association of Realtors because there was growing evidence that adults in the twenty-five to thirty-five age group were not entering the real estate field. The survey would ask two questions: Had the agency hired anyone in that age group as an agent, secretary, or receptionist in the last six months, and if so, were they a male or female?

He'd need another plan for checking out health clubs and gyms. Those survey questions wouldn't work there, since most of the people who joined them were in that age group. It meant that locating Farrell through the clubs would be riskier.

He would have to actually go to them, pretend he was interested in joining, then flash Farrell's picture. It was an old photo, cut from her college yearbook, but it still looked like her. He would claim that she was his daughter and had left home after a family misunderstanding. He was trying to find her because her mother was sick with worry about her.

Checking out the health clubs would be a long shot, but fortunately there were not too many in the metro area, so it wouldn't take him too long.

At five of ten, Sandy was ready to go out for a

walk. The mall was dark now, the windows of the toney stores no longer glittering.

Sandy knew that the Mississippi River was within walking distance. He turned right and headed in that direction, a solitary figure who to a casual viewer would appear to be a man in his sixties who probably ought not to be walking alone at night.

A casual observer would have no idea how misdirected that concern was, since on that walk, Sandy Savarano began to experience the curious thrill that came to him whenever he began to stalk a victim and sensed that he was approaching the habitat of the hunted.

32

On Tuesday morning, Lacey was waiting in front of Royce Realty when Millicent Royce arrived at nine o'clock.

"The pay isn't *that* good," Millicent Royce said with a laugh.

"It's what we agreed on," Lacey said. "And I can tell I'll like the job."

Mrs. Royce unlocked and opened the door. The warmth of the interior greeted them. "A Minnesota chill in the air," Royce said. "First things first, I'll put the coffee on. How do you like yours?"

"Black, please."

"Regina, my assistant who just left to have a baby, used two heaping teaspoonsful of sugar and never gained an ounce. I told her it was serious cause for simple hatred."

Lacey thought of Janey Boyd, a secretary at Parker and Parker, who always seemed to be munching a cookie or a chocolate bar but remained a size six. "There was a girl like that at—" She stopped herself. "At the doctor's office," she finished, then quickly added. "She didn't stay long. Just as well. She was setting a bad example."

Suppose Millicent Royce had picked up on that and suggested calling a coworker for a personal reference. Be careful, Lacey told herself, *be careful.*

The first phone call of the day came right then and was a welcome interruption.

At twelve Lacey left for the luncheon date with Kate Knowles. "I'll be back by two," she promised, "and after this, I'll have a sandwich at the desk so if you want to make outside appointments, I'll be here."

She arrived at the Radisson at 12:25 to find that Kate was already at the table, munching on a roll. "This is breakfast and lunch for me," she told Lacey, "so I started. Hope you don't mind."

Lacey slid into the seat opposite her. "Not at all. How's the show going?"

"Great."

They both ordered omelets, salads, and coffee. "The necessaries out of the way," Kate said with a grin. "I have to admit I'm getting curious. I was talking to Tom this morning and told him we were having lunch. He said he wished he could join us and sent his best to you."

Kate reached for another roll. "Tom was telling me that you just decided to pick up and move here, that you'd only been here once on a visit as a kid. What makes a place stick in your mind like that?"

Answer the question with a question.

"You're on the road a lot with shows," Lacey said. "Don't you remember some cities better than others?"

"Oh, sure. The good ones, like here, and the not-so-good ones. Let me tell you about the all-time not-so-good one . . ."

Lacey found herself relaxing as Kate told her story, her timing perfect. So many show business people are like that, Lacey thought nostalgically. Dad had the same talent; he could make a grocery list sound interesting.

Over a second cup of coffee she managed to

steer the conversation to the friend named Bill that Kate had mentioned. "You talked the other night about someone you're dating," she began. "Bill something, wasn't it?"

"Bill Merrill. Nice guy. Could even be Mr. Right, although the way things are going I may never know. I'll keep trying, though." Kate's eyes brightened. "The trouble is that I'm on the road so much, and he travels all the time too."

"What does he do?"

"He's an investment banker and practically commutes to China."

Don't let him be in China now, Lacey prayed. "Which bank is he with, Kate?"

"Chase."

Lacey had learned to watch for the flicker of curiosity that signaled she was being studied. Kate was smart. She sensed now that she was being probed for information. I've got what I need to know, Lacey thought. Get back to letting Kate do the talking.

"I guess the best of all possible worlds for you is to get a Broadway hit that runs for ten years," she suggested.

"Now you're talking," Kate said with a grin. "That would be having my cake and eating it too. I'd love to be able to stay put in New York.

Primarily because of Bill, of course, but there's no question that Tom's going to end up there in the next few years. He's clearly headed for success, and New York will be where he lands. That really would be the icing on the cake for me. We're both only children, so we've been more like siblings and best friends than cousins. He's always been there for me. Plus Tom's just naturally the kind of guy who seems to sense when people need help."

I wonder if that's why he asked me out last week and called me last night? Lacey thought. She signaled for a check. "I've got to run," she explained quickly. "First full day on the job."

At a pay phone in the lobby, she called and left a message for George Svenson. "I have new information concerning the Heather Landi case that I must give directly to Mr. Baldwin at the U.S. Attorney's office."

When she hung up, she hurried through the lobby, aware she was already late getting back to the agency.

Less than a minute later, a hand with brown

age spots picked up the receiver that was still warm from her touch.

Sandy Savarano never made phone calls that could be traced. His pockets were filled with quarters. His plan was to make five calls here, then go to a different location and make five more until his list of local real estate offices was exhausted.

He dialed, and when someone answered, "Downtown Realty," he began his spiel. "I won't take much of your time," he said. "I'm with the National Association of Realtors. We're conducting an informal survey . . ."

33

As U.S. Attorney Gary Baldwin told NYPD Detective Ed Sloane, he did not suffer fools gladly. He had been infuriated by the phone call from Sloane the previous afternoon, informing him that several pages of Jimmy Landi's copy of his daughter's journal apparently had vanished while it was in the police station. "How is it you managed to not lose the whole thing?" he had raged. "That's what happened to the original."

When Sloane phoned again twenty-four hours later, it gave Baldwin a second chance to air his grievances: "We're busting our chops going over the copy of the journal you gave us, and we find that we don't have several pages that obviously were of some importance, since someone took the risk of stealing them from under your nose! Where'd you leave the journal when you got it? On the bulletin board? Where'd you leave the copy? On the *street?* Did you hang out a sign on it? *'Evidence in a murder case. Feel free to take'?"*

As he listened to the tirade, Detective Ed Sloane's thoughts about what he would like to do to Baldwin yanked him back to his Latin 3 Class at Xavier Military Academy. When he preached on a grave sin, St. Paul had cautioned, *"Ne nominatur in vobis"*—Let it not be named among you.

It fits, Sloane thought, because what I'd like to do to you would be better off unnamed. But he too was incensed by the fact that the original journal, as well as possibly several pages from the copy, had disappeared from *his* locked evidence box in *his* cubby, which was located in the squad room.

Clearly it was *his* fault. He carried the keys to the box and the cubby on the heavy key ring that he kept in his jacket pocket. And he was always taking off his jacket, so virtually anybody could have taken the key ring out of his pocket, made duplicates, then returned the keys before he had even noticed that they were missing.

After the original journal vanished, the locks

had been changed. But he hadn't changed his habit of forgetting to take his keys out of the jacket that was draped on the back of his desk chair.

He focused once more on the phone conversation. Baldwin had finally run out of breath, so Sloane grabbed the opportunity to get in a word. "Sir, I reported this yesterday because you should know about it. I'm calling now because, frankly, I'm not at all sure Jimmy Landi is a reliable witness in this instance. He admitted yesterday that he barely even scanned the journal when Ms. Farrell gave it to him. Plus he only had it a day or so."

"Oh, the journal's not that long," Baldwin snapped. "It could be read carefully in just a few hours."

"But he didn't, and that's the point," Sloane said emphatically, as he nodded his thanks to Nick Mars, who had just placed a cup of coffee on his desk. "He's also threatening to be difficult, saying he's going to bring in his own investigator. And Landi's partner, Steve Abbott, came to the meeting with him and was throwing his weight around on Jimmy's behalf."

"I don't blame Landi," Baldwin snapped. "And another investigator on this case could be a good idea, especially since you don't seem to be getting anywhere."

"You know that's not so. He'd just get in the way. But at this point it looks like it's not going to happen. Abbott just called me," Sloane said. "In a way, he apologized. He said that thinking it over, it's possible that Landi was mistaken about the pages he thinks are missing. He said the night Jimmy got the journal from Lacey Farrell, it was so tough on him to try to read it that he put it aside. The next night he got smashed before he looked at it. Then a day later we took his copy from him."

"It's possible he's mistaken about the missing pages, but we'll never know, will we?" Baldwin said, his voice cold. "And even if he *is* wrong about the missing unlined pages, the original journal clearly was taken while in your possession, which means you've got someone in the precinct who's working both sides of the street. I suggest you do some housecleaning up there."

"We're working on it." Ed Sloane did not think it necessary to tell Baldwin that he had been setting traps for the culprit by talking cryptically around the station house about new evidence in the Waring case that he had stored in his cubby.

Baldwin concluded the conversation. "Keep me posted. And try to hang on to any other evidence that may come up in the case. Think you can do that?"

"Yes, I do. And as I remember it, sir, *we* were the ones who found and identified Savarano's fingerprint on the door to Farrell's apartment after the break-in," Sloane shot back. "I think *your* investigators were the ones who certified that he was dead."

A click of the phone in the U.S. Attorney's office proved to Detective Ed Sloane that he had succeeded in getting to the thin-skinned Baldwin. Score one for the good guys, he thought.

But it was a hollow victory, and he knew it.

For the rest of the afternoon, Gary Baldwin's staff endured the fallout from his frustration over the bungled investigation. Then his mood changed suddenly when he received word that the secured witness, Lacey Farrell, had new information for him. "I'll wait as long as it takes, but make sure you get her call through to me tonight," he told George Svenson in Minneapolis.

Following the call, Svenson drove to Lacey's

apartment building and waited for her in his car. When she got home from work, he didn't even give her a chance to go inside. "The man is jumping up and down waiting to talk to you," he said, "so we're going to do this *now.*"

They drove off in his car. Svenson was a quiet man by nature, and he did not seem to find the need to make small talk. During her indoctrination period in the safe site in Washington, Lacey had been tipped off that federal marshals hated the witness protection program, hated dealing with all those misplaced persons. They felt they had been stuck with what was, in essence, a baby-sitting job.

From day one in Minneapolis, Lacey had decided that while it was not pleasant to be dependent on a stranger, she was determined not to give him cause to consider her anything more than a minimal nuisance. In the four months she had been there, her single extraordinary request to Svenson had been for permission to do her furniture shopping at garage sales rather than at department stores.

Lacey now had a feeling that she had earned Svenson's grudging respect. As he drove through the gathering evening traffic to the secure phone, he asked her about her job.

"I like it," Lacey told him. "I feel like a whole person when I'm working."

She took his grunt as a sign of approval and agreement.

Svenson was the only person in the entire city to whom she could have talked about how she had almost burst into tears when Millicent Royce showed her a picture of her five-year-old granddaughter, dressed in a ballet recital costume. It had reminded her so much of Bonnie, and she had suffered an almost overwhelming wave of homesickness. But of course she *wouldn't* tell him.

Looking at the picture of a child Bonnie's age had made Lacey long to see her niece again. An old, turn-of-the-century song had been playing in her head since she saw the picture: *My bonnie lies over the ocean, my bonnie lies over the sea . . . bring back, bring back, oh bring back my bonnie to me . . .*

But Bonnie isn't over the ocean, Lacey told herself. She's about a three-hour flight away, and I'm about to give the U.S. Attorney information that may help get me on a plane home soon.

They were driving past one of the many lakes that were dotted throughout the city. The latest snow was nearly a week old but still appeared pristine white. Stars were beginning to come out, clear and shining in the fresh evening air. It *is* beautiful here, Lacey thought. Under different circumstances, I could very well understand why someone would choose to live here, but I want to go home. I *need* to go home.

For tonight's call they had set up a secure line in a hotel room. Before he put the call through, Svenson told Lacey that he would wait in the hotel lobby while she was talking to Baldwin.

Lacey could tell that the phone at the other end was picked up on the first ring; she could even hear Gary Baldwin identify himself.

Svenson handed her the phone. "Good luck," he murmured as he left.

"Mr. Baldwin," she began, "thank you for getting back to me so quickly. I have some information that I think may be very important."

"I hope so, Ms. Farrell. What is it?"

Lacey felt a stab of resentment and irritation. It wouldn't hurt to ask how it's going with me, she thought. It wouldn't hurt to be civil. I'm not here because I want to be. I'm here because *you* haven't been able to catch a killer. It's not *my* fault I wound up a witness in a murder case.

"What it is," she said, forming her words deliberately and slowly, as though otherwise he might not understand what she was telling him, "is that I have learned that Rick Parker—remember him? he was one of the Parkers of the Parker and Parker I used to work for—was in the same ski lodge as Heather Landi only hours before Heather died, and that she seemed frightened, or at least very agitated, when she saw him."

There was a long pause; then Baldwin asked, "How did you possibly come by that information in Minnesota, Ms. Farrell?"

Lacey realized suddenly that she had not thought this revelation through before making the phone call. She had never admitted to anyone that she had made herself a copy of Heather Landi's journal before she turned it over to Detective Sloane. She already had been threatened with prosecution because she had taken the original journal pages from Isabelle's apartment. She knew they never would believe that she had made a secret copy of it only to honor her promise to Isabelle to read it.

"I asked you how you came by that information, Ms. Farrell," Baldwin said, his voice reminding Lacey of a particularly prickly principal she had once had at school.

Lacey spoke carefully, as though wending her way through a minefield. "I have made a few friends out here, Mr. Baldwin. One of them invited me to a party for the road company production cast of *The King and I.* I chatted with Kate Knowles, an actress in the group, and—"

"And she just *happened* to say that Rick Parker was in a skiing lodge in Vermont just hours before Heather Landi died. Is *that* what you're telling me, Ms. Farrell?"

"Mr. Baldwin," Lacey said, knowing that her voice was rising, "will you please tell me what you are suggesting? I don't know how much you know about my background, but my father was a Broadway musician. I've attended, and enjoyed, many, many musicals. I know the musical theater, and I know theater people. When I spoke to Kate Knowles, it came up that she had been in a revival of *The Boy Friend* that ran off-Broadway two years ago. We talked about it. I saw that show, with Heather Landi in the lead."

"You never told us that you knew Heather Landi," Baldwin interrupted.

"There was nothing to tell," Lacey protested.

"Detective Sloane asked me if I knew Heather Landi. The answer I gave him, which happens to be the truth, is that, no, I didn't *know* her. I, like hundreds and perhaps thousands of other theater-goers, saw her perform in a musical. If I see Robert De Niro in a film tonight, should I tell you that I *know* him?"

"All right, Ms. Farrell, you've made your point," he said without a trace of humor in his voice. "So the subject of *The Boy Friend* came up. Then what?"

Lacey was gripping the phone tightly with her right hand. She pressed the nails of her left hand into her palm, reminding herself to stay calm. "Since Kate was in the cast, it seemed obvious to me that she must have known Heather Landi. So I asked her, and then got her to talk about Heather. She freely told me that Isabelle Waring had asked everyone in the cast if Heather had seemed upset in the several days before she died, and if so, did they have any idea what the cause could have been."

Baldwin sounded somewhat mollified. "That was smart of you. What did she say?"

"She said the same thing that I gather Isabelle heard from all Heather's friends. Yes, Heather was troubled. No, she never told anyone *why* she was troubled. But then—and this is the reason for my call to you—Kate told me that she was thinking of calling Heather's mother with one thing she had remembered. Of course, she's been on the road and didn't know that Isabelle was dead."

Once again Lacey spoke slowly and deliberately. "Kate Knowles has a boyfriend. He lives in New York. His name is Bill Merrill. He's an investment banker with Chase. Apparently he is a friend of Rick Parker, or at least knows him. Bill told Kate he had been chatting with Heather in the après-ski bar of the big lodge in Stowe the afternoon before she died. When Rick came in, though, she apparently broke off their conversation and left the bar almost immediately."

"He's sure this was the afternoon before Heather died?"

"That's what Kate said. Her understanding is that Heather was very upset when she spotted Rick. I asked if she had any idea why Heather would react so strongly, and Kate told me that apparently Rick had pulled something on Heather when she first moved to New York, four years ago."

"Ms. Farrell, let me ask you something. You worked for Parker and Parker for some eight years. With Rick Parker. Is that right?"

"That's right. But Rick was in the West Side office until three years ago."

"I see. And through this whole thing with Isabelle Waring, he never communicated to you that he knew, or might have known, Heather Landi?"

"No, he did not. May I remind you, Mr. Baldwin, that I'm where I am because Rick Parker gave me the name of Curtis Caldwell, who supposedly was from a prestigious law firm? Rick is the only one in the office who spoke, or *supposedly* spoke, to that man who turned out to be Isabelle Waring's killer. Wouldn't it have been natural in the weeks I was showing that apartment, and telling Rick about Isabelle Waring and her obsession over her daughter's death, for him to have said he knew Heather? I certainly think so," she said emphatically.

I turned the journal over to the police the day after Isabelle died, Lacey thought. I told them at the time that I had given a copy to Jimmy Landi, as I promised. Did I say anything about Isabelle asking me to read it? Or did I say I'd glanced at it? She rubbed her forehead with her palm, trying to force herself to remember.

Don't let them ask me who my date for the show was, she thought. Tom Lynch's name is in the journal, and they're sure to recognize it. It won't take them long to learn that all this wasn't a coincidence.

"Let me get this straight," Baldwin said. "You say the man who saw Rick Parker in Stowe is an investment banker named Bill Merrill who works for Chase?"

"Yes."

"Was all this information just volunteered at this casual meeting with Ms. Knowles?"

Lacey's patience snapped. "Mr. Baldwin, in my effort to get this information for you I manipulated a luncheon with a very nice and talented actress whom I would enjoy having as a friend. I've lied to her as I have to every living soul I've met in Minneapolis, other than George Svenson, of course. It's to my best interests to pick up any information I can that might lead to my having the chance to become a normal, truthful human being again. If I were you, I think I'd be much more concerned with investigating Rick Parker's link to Heather Landi than acting as if I'm making things up."

"I wasn't suggesting anything of the sort, Ms. Farrell. We'll follow up on this information immediately. However, you must admit that not too many witnesses in the protection program manage to bump into the friend of a dead woman whose mother's murder was the cause of their being in the program."

"And not too many mothers get murdered because they're not convinced their daughter's death was an accident."

"We'll look into this, Ms. Farrell. I'm sure you've been told this already, but it's very important. I insist that you be extremely careful not to let your guard down. You say you have new friends, and that's fine, but watch what you say to them. Always, always, *just be careful.* If even *one* person knows where you can be reached, we will have to relocate you."

"Don't worry about me, Mr. Baldwin," Lacey said, as with a sinking heart she thought again about telling her mother she was in Minneapolis.

As she hung up the phone and turned to leave the room, she felt as though the weight of the world was pressing on her shoulders. Baldwin had practically dismissed what she told him. He had seemed not to believe there was any significance to Rick Parker having had a connection to Heather Landi.

There was no way Lacey could have known

that the moment he replaced the receiver, U.S. Attorney Gary Baldwin said to his assistants, who were monitoring the phone call, "The first real break! Parker is in this up to his neck." He paused, then added, "And Lacey Farrell knows more than she's telling."

34

I guess I was wrong about Alice, Tom Lynch thought as he showered after working out at the Twin Cities Gym. Maybe she *was* sore that I didn't stick by her at the party. For the second day in a row she had not shown up at the gym. Nor had she returned his phone call.

But Kate had called to tell him about her lunch with Alice, and Alice had been the one who made the date, so at least she likes *somebody* in the family, he told himself.

But why didn't she call me back, even if it was to say she couldn't make it, or that she didn't get the message in time to make dinner last night? he wondered.

He stepped out of the shower and vigorously toweled himself dry. On the other hand, Kate also mentioned that Alice was starting a new job. Maybe *that's* why she hadn't gotten back to him, he decided.

Or maybe there was another guy in the picture?

Or maybe she was sick?

Knowing that Ruth Wilcox missed nothing, Tom stopped at her office on the way out. "No sign of Alice Carroll again today," he said, trying to sound casual. "Or maybe she comes in at a different time now?"

He saw the spark of interest in Ruth's eyes. "As a matter of fact, I was just about to give her a call to see if something was wrong," she said. "She's been so faithful, coming in every day for two weeks, that I figure something must be up."

Ruth smiled slyly. "Why don't I call her right now? If she answers, should I tell her you're asking for her, and put you on?"

Oh boy! Tom thought ruefully. It'll be all over the gym that something's brewing between Alice and me. Well, you started it, he reminded himself. "You're a regular Dolly Levi, Ruth," he said. "Sure, if she answers, put me on."

After four rings, Ruth said, "What a shame. She must be out, but the answering machine is on. I'll leave a message."

Her message was that she and a certain very attractive gentleman were wondering where Alice was keeping herself.

Well, at least that will smoke her out, Tom thought. If she's not interested in going out with me, I'd like to know it. I wonder if there is some kind of problem in her life?

When he went out, he stood on the street for a few minutes, debating what he wanted to do. Had he run into Alice at the gym, he would have asked her to go to dinner and a movie, or that at least had been his plan. The film that had been awarded first prize at the Cannes Film Festival was playing at the Uptown Theatre. He knew he could always go alone, but he just didn't feel like seeing it by himself.

He was getting cold, standing on the sidewalk, trying to decide. Finally he shrugged and said aloud, "Why not?" He would drive over to where Alice lived. With luck she would be there and he would ask her if she wanted to go to the movie with him.

From his car phone he tried her number again

and got the answering machine. She wasn't home yet. He parked at the curb outside her building and studied it, remembering that Alice lived on the fourth floor and her windows were directly over the main entrance.

Those windows were dark. I'll wait awhile, Tom decided, and if she doesn't show up, I'll get something to eat and skip the movie.

Forty minutes passed. He was about to leave when a car pulled into the semicircular driveway and stopped. The passenger door opened, and he saw Alice get out and dart into the apartment building.

For a moment the car was illuminated by the overhead light. Tom could see that it was a dark green Plymouth; it appeared to be five or six years old, the very essence of nondescript. He caught a glimpse of the driver and was pleased to note that he obviously was an older man. Certainly he would be an unlikely romantic partner for Alice.

The intercom was in the foyer. Tom pushed 4F.

When Alice answered, she obviously thought it was the man who had just dropped her off. "Mr. Svenson?"

"No, Alice, it's Mr. Lynch," Tom said, his tone one of mock formality. "May I come up?"

When Lacey opened the door, Tom could see that she looked drained, even stunned. Her skin was pale, almost alabaster white. The pupils of her eyes seemed enormous. He did not waste time on preliminaries. "Obviously something's terribly wrong," he said, alarm in his voice. "What is it, Alice?"

The sight of his tall, rangy figure filling the doorway, the concern in his eyes, in his whole expression, the realization that he had sought her out when she ignored his call, almost unhinged Lacey.

It was when he called her Alice that she managed to rein herself in, to regain at least a modicum of control. In the twenty-minute ride from the secure phone back to the apartment, she had exploded at George Svenson. "What is the *matter* with that Baldwin? I give him information that *has* to be useful in this case, and he treats me as if I'm a criminal! He just dismissed me, treated me like a child. For two cents I'd go home and walk down Fifth Avenue with a sign on me saying 'Rick Parker is a no-good, spoiled jerk who must have done something terrible to Heather Landi when she was a twenty-year-old kid just arriving in New York, because four years later she was still obviously spooked by him. Anyone with any information please come forward.' "

Svenson's response had been, "Take it easy, Alice. Calm down." And in fact he had the kind of voice that could soothe a lioness, let alone Lacey. It came with the job, of course.

During the drive home a new fear had hit Lacey. Suppose Baldwin had someone on his staff talk to her mother or Kit to be sure she hadn't told them where she was living. They would see through Mom in a minute, she thought. She would never be able to fool them. Unlike me, she's never learned to be an accomplished liar. If Baldwin thought Mom knew, he would relocate me, I know it. I can't go through the whole business of starting over again.

After all, here in Minneapolis she had a semblance of a job, and at least the beginnings of something resembling a personal life.

"Alice, you haven't invited me in. You might as well. I have no intention of leaving."

And it was here that she had met Tom Lynch.

Lacey attempted a smile. "Please come in. It's nice to see you, Tom. I was just about to pour myself a much needed glass of wine. Will you join me?"

"I'd be glad to." Tom took off his coat, and

tossed it on a chair. "How about I do the honors?" he asked. "Wine in the refrigerator?"

"No, as a matter of fact it's in the wine cellar. That's just beyond my state-of-the-art kitchen."

The Pullman kitchen in the tiny apartment consisted of a small stove and oven, a miniature sink, and a bar-sized refrigerator.

Tom raised his eyebrows. "Shall I lay a fire in the great room?"

"That would be nice. I'll wait on the verandah." Lacey opened the cabinet and poured cashews into a bowl. Two minutes ago I was within an inch of going to pieces, she thought. Here I am, actually joking with someone. Clearly Tom's presence had made the difference.

She sat in a corner of the couch; he settled in the overstuffed chair and stretched out his long legs. He lifted his glass to her in a toast, "Good to be with you, Alice." His expression became serious. "I have to ask you a question, and please be honest. Is there another man in your life?"

Yes, there is, Lacey thought, but not the way you're thinking. The man in my life is a killer who's stalking me.

"*Is* there someone, Alice?" Tom asked.

Lacey looked at Tom for a long minute. I could love you, she thought. Maybe I've already started to love you. She remembered the bullets whistling past her head, the blood spurting from Bonnie's shoulder.

No, I can't risk that. I'm a pariah, she thought. If Caldwell, or whatever his name is, learns where I am, he'll follow me here. I can't expose Tom to danger.

"Yes, I'm afraid there *is* someone in my life," she told him, struggling to keep her voice steady.

He left ten minutes later.

35

Rick Parker had taken more than a dozen prospective buyers to look at the Waring apartment. A few times he had seemed to be on the verge of a sale, but each time the potential buyer had pulled back from making an offer. Now he had another strong possibility, Shirley Forbes, a fiftyish divorcée. She had been to see the place three times, and he had arranged to meet her there again at ten-thirty.

This morning, as he had walked in the door of the office, his phone was ringing. It was Detective Ed Sloane. "Rick, we haven't talked in a couple of weeks," Sloane said. "I think you'd better come in and see me today. I just want to see if maybe by now your memory has improved a little."

"I have nothing to remember," Rick snapped.

"Oh yes you do. Twelve o'clock. Be here."

Rick jumped as Sloane abruptly broke off their connection. He sat heavily in his chair and began rubbing his forehead, which increasingly seemed to be covered with icy beads of perspiration. The savage pounding going on inside his head made him feel as though his skull was about to explode.

I'm drinking too much, Rick told himself. I've got to slow down.

He had made the rounds of his favorite bars last night. Did something happen? he wondered. He vaguely remembered that he had ended up at Landi's for a nightcap, although it wasn't on his usual circuit. He had wanted to see Heather's portraits in the murals.

I had forgotten they were painted out, he thought. Did I do something stupid while I was there? Did I say anything to Jimmy about the paintings? *Did I say anything about Heather?*

The last thing he needed this morning was to go back into Heather's apartment just before he had to go talk to Sloane, but there was no way he could postpone the appointment. Shirley Forbes had made a point of telling him she would be coming there from a doctor's appointment. He knew that all his father would need to hear was that he had let another potential sale of that apartment slip through his fingers.

"Rick."

He looked up to see R. J. Parker Sr. standing over his desk, scowling at him. "I was in Landi's for dinner last night," his father told him. "Jimmy wants that apartment sold. I said you had someone coming back this morning who's definitely interested. He said he'd gladly settle for a hundred thousand less than the six hundred he's been asking, just to get rid of it."

"I'm on my way to meet Mrs. Forbes now, Dad," Rick said.

My God! he thought. *R. J. was in Landi's last night. I could have bumped into him!* The very idea of such a disastrous encounter increased the pounding in his head.

"Rick," his father said, "I don't think I have to tell you that the sooner that place is off our hands, the less chance Jimmy has of finding out—"

"I know, Dad, I know." Rick pushed his chair back. "I've got to go."

"I'm sorry. It's exactly what I want, but I just know I'd never spend a comfortable moment alone here. I'd keep thinking of the way that poor woman died, trapped and defenseless."

Shirley Forbes announced her decision as she and Rick stood in the bedroom where Isabelle Waring had died. The apartment had been left with everything still in place. Forbes looked around the room. "I looked up all the newspaper accounts of the murder on the Internet," she said, dropping her voice as though confiding a secret. "From what I understand, Mrs. Waring was propped up against *that* headboard."

Her eyes unnaturally wide behind oversized glasses, Mrs. Forbes pointed to the bed. "I've read all about it. She was resting right here in her own bedroom, and someone came in and shot her. The police think she tried to get away, but her killer was blocking the door, so she shrank back on the bed and put her hand up to protect herself. That's why her hand was so bloody. And then that real estate agent came in, just in time to hear her beg for her life. Just think, that agent could have been killed too. That would have been two murders in this apartment."

Rick turned abruptly. "Okay. You've made your point. Let's go."

The woman followed him through the sitting room and down the stairs. "I'm afraid I've upset you, Mr. Parker. I'm so sorry. Did you know either Heather Landi or Mrs. Waring?" Rick wanted to rip off those idiotic glasses and grind them under his feet. He wanted to push this stupid woman, this voyeur, down the stairs. That's all she was, he decided—a voyeur, wasting his time, churning up his guts. She probably had looked at this place *only* because of the murder. She had no intention of buying.

He had other listings to offer her, but to hell with them, he decided. She saved him the trouble of telling her to get out by saying, "I really must rush now. I'll call you in a few days to see if anything else has come up."

She was gone. Rick went into the powder room, opened the door of the linen closet, and extracted a bottle from its hiding place. He carried the bottle into the kitchen, got out a glass, and half filled it with vodka. Taking a deep sip, he sat down on a bar stool at the counter that separated the kitchen from the dining area.

His attention became riveted on a small lamp

at the end of the counter. The base was a teapot. He remembered it all too well.

"It's my Aladdin's lamp," Heather had said that day when she spotted it in a secondhand store on West Eightieth. "I'll rub it for luck," she had said. Then, holding it up, she had closed her eyes, and chanted in a somber voice: "Powerful genie, grant me my wish. Let me get the part I auditioned for. Put my name up in lights." Then in a worried voice she had added, "And don't let Baba be too mad at me when I tell him I bought a co-op without his permission."

She had turned to Rick with a frown and said, "It's my money, or at least he told me I could use it for whatever I wanted, but at the same time I know he wanted to have a say in where I live here. He's worried enough as it is about my deciding to leave college early and move here and be on my own."

Then she had smiled again—she had a wonderful smile, Rick remembered—and rubbed the lamp once more. "But maybe he won't mind," she had said. "I bet finding this 'magic' lamp is a sign that everything will be fine."

Rick looked at the lamp, now sitting on the counter. Reaching for it, he yanked out the cord as he picked it up.

The next week, Heather had begged him to cancel the sale and give back her deposit. "I told my mother on the phone that I'd seen a place I loved. She was so upset. She told me that as a surprise my father had already bought an apartment for me on East Seventieth at Fifth Avenue. I can't let him know that I've bought another one without his permission. You just don't know him, Rick," she pleaded. "Rick, please, your family *owns* the agency. You can help me."

Rick aimed the lamp at the wall over the sink and threw it with all the force he could muster.

The genie in the lamp had gotten Heather the part in the show. After that he hadn't helped her very much.

Undercover detective Betty Ponds, the woman Rick Parker knew as Shirley Forbes, reported to Detective Sloane at the 19th Precinct. "Parker's so jumpy that he's twitching," she said. "Before too long, he'll crack like a broken egg. You should have seen the look in his eyes when I described how Isabelle Waring died. Rick Parker is scared silly."

"He has a lot more to be worried about,"

Sloane told her. "The Feds are talking right now to a guy who can place Parker in Stowe the afternoon before Heather Landi died."

"What time do you expect him?" Ponds asked.

"Noon."

"It's almost that now. I'm out of here. I don't want him to see me." With a wave she left the squad room.

Twelve-fifteen and twelve-thirty came and went. At one o'clock Sloane phoned Parker and Parker. He was told that Rick had not returned to the office since leaving for a ten-thirty appointment.

By the next morning it was clear that Rick Parker had disappeared, voluntarily or otherwise.

36

It had become clear to Lacey that she could not continue to go to the Twin Cities Gym, because she would just keep running into Tom Lynch. Even though she had told him there was someone else in her life, she was sure that if they saw each other day after day at the gym, inevitably they would end up going out together, and there was just no way she could tolerate the constant fabrication and the web of lies she would have to spin.

There was no question she liked him, and no question that she would like to get to know him. She could imagine sitting across a table from him, and over a plate of pasta and a glass of red wine, telling him about her mother and father, about Kit and Jay and the children.

What she could *not* imagine was inventing stories about a mother who supposedly lived in England, about the school she never attended, about her nonexistent boyfriend.

Kate Knowles had said that Tom loved New York and would end up there eventually. How *well* did he know it? Lacey wondered. She thought of how much fun it would be to take him on one of the Jack Farrell tours of the city, "East Side, West Side, all around the town."

In the days that immediately followed Tom's visit to her apartment, Lacey found that when she finally got to sleep, she had vague dreams of him. In those dreams, the doorbell of her apartment would ring and she would open the door and he would say, just as he had on the intercom that last night, "No, Alice, it's Mr. Lynch."

But on the third night, the dream changed. This time, as Tom came down the corridor, the elevator door opened and Curtis Caldwell stepped out, the pistol in his hand aimed at Tom's back.

That night Lacey awoke with a scream, trying to warn Tom, trying to pull him into the apartment, to bolt the door so they both could be safe inside.

Given her generally distressed state, the job with Millicent Royce was a lifesaver. At Millicent's invitation, Lacey had been out with her on several sales calls, either to show houses to a prospective client or to obtain new listings.

"It will be more interesting for you if you get to know the area well," Mrs. Royce told her. "Did you ever hear it said that real estate is all about location?"

Location, location, location. In Manhattan a park or river view dramatically increased the price of an apartment. Lacey found herself longing to swap stories with Millicent about some of the eccentric clients she had dealt with over the years.

The evenings were the hardest times. They stretched long and empty in front of her. On Thursday night she made herself go to a movie. The theater was half empty, with rows of unoccupied seats, but just before the film began, a man came down the aisle, went past her row, turned, looked around, and chose the seat directly behind her.

In the semidarkness she could only tell that he was of medium height and slender. Her heart began to race.

As the credits rolled on the screen, Lacey could hear the creaking of the seat behind her as he settled into it, she could smell the popcorn he was carrying. Then suddenly she felt his hand tap her shoulder. Almost paralyzed with fright as she was, it took what felt to be a superhuman effort to turn her head to look at him.

He was holding a glove. "This yours, ma'am?" he asked. "It was under your chair."

Lacey did not stay to see the film. She found it impossible to concentrate on what was happening on the screen.

On Friday morning, Millicent asked Lacey what she would be doing over the weekend.

"Mostly hunting for a gym or health club," Lacey said. "The one I joined is fine, but it doesn't have a squash court, and I really miss that."

Of course, that's not the *real* reason I won't go to Twin Cities Gym anymore, she thought, but for once, it isn't a totally dishonest answer.

"I've heard there's a new health club in Edina that's supposed to have a great squash court," Millicent told her. "Let me find out about it."

In a few minutes she came back to Lacey's

desk with the smile of someone who has achieved a goal. "I was right. And because they're new, there's a discount for joining right now."

When Millicent left later for her appointment, Lacey called George Svenson. She had two requests for him: she wanted to speak to U.S. Attorney Gary Baldwin again. "I deserve to know what's happening," she said.

Then she added, "People are getting too curious at the Twin Cities Gym. I'm afraid I've got to ask you to advance the registration fee for a different one."

Beggar, she thought despairingly as she waited for his answer. I'm not only a liar but a beggar!

But Svenson did not hesitate: "I can okay that. The change will do you good."

37

Lottie Hoffman read the New York papers every morning over her solitary breakfast. For forty-five years, up until a little over a year ago, she and Max had shared them. It was still unreal to Lottie that on that day in early December, Max had gone out for his usual early morning walk and never returned.

An item on page three of the *Daily News* caught her eye: Richard J. Parker Jr., wanted for questioning in the murder of Isabelle Waring, had disappeared. What had happened to him? she wondered nervously.

Lottie pushed her chair back and went to the desk in the living room. From the middle drawer, she took out the letter Isabelle Waring had written

Max the very day before she had been murdered. She read it once again.

Dear Max,

I tried to phone you today, but your number is unlisted, which is why I am writing. I am sure that you must have heard that Heather died in an accident last December. Her death was a tremendous loss to me, of course, but the circumstances of her death have been especially troublesome.

In clearing out her apartment I have come across her journal, and in it she refers to her intention of meeting you for lunch. That was only five days before her death. She does not mention either you or the lunch date after that. Instead the next two entries in the journal indicate that she was clearly distraught, although there is no indication of what was actually bothering her.

Max, you worked at Jimmy's restaurant for the first fifteen years of Heather's life. You were the best captain he ever had, and I know how much he regretted your leaving him. Remember, when Heather was two and you did magic tricks to make her sit still for the artist who was painting her into the mural? Heather loved and trusted you, and it is my hope that she may have confided in you when you saw her.

In any event, will you please phone me? I'm staying in Heather's apartment. The number is 555-2437.

Lottie returned the letter to the drawer and went back to the table. She picked up her coffee cup, then realized that her right hand was trembling so much that she had to steady the cup with the fingers of her left hand. Since that terrible morning, when she had answered the doorbell to find a policeman standing there . . . well, ever since that terrible morning she had felt every one of her seventy-four years.

She thought back to that time. I called Isabelle Waring, she remembered nervously. She was so shocked when I told her that Max had been killed by a hit-and-run driver only two days before Heather's death. At that time, I still thought his death was an accident.

She remembered that Isabelle had asked if she had any idea what Max and Heather might have talked about.

Max had always said that in his business you heard a lot, but you learned to keep your mouth shut. Lottie shook her head. Well, he must have broken that rule when he talked to Heather, she decided, and now I know it cost him his life.

She had tried to help Isabelle. I told her what I knew, she thought. I told her that I'd never met Heather, although I had gone with my senior citizen group to see the production of *The Boy Friend* when she was appearing in it. Then sometime soon after that, Lottie had gone on a day outing with the same group to Mohonk Mountain House, the resort in the Catskills. She had seen Heather there a second—and last—time. I took a walk along the trails, she remembered, and I saw a couple in ski clothes with their arms around each other. They were in a gazebo, all lovey-dovey. I recognized Heather, but not the guy she was with. That night she had told Max about it.

He asked about Heather's boyfriend, she remembered. When I described him, Max knew who I was talking about and became terribly upset. He said that what he knew about that man would curl my hair. He said the man had been very careful, that there wasn't a breath of suspicion against him, but Max said he was a racketeer and a drug dealer.

Max didn't tell me the man's name, Lottie thought, and before I could describe him to Isabelle Waring when she had called that night, Isabelle had said, "I hear someone downstairs. It must be the real estate agent. Give me your number. I'll call you right back."

Lottie remembered how Isabelle had repeated the number several times, then hung up the phone. I waited for the call all evening, Lottie thought, and then I heard the eleven-o'clock news.

It was only then that the full impact of what must have happened had hit her. Whoever had come in while she and Isabelle were on the phone must have been Isabelle Waring's murderer. Isabelle was dead because she would not stop looking for the reason for Heather's death. And now Lottie was convinced that Max was dead because he had warned Heather away from the man she was seeing.

And if I saw that man, I could identify him, she thought, but thank the Lord no one knows that. If there was one thing Lottie was sure of, it was that whatever Max told Heather when he cautioned her, he had not involved Lottie. She knew Max would never have put her in danger.

Suppose the police should ever come to her, she wondered suddenly. What would Max want her to do?

The answer was very calming, and it came to her as clearly as if he were sitting across the table from her. "Do absolutely nothing, Lottie," he cautioned. "Keep your mouth shut."

38

Sandy Savarano was finding his search was taking more time than he had expected. Some real estate agencies answered his questions willingly. The ones that told him they had hired young women between the ages of twenty-five and thirty-five all had to be checked out, which meant on-site surveillance. Other agencies refused to give him information on the phone, which meant they had to be checked out too.

In the mornings he would drive to the agencies and look them over, giving the most attention to the small mom-and-pop businesses. Usually they were storefront offices where he could walk past and by merely looking inside see what was going on. Some were obviously two-person operations.

To the ones that turned out to be more elaborate, prosperous-looking setups, he gave scant attention. They wouldn't be the kind to take on someone without a thorough background check.

The late afternoons he spent covering the health clubs and the gyms. Before he went into one of them, he would park for a time outside, looking at the people who were going in and out.

Sandy had no doubt that eventually he would find Lacey Farrell. The kind of job she would probably look for, and the kind of recreation she would rely on, were more than enough to lead him to her. A person didn't change her habits just because she changed her name. He had tracked down his quarry in the past with a lot less to go on. He would find her. It was just a matter of time.

Sandy liked to think about Junior, an FBI informant he had tracked to Dallas. The one good clue he had was that the guy was a nut for sushi. The problem was that sushi had become very trendy, and a lot of Japanese restaurants had opened in Dallas recently. Sandy had been parked outside a restaurant named Sushi Zen, and Junior had come out.

Sandy liked to remember the look on Junior's face when he had seen the car's tinted window slide down and had realized what was going to happen. The first bullet had been aimed at his gut. Sandy wanted to wake up all those raw fishies. The second had been directed at his heart. The third, to his head, had been a mere afterthought.

Late Friday morning, Sandy drove to check out Royce Realty in Edina. The woman he had spoken to on the phone had seemed one of those firm, schoolmarm types. She had answered his initial questions freely enough. Yes, she had a young woman working for her, age twenty-six, who was planning to take her Realtor certification test but had left to have a baby.

Sandy had asked if that young woman had been replaced.

It was the pause that interested him. It indicated neither denial nor confirmation. "I have a candidate in mind," was what Mrs. Royce finally told him. And yes, she was in the twenty-five to thirty-five age category.

When he reached Edina, Sandy parked his car in the supermarket lot across the street from the Royce office. He sat there for about twenty minutes, taking in details of the area. There was a delicatessen, next door to the agency, which had a fair amount of traffic. A hardware store halfway down the block also looked busy. He saw no one, however, either going into or coming out of Royce Realty.

Finally Sandy got out of the car, crossed the street, and sauntered past the agency, casually glancing inside. Then he stopped as though to examine the contents of a flyer prominently displayed in the agency window.

He could see that there was a desk in the reception area. Neatly stacked papers suggested that it was usually occupied. He could see beyond to where a largish woman with gray hair was sitting at a desk in a private office.

Sandy decided to go in.

Millicent Royce looked up as the door chimes signaled the arrival of a visitor. She saw a conservatively dressed gray-haired man in what she judged to be his late fifties. She went out to greet him.

His story was simple and direct. He said he was Paul Gilbert, visiting the Twin Cities on business for 3M—"That's Minnesota Mining and Manufacturing," he explained with an apologetic smile.

"My husband worked there all his adult life," Millicent answered, not quite understanding why it should irritate her that this stranger had assumed she would not understand what 3M stood for.

"My daughter's husband is being transferred here, and my daughter was told that Edina is a lovely place to live," he told her. "She's pregnant, so I thought that while I'm here I could do a little house hunting for her."

Millicent Royce dismissed her feeling of pique. "Aren't you the good father!" she said. "Now let me just ask you a few questions so I can get some idea of what your daughter is hoping to find."

Sandy smoothly gave appropriate answers about his supposed daughter's name, address, and family needs, which included "a kindergarten for her four-year-old, a good-sized back yard, and a large kitchen—she loves to cook." He left half an hour later with Millicent Royce's card in his pocket, and her promise to find just the right house. In fact, she told him she had one just coming on the market that might be perfect.

Sandy went back across the street and again sat in the car, his eyes fixed on the entrance to the agency. If there was someone using the reception desk, she was probably at lunch, he figured, and would return soon.

Ten minutes later, a young blond woman in her twenties went into the agency. Customer or receptionist? Sandy wondered. He got out of the car and again crossed the street, taking care to stay out of view of anyone inside the real estate office. For several minutes he stood in front of the delicatessen, reading the lunch specials. From the corner of his eye he could glance from time to time into the Royce agency.

The young blond woman was sitting at the reception desk, talking animatedly to Mrs. Royce.

Unfortunately for Sandy, he could not read lips. Had he been able to, he would have heard Regina saying, "Millicent, you have no idea how much easier it was to sit behind this desk than to take care of a colicky baby! And I have to admit that your new assistant keeps it a lot neater than I did."

Irritated at having wasted so much time, Sandy walked quickly back to his car and drove away. Another washout, he thought. Since there were other possibilities to track down in the area, he decided to continue to make the rounds of suburban agencies. He wanted to be back in downtown Minneapolis by late afternoon, though. That was a good time to look into the health clubs.

The next club on his list was the Twin Cities Gym on Hennepin Avenue.

39

"Now Bonnie, don't be like that. You know you do *so* like Jane to mind you," Kit said persuasively. "Daddy and Nana and I are just going to dinner in New York. We won't be late, I promise. But now Mommy has to finish getting dressed."

Heartsick, she looked at her daughter's woebegone face. "Don't forget, Nana promised that next week, when Lacey phones, you can talk to her."

Jay was putting on his tie. Kit's eyes met his over Bonnie's head. Her look implored him to think of something to say to their daughter.

"I've got an idea for Bonnie," he said cheerfully. "Who wants to hear it?"

Bonnie did not look up.

"I want to hear it," Kit volunteered.

"When Lacey comes home, I'm going to send her and Bonnie—just the two of them—to Disney World. How does that sound?"

"But when is Lacey coming home?" Bonnie whispered.

"Very soon," Kit said heartily.

"In time for my birthday?" There was the sound of hope in the little girl's voice.

Bonnie would be five on March 1st.

"Yes, in time for your birthday," Jay promised. "Now go on downstairs, sweetheart. Jane wants you to help her make brownies."

"My birthday isn't that far away," a much happier Bonnie said, as she sprang up from beside Kit's dressing table.

Kit waited until she heard Bonnie's footsteps going down the stairs. "Jay, how *could* you . . . ?

"Kit, I know it was a mistake, but I had to say *something* to cheer her up. We can't be late for this dinner. I don't think you understand how I've sweated this order for Jimmy Landi's casino. For a long time I've been closed out there completely. As it is, I got underbid on some of the biggest orders. Now that I'm back in with them, I can't let anything go wrong."

He pulled on his jacket. "And, Kit, remember

that Jimmy just found out from some private detective he hired that Lacey is my sister-in-law. In fact, Alex said that's why Landi called him to set up the dinner."

"Why Alex?"

"Because he also found out that Alex is dating your mother."

"What *else* does he know about us?" Kit asked angrily. "Does he know that my sister could have been killed if she'd gone into that apartment five minutes earlier? Or when she was shot at on our doorstep? Does he know that our child is recovering from a bullet wound and is under treatment for depression?"

Jay Taylor put his arm around his wife's shoulders. "Kit, please! It'll be okay, I promise. But we have to go. Don't forget, we've got to pick up your mother."

Mona Farrell had carried the phone to the window and was looking outside when she saw the car pull up. "They're here, Lacey," she said. "I'm going to have to go."

They had been talking for nearly forty minutes. Lacey knew that Deputy Marshal Svenson would be getting impatient, but she had been especially reluctant to break the connection tonight. It had been such a long day, and the weekend stretched endlessly before her.

Last Friday at this time she had been looking forward to her date with Tom Lynch. There was nothing for her to look forward to now.

When she had asked about Bonnie, she could tell from her mother's overly cheerful reassurances that Bonnie was still not doing well.

Even less reassuring had been the news that her mother, Kit, and Jay were having dinner tonight with Jimmy Landi at Alex Carbine's restaurant. As she started to say good-bye, Lacey cautioned, "Mom, for heaven's sake, be careful not to tell anyone where I am. You've got to *swear* to me—"

"Lacey, don't you think I understand the danger I'd put you in? Don't worry. No one will learn anything from me."

"I'm sorry, Mom, it's just—"

"It's all right, dear. Now I really do have to go. I can't keep them waiting. What have you got on for tonight?"

"I'm signed up at a new gym. It has a great squash court. Should be fun."

"Oh, I know how much you love to play

squash." Mona Farrell was genuinely pleased as she murmured, "Love and miss you, dear. Goodbye."

She hurried down to the car, thinking that at least she could tell Kit and Jay and Alex what Lacey was doing for recreation.

40

On Friday evening, Tom Lynch was planning to have an after-theater drink with his cousin, Kate. Her show was completing its Minneapolis engagement, and he wanted to say good-bye to her. He was also hoping that she might pick up his spirits.

Ever since Alice Carroll had told him that there was another man in her life, he had been depressed, and as a result everything seemed to be going wrong. The producer of his radio program had had to signal him several times to pick up his delivery, and even he was aware that he had sounded downright flat during several author interviews.

A touring production of *Show Boat* was opening at the Orpheum on Saturday night, and Tom's fingers itched to dial Alice's number and invite her to see it with him. He even found himself planning what he would say to her: "This time *you* can have the extra slice of pizza."

On Friday evening he decided to go over to the gym and work out for a while. He wasn't meeting Kate until eleven o'clock, and there was absolutely nothing else he could think of to do with his time.

He admitted to himself that he actually was harboring the secret hope that Alice might come into the gym, that they would start talking, and she would admit that she had serious doubts about this man in her life.

When he came out of the men's locker room, Tom looked around, but it was clear that Alice Carroll wasn't there, and, in fact, he already knew that she hadn't been there all week.

Through the glass that surrounded the manager's office, he could see Ruth Wilcox in deep conversation with a gray-haired man. As he watched, Ruth shook her head several times, and he thought he detected a slight expression of distaste on her face.

What does he want, a discount? Tom asked himself. He knew he should start to jog, but he had to ask Ruth if she had heard anything from Alice.

"Have I got news for you, Tom!" Ruth confided. "Close the door. I don't want anyone else to hear this."

Somehow Tom knew that the news had to do with Alice and the gray-haired man who had just left.

"That guy is looking for Alice," Ruth told him, her voice snapping with excitement. "He's her father."

"Her father! That's crazy. Alice told me her father died years ago."

"Maybe that's what she told you, but that man is her father. Or at least he says he is. He even showed me her picture and asked if I'd seen her."

Tom's instincts as a newsman were aroused. "What did you tell him?" he asked cautiously.

"I didn't say anything. How do I know he wasn't a bill collector or something? I said that I couldn't be sure. Then he told me that his daughter and his wife had had a terrible misunderstanding, and that he knew his daughter had moved to Minneapolis four months ago. His wife is very sick and desperate to make amends before she dies."

"That sounds phony as hell to me," Tom said flatly. "I hope you didn't give him any information."

"No way," Ruth said positively. "All I told him was to leave his name and if I happened to find that young lady was among our clients I'd ask her to call home."

"He didn't give you *his* name, or tell you where he's staying?"

"No."

"Didn't you think that was strange?"

"The gentleman said that he'd appreciate it if I didn't tell his daughter he was looking for her. He doesn't want her to disappear again. I felt so sorry for him. He had tears in his eyes."

If there's one thing I know about Alice Carroll, Tom thought, it is that no matter how big a misunderstanding, she's not the kind who would turn her back on a terminally ill mother.

Then another possibility occurred to him, one that he found enticing. If she wasn't telling the truth about her background, maybe the man she claimed to be involved with doesn't exist, he thought. He felt better already.

41

Detective Ed Sloane worked the eight-to-four day shift, but at five-thirty on Friday evening he was still in his office at the 19th Precinct, with Rick Parker's file spread out on his desk. He was glad that it was Friday. He hoped that at least over the weekend, he might have some peace from the Feds.

It had been a grueling last couple of days. Since Tuesday, when Rick Parker had not shown up for his appointment, the rocky relationship between the NYPD and the U.S. Attorney's office had become openly hostile.

It drove Sloane nuts that it was only when two federal agents showed up, looking for Parker, that Gary Baldwin finally admitted they had a witness who could place Rick at a ski lodge in Stowe the afternoon before Heather Landi died.

Baldwin didn't share that information, Sloane thought, but when he learned that I was putting heavy pressure on Parker, he had the nerve to complain to the district attorney.

Fortunately the DA stood by me, Sloane thought grimly. In a face-to-face confrontation, the DA had reminded Baldwin that the NYPD had an unsolved homicide that had occurred in the 19th Precinct, and it was their intention to solve it. He also made it clear that if the federal law enforcement officials wished to cooperate and share information, they might all be better off, but the NYPD was running the case, not the Feds.

The fact that the DA had gone to bat for him, even though he had had to sit and listen as Baldwin reminded him that vital evidence had disappeared from Sloane's locked cubby, had given Sloane a driving need to be the one who eventually pulled Rick Parker in.

Unless he was already dead, of course, Sloane reminded himself, which was a distinct possibility.

If not, Rick's disappearance was a sure sign that they were on the right track. It certainly cast in a new light the fact that he had never been able to explain how Isabelle Waring's murderer was able to pass himself off so easily as a lawyer with a prestigious law firm that just *happened* to be a major Parker and Parker client.

Now they knew that Parker had been at the ski lodge, and that Heather Landi was spooked when she had seen him there, only hours before her death.

In the four months since Isabelle Waring's murder, Sloane had put together an extensive curriculum vitae on Rick Parker. I know more about him than he knows about himself, Sloane thought, as once again he read through the thick file.

Richard J. Parker Jr. Only child. Thirty-one years old. Kicked out of two prestigious prep schools for possession of drugs. Suspicion, but no proof, of selling drugs—witness probably paid off to recant. Took six years to finally finish college at age twenty-three. Father paid for damages to fraternity house during wild party.

Always plenty of spending money through school years, Mercedes convertible as a 17th birthday present, Central Park West apartment as college graduation gift.

First and only job at Parker and Parker. Five years in the West 67th Street branch office, three years to present in East 62nd Street main office.

It hadn't been hard for Sloane to learn that Rick's coworkers on the West Side had despised him. One former employee of Parker and Parker told Sloane, "Rick would be out partying all night, show up with a hangover or still high on coke, and then start throwing his weight around in the office."

Five years ago Rick's father had elected to settle a sexual assault complaint brought against Rick by a young secretary, rather than have a public scandal. Following that episode, Parker Sr. had pulled the rug out from under his son.

The income from Rick's trust fund had been frozen, and he had been put on exactly the same base salary plus sales commission as his fellow employees.

Papa must have taken a course on tough love, Sloane thought with a touch of sarcasm. There was one problem with that scenario, however: Tough love doesn't support a cocaine habit. Once again he skimmed through the file. So where's

Rick been getting his money for drugs, and if he's still alive, who's paying for him to hide out?

Sloane pulled another cigarette from the ever-present pack in his shirt pocket.

The curriculum vitae for Richard J. Parker Jr. revealed one consistent pattern. For all his bluster and desk pounding, Parker Sr. always came through in the end when his son was in real trouble.

Like now.

Ed Sloane grunted and got up. Theoretically he was off for the weekend, and his wife had big plans for him to clean out the garage. But he knew that those plans would have to be changed; the garage would have to wait. He was going to drive up to Greenwich, Connecticut, and have a little chat with R. J. Parker Sr. Yes, it definitely was time for him to visit the palatial estate where Rick Parker had been raised, and had been given everything that money could buy.

42

On Friday evenings, the traffic from New Jersey into New York City was as heavy as the commuter traffic headed in the other direction. It was a dinner-and-theater night for many people, and Kit could see the strained expression on her husband's face as they inched their way across the George Washington Bridge. She was glad he had not said anything to her mother about how they should have left earlier.

Lacey had once asked her, "How can you stand it when he snaps at you for something that isn't your fault?"

I told Lacey that I didn't let it bother me, Kit remembered. I understand. Jay is a world-class worrier, and that's his way of expressing it. She glanced at him again. Right now he's worried because we are going to be late for dinner with an important client, she thought. I know he's worried sick about Bonnie, and by now he's churning about the fact that he's made a promise to her that he can't keep.

Jay sighed heavily as they finally turned off the bridge and onto the ramp leading to the West Side Highway. Kit was relieved to see that the cars ahead of them seemed to be moving downtown in a steady flow.

She put a comforting hand on her husband's arm, then turned to look in the backseat. As usual after speaking with Lacey, her mother had been on the verge of tears. When she got in the car, she had said, "Let's not talk about it."

"How's it going, Mom?" Kit asked.

Mona Farrell attempted a smile. "I'm all right, dear."

"Did you explain to Lacey why I wasn't able to talk to her tonight?"

"I told her we were going into New York and you wanted to be sure Bonnie had her dinner before you left. She certainly understood."

"Did you tell her we were meeting Jimmy Landi?" Jay asked.

"Yes."

"What did she say?"

"She said—" Mona Farrell stopped herself before she blurted out that Lacey had cautioned her not to tell where she was living. Kit and Jay did not know that Lacey had confided that information to her.

"She said that she was surprised," Mona finished lamely, feeling uncomfortable.

"So Alex has made you a captain, Carlos?" Jimmy Landi greeted his former employee as he sat down at the reserved table in Alex's Place.

"Yes, he did, Mr. Landi," Carlos said with a big smile.

"If you'd waited a while, Jimmy would have promoted you," Steve Abbott said.

"Or maybe I wouldn't," Jimmy said shortly.

"In any case it's a moot point," Alex Carbine told him. "Jimmy, this is your first time here. Tell me what you think of the place."

Jimmy Landi looked around him, studying the attractive dining room with its dark green walls brightened by colorful paintings in ornate gold frames.

"Looks like you got your inspiration from the Russian Tea Room, Alex," he commented.

"I did," Alex Carbine agreed pleasantly. "Just as you paid homage to La Côte Basque when you opened *your* place. Now, what are you having to drink? I want you to try my wine."

Jimmy Landi isn't the kind of man I had anticipated, Kit thought as she sipped a glass of chardonnay. Jay had been so worried about not keeping him waiting, but he certainly didn't seem upset that we were a couple of minutes late. In fact, when Jay apologized, Landi said, "In my place I *like* people to be late. Whoever's waiting has another drink. It adds up."

Despite his apparent good humor, Kit sensed that Jimmy Landi was extremely tense. There was a drawn look to his face, along with an unhealthy pallor. Perhaps it's just that he's grieved so much for his daughter, she decided. Lacey had told them that Heather Landi's mother had been heartbroken over their daughter's death. It made sense that Heather's father would have the same reaction.

When they had been introduced, Mona had said to Jimmy, "I know how much you've been through. My daughter—"

Alex interrupted, holding up his hand. "Why don't we wait until later to talk about that, dear?" he said smoothly.

Kit instinctively liked Jimmy's partner, Steve Abbott. Alex had told them that he had become something of a surrogate son to Jimmy, and that they were very close. Not in appearance, though, Kit decided. Abbott is *really* good-looking.

As dinner progressed, Kit could see that Steve and Alex were deliberately keeping the conversation away from any mention of either Lacey or Isabelle Waring. Between them they got Landi to tell some amusing stories about encounters with some of his celebrity clients.

Landi was, in fact, a first-class raconteur, a trait that Kit decided combined with his earthy, peasant appearance to make him oddly attractive. He also seemed genuinely warm and interested in them.

On the other hand, when he noticed a waiter looking impatiently at a woman who was obviously hemming and hawing over her entrée selection, his face darkened.

"Fire him, Alex," he said sharply. "He's no good. He'll never be any good."

Wow! Kit thought. He *is* tough! No wonder Jay is afraid of stepping on his toes.

Finally it was Jimmy who abruptly began to discuss Lacey and Isabelle Waring. As soon as coffee was served he said, "Mrs. Farrell, I met your daughter once. She was trying to keep her promise to my ex-wife by delivering my daughter's journal to me."

"I know that," Mona said quietly.

"I wasn't very nice to her. She'd brought me a copy of the journal instead of the original, and at the time I thought she had a hell of a nerve to decide to give the original to the cops."

"Do you still feel that way?" Mona asked, then didn't wait for an answer. "Mr. Landi, my daughter has been threatened with prosecution for withholding evidence because she tried to fulfill Isabelle Waring's dying wish."

Dear God, Kit thought. Mom is ready to explode.

"I learned about this only two days ago," Landi said brusquely. "I finally had the brains to hire a private detective when I saw that I'd been given the runaround by the cops. He's the one who found out that the cock-and-bull story they'd given me about a professional thief unintentionally killing Isabelle was so much hogwash."

Kit watched as Landi's complexion darkened to beet red.

It was obvious that Steve Abbott had noticed too. "Calm down, Jimmy," he urged. "You'll make a lousy patient if you have a stroke."

Jimmy shot a wry glance at him, then looked back at Mona. "That's just what my daughter used to tell me," he said. He swallowed the rest of the espresso in his cup. "I know your daughter's in that witness protection plan," he said. "Pretty lousy for her and for all of you."

"Yes, it is," Mona said, nodding in agreement.

"How do you stay in touch with her?"

"She calls once a week," Mona said. "In fact the reason we were a few minutes late is because I was talking to her until Jay and Kit picked me up."

"You can't call her?" Jimmy asked.

"Absolutely not. I wouldn't know where to reach her."

"*I* want to talk to her," Jimmy said abruptly. "Tell her that. The guy I hired tells me she spent a lot of time with Isabelle in the days before she died. I have a lot of questions I want to ask her."

"Mr. Landi, that request would have to be made through the U.S. Attorney's office," Jay said, breaking his silence on the matter. "They talked with us before Lacey went into the program."

"What you're saying is they'll probably turn me down," Jimmy growled. "All right, maybe there's another way. You ask her this question for me. Ask her if she remembers if there were a couple of unlined pages with writing on them at the end of Heather's journal."

"Why is that important, Jimmy?" Alex Carbine asked.

"Because if there *were,* it means that none of the evidence delivered to that precinct is going to be safe; it's going to be doctored or disappear. And I gotta find a way to do something about it."

Jimmy waved away Carlos, who was standing behind him with the coffee carafe. Then he stood and extended his hand to Mona. "Well, that's it, I guess. I'm sorry for you, Mrs. Farrell. I'm sorry for your daughter. From what I hear she was very nice to Isabelle, and she tried to be helpful to me. I owe her an apology. How is she doing?"

"Lacey is a trouper," Mona said. "She never complains. In fact she's always trying to cheer me up." She turned to Kit and Jay. "I forgot to tell you two in the car that Lacey just joined a brand-new health club, apparently one that has a fabulous squash court." She turned back to Landi. "She's always been a demon for exercise."

43

After completing her call to her mother and hanging up, Lacey met George Svenson in the lobby of the motel and walked wordlessly with him to the car.

She thought briefly about what she would do for the rest of the evening that stretched out ahead of her. One thing was certain—she simply could not spend all that time alone in the empty apartment. But what should she do? She was not particularly hungry and didn't like the idea of going to a restaurant alone. After the experience at the movie Thursday night, she also could not bear the idea of sitting alone in a darkened movie theater.

In a way, she would have enjoyed seeing the final Minneapolis performance of *The King and I,* if she could get a ticket, but was sure that the overture would completely unravel her. She had a mental image from years ago of looking down into the orchestra pit for her father.

Dad, I miss you, she thought as she got into Svenson's car.

But a voice inside her head came back with a reply.

Be honest, Lacey, my girl, you're not grieving for me at the moment. Face it—you've met some-one you want, but you're using my image to block out his. Admit it. It's not my face you're chasing, and not my image you're running away from.

Svenson was silent the entire drive, leaving her to her thoughts. Finally Lacey asked him if he had heard anything more from Gary Baldwin.

"No, I haven't, Alice," he replied.

It irritated Lacey that the one human being with whom she had even this much honest contact would not call her by her own name.

"Then kindly pass the word to the Great One that I want to know what is going on. I gave him some important information Tuesday night. As a simple courtesy, he could keep me informed of developments. I don't think I can live like this much longer."

Lacey bit her lip and slumped back in the seat.

As always when she vented her anger on Svenson, she felt embarrassed and childish. She was sure he wanted to be home with his wife and three teenage daughters, not out dragging her around to motels to make phone calls.

"I had money put in your account, Alice. You can join the new health club tomorrow morning."

It was Svenson's way of telling her that he understood how she felt.

"Thanks," she murmured, then realized she wanted to shout, *"Please, just once, call me Lacey! My name is Lacey Farrell!"*

When they reached her apartment building, she went into the lobby, still undecided about what to do. For several long moments she stood irresolutely in front of the elevator, then turned abruptly. Instead of going upstairs, she went out again, but this time got into her own car. She drove around aimlessly for some time, finally turning in the direction of Wayzata, the community in which she had attended the *King and I* cast party. Once there she looked for a small restaurant she remembered passing that night, and took some comfort in the fact that despite her less than sterling sense of direction, she found it easily. Maybe I'm finally getting the feel and sense of this area, she thought. If I'm going to be in the real estate business out here for any length of time, I'll definitely need it.

The restaurant she had chosen might have been on West Fourth Street in New York's Greenwich Village. As soon as she opened the door, she smelled the welcoming aroma of baking garlic bread. There were about twenty tables, each covered with a red-and-white-checked tablecloth, and each sporting a candle.

Lacey glanced around. The place was clearly crowded. "It looks like you're full," she said to the hostess.

"No, as a matter of fact, we just got a cancellation." The hostess led her to a corner table that had not been visible from the desk.

As she waited to be served, Lacey nibbled at warm, crunchy Italian bread and sipped red wine. Around her, people were eating and chatting, obviously enjoying themselves. She was the only solitary diner.

What was different about this place? she wondered. Why did she feel different in here?

With a start, Lacey realized she had put her finger on something she had either been avoiding or not recognizing. Here, in this small restaurant, where she could see whoever came in the door without being immediately seen herself, she felt safer than she had all week.

Why was that? she wondered.

It's because I told Mom where I am, she admitted to herself ruefully.

The warnings she had received in the safe site echoed in her head. *It's not that your family would knowingly give you away,* she was told. *It's remarks they might unconsciously make that could jeopardize your safety.*

She remembered how her dad had always joked that if Mom ever wrote her memoirs, they ought to title it *In Deepest Confidence,* because Mom never *could* keep a secret.

Then she thought of how shocked her mother had sounded when Lacey warned her not to drop anything to Jimmy Landi about where she was living. Maybe it will be okay, Lacey thought, praying that her mother had taken the warning seriously.

The salad greens were crisp, the house dressing tangy, the linguine with clam sauce delicious, but the feeling of safety was short-lived, and when Lacey left the restaurant and drove home, she was haunted by the sense that something or someone was closing in on her.

Tom Lynch had left her a message. "Alice, it's imperative that I see you tomorrow. Please call me back." He left his number.

If only I could call him, Lacey thought.

Ruth Wilcox had phoned as well: "Alice, we miss you. Please come in over the weekend. I want to talk to you about a gentleman who was inquiring about you."

Ruth, still playing the matchmaker, Lacey thought wryly.

She went to bed and managed to fall asleep, but then drifted promptly into a nightmare. *In it she was kneeling beside Isabelle's body. A hand touched her shoulder . . . She looked up and saw Isabelle's murderer, his pale blue eyes staring down at her, the pistol he was holding pointed at her head.*

She bolted up in bed, trying to scream. After that, it was no use. There was no more sleep for the rest of the night.

Early in the morning Lacey made herself go out for a jog but found she could not resist casting frequent glances over her shoulder to make certain she was not being followed.

I'm turning into a basket case, she acknowledged when she got back to the apartment and bolted the door.

It was only nine o'clock in the morning, and she had absolutely no plans of any kind for the rest of the day. Millicent Royce had said that often on weekends she had appointments to show houses and Lacey was welcome to go along with her. Unfortunately, though, there were none scheduled this weekend.

I'll have some breakfast, then try the new club, Lacey decided. At least it will be something to do.

She got to the Edina Health Center at ten-fifteen and was waved to a seat in the business office. She fished in her tote bag for her completed registration forms as the manager wound up a phone call by saying, "Yes, indeed, sir. We're a brand-new facility and have a wonderful squash court. Do come right over and take a look."

44

On Saturday morning, Detective Ed Sloane drove from his home in the Riverdale section of the Bronx to the meeting he had insisted on having with Richard J. Parker Sr., in Greenwich, Connecticut. On the way, he noted that the snow, which had been so picture perfect only a few days ago, was already disintegrating into piles of graying slush. The sky was overcast, and rain was predicted, although the forecast said it would turn into sleet as the temperatures dropped.

It's just another lousy winter day, the kind when the smart people who could afford it became snowbirds and flew south, Sloane told himself.

Or to Hawaii. That was the trip he was saving

for. He planned to take Betty there on their thirtieth anniversary, which was two years away.

He wished they were leaving tomorrow. Maybe even today.

Although with what was going on at the precinct, he knew he couldn't have gotten away. It haunted Sloane that evidence that might have been crucial to solving the murder of Isabelle Waring had been lost. It was bad enough, he thought, that Lacey Farrell had originally taken the journal from the crime scene. Infinitely worse was the fact that some still unknown perpetrator —most likely a "bad cop"—had stolen the journal from his own cubby. And probably had stolen pages from the copy that Jimmy Landi had turned over, he reminded himself.

The thought that he might be working, eating, and drinking with a cop who worked both sides of the street disgusted him physically.

As he turned off the Merritt Parkway at Exit 31, Ed thought about the sting he had set into motion in the squad room, aimed at catching whoever had been taking things out of the evidence box. He had begun to make a production out of taking his keys out of his suit jacket and locking them in his desk.

"I'm damned if I'll lose anything else out of

my cubby," he had announced grimly to whoever happened to be in the squad room. With the captain's help, he had concocted the story that a piece of evidence locked in his cubby just *might* turn out to be the key to solving Isabelle Waring's murder. His entry describing the supposed evidence in the precinct's evidence log was deliberately ambiguous.

A hidden ceiling camera was now trained on his desk. Next week he would start reverting to his old habit of leaving his keys in his jacket on the back of his desk chair. He had a feeling that with the kind of fake information he was passing around, there was a good chance he would smoke out his quarry. Surely whoever killed Isabelle Waring had to be behind the thefts from the squad room and would be seriously worried about potential new evidence. Sloane found it hard to believe, though, that someone like Sandy Savarano would be behind the thefts himself. He was just a trigger man. No, he thought, chances were there was somebody with clout and lots of money who was calling the shots. And when he heard about this new evidence, he would order it destroyed.

Ed Sloane's dilemma was that, much as he wanted to expose a bad cop, he knew it might well turn out to be one of the guys who over the past twenty-five years had at one time or another pulled him out of a tight spot. This kind of thing was never easy.

The Parker estate was situated on Long Island Sound. The handsome pale-red-brick mansion was turreted at either end, and old enough to have acquired a mellow patina, set off by the patches of snow still covering the extensive grounds.

Sloane drove through the open gates and parked to the side of the semicircle at the main entrance, thinking as he did so that he doubted too many five-year-old Saturns had stopped there.

As he went up the flagstone walk, his eyes darted from one window to another, half hoping to catch Rick Parker looking out at him.

A very attractive young woman in a maid's uniform admitted him, and when he gave his name, told him he was expected. "Mr. Parker is waiting for you in his study," she said. There was a hint of intimacy in the way she spoke. Ed had the feeling she had just left the study.

As he followed her down a wide, carpeted foyer, he reviewed what he knew of Parker Sr. He had heard that he had the reputation of being a womanizer, and wondered as he looked at the attractive young woman ahead of him if Parker was fool enough to try anything in his own home.

He just might be that damned foolish, Sloane decided a few minutes later. He found Mr. Parker sitting on a leather couch, sipping coffee; there was another cup beside his, half filled.

Parker neither got up to greet him nor did he offer him coffee. "Sit down, Detective Sloane." It was not so much an invitation as an order.

Sloane knew that the next thing he would hear was that Parker was very busy, so this couldn't take more than a few minutes.

He heard exactly that.

Noticing that the maid was still in the room, Sloane turned to her. "You can come back as soon as I leave, miss," he said crisply.

Richard Parker jumped up, his expression one of indignation. "Who do you think—"

Sloane interrupted him. "I think, Mr. Parker, that you should know from the outset that I'm not one of your lackeys. This is not some real estate transaction, some big deal that you're running. I am here to talk to you about your son. He is well on the way to being considered a suspect in not one, but *two* murder cases."

He leaned forward and tapped the coffee table

for emphasis. "Isabelle Waring did not believe that her daughter's death was an accident. Evidence points to the fact that Mrs. Waring died at the hands of a professional killer, one known to us, and known as well to have worked for a drug cartel. That, by the way, isn't general knowledge, yet, but I'm letting you in on it. You are certainly aware that your son was the one who cleared the way for the killer to get into Isabelle Waring's apartment. That alone makes him an accessory before the fact. A bench warrant on that charge is about to be issued for his arrest.

"But here's another piece of information you should know about your son, or perhaps you know it already. Rick was in Stowe the afternoon before Heather Landi died, and we have an eyewitness who can testify that she appeared to be frightened of him and ran out of the ski lodge when he showed up." Sloane stopped and looked at the man sitting tensely before him.

Red patches mottled Parker's face, revealing his agitation, but his voice was icy calm when he said, "Is that all, Detective?"

"Not quite. Your pride and joy, Richard J. Parker Jr., is a drug addict. You've apparently stopped paying his bills, but he's still getting the drugs somehow. Chances are, that means he owes someone a lot of money. That could be a very dangerous situation. My advice to you is to hire a criminal lawyer for him and tell him to surrender to us. Otherwise you might face charges yourself."

"I don't know where he is." Parker spat out the words.

Sloane stood up. "I think you do. I warn you. He's potentially in great danger. He wouldn't be the first person who got in over his head, and who paid the price by disappearing. Permanently."

"My son is in a drug rehabilitation clinic in Hartford," Priscilla Parker said.

Detective Sloane turned, startled by the unexpected voice.

Priscilla Parker was standing in the doorway. "I drove him there last Wednesday," she said. "My husband is being honest when he says he doesn't know where his son is. Rick came to me for help. His father was otherwise occupied that day." Her eyes rested on the second coffee cup, then she looked at her husband, contempt and loathing written clearly on her face.

45

After she had given the manager at the Edina Health Club the completed registration forms and her check, Lacey went directly to the squash court and began hitting balls against the wall. She quickly realized that the combination of the previous sleepless night and an earlier long jog had left her exhausted. She kept missing easy returns, and then she fell, badly wrenching her ankle, all in an attempt to connect with a ball she had no chance of hitting. It was typical of her life right now.

Disgusted with herself and close to tears, she limped off the court and collected her coat and tote bag from the locker.

The door to the manager's office was partially

open. Inside, a young couple was sitting at the manager's desk, and a gray-haired man was waiting to speak to her.

Lacey could feel her ankle swelling already. For a moment she paused in front of the open door, debating whether to ask the manager if the club kept elastic bandages in its medical supply kit. Then she decided to go straight home and put ice on her ankle instead.

As much as she had wanted to get out of her apartment this morning, Lacey realized that all she wanted now was to be back inside, with the door locked and bolted.

Earlier that morning, when Lacey had gone out jogging, a smattering of clouds dotted the sky. Now they were filling it, moving so close together as to be seamless. Driving from Edina to Minneapolis, Lacey could tell that a heavy snowfall was imminent.

She had a designated parking spot behind her apartment building. She pulled into the space and turned off the engine. She sat for a moment in the silence. Her life was a total mess. Here she was, hundreds of miles away from her family, living an existence that could not be called a life, alone and lonely. She was trapped in a lie, having to pretend to be someone other than herself—and why? Why? Just because she had been a witness to a crime. Sometimes she wished the killer had seen her there in the closet. She had no desire to die, but it would have been easier than living this way, she thought desperately. I've got to do something about this.

She opened the door and got out of the car, careful to favor her throbbing right ankle. As she turned to lock the door, she felt a hand on her shoulder.

It was the same emotion she experienced in the nightmare, life moving in slow motion as she tried to scream, but no sound would come. She lunged forward, trying to break away, then gasped and stumbled as a flash of pain like the sting of a hot branding iron seared her ankle.

An arm went around her, steadying her. A familiar voice said contritely, "Alice, I'm sorry! I didn't mean to frighten you. Forgive me."

It was Tom Lynch.

Limp with relief, Lacey sagged against him. "Oh Tom . . . Oh God . . . I . . . I'm all right, I just . . . I guess you startled me."

She started to cry. It was so good to feel herself

firmly encircled and protected by his arm. She stood there for several moments, not moving, feeling a sense of relief wash over her. Then she straightened and turned to face him. She couldn't do this—not to him, not to herself. "I'm sorry you bothered to come, Tom. I'm going upstairs," she said, making herself breathe normally, wiping away the tears.

"I'm coming with you," he told her. "We have to talk."

"We have nothing to talk about."

"Oh but we do," he said. "Starting with the fact that your father is looking all over Minneapolis for you because your mother is dying and wants to make up with you."

"What . . . are . . . you . . . talking . . . about?" Lacey's lips felt rubbery. Her throat constricted to the point where she could barely force the words out of her mouth.

"I'm talking about the fact that Ruth Wilcox told me yesterday afternoon some guy had showed up at the gym with your picture, looking for you and claiming to be your father."

He's in Minneapolis! Lacey thought. *He's going to find me!*

"Alice, look at me! Is it *true?* Was that your father looking for you?"

She shook her head, desperate now to be free of him. "Tom, please. Go away."

"I will *not* go away." He cupped her face in his hands, forcing her to look up at him.

Once again, Jack Farrell's voice echoed in Lacey's mind: *You put my face in front of the one you want,* he said. *Admit it.*

I admit it, she thought, looking up at the firm line of Tom's jaw, the way his forehead was creased with concern for her—the expression in his eyes.

The look you give someone special. Well, I won't let anything happen to you because of it, she promised.

If Isabelle Waring's murderer had been able to coax my address out of Ruth Wilcox at Twin Cities Gym, I probably wouldn't be alive right now, she thought. So far, so good. But where else was he showing her picture?

"Alice, I know you're in trouble, and no matter what it is, I'll stand by you. But I can't be in the dark anymore," Tom's voice urged. "Can't you understand that?"

She looked at him. It was such a strange sensation, seeing this man in front of her who clearly had special feelings for her—love? Maybe. And he was exactly the person she had hoped to meet someday. But not now! Not here! Not in this situation. *I cannot do this to him,* she thought.

A car drove into the parking area. Lacey's instinct was to pull Tom down, to hide with him behind her car. I have to get away, she thought. And I have to get Tom away from me.

As the approaching car came into full view she saw that the driver was a woman whom she recognized as living in the building.

But who would be driving the next car to come into the parking lot? she wondered angrily. It could be him.

The first flakes of snow were beginning to fall.

"Tom, please go," she begged. "I have to call home and talk to my mother."

"Then that story is true."

She nodded, careful not to look at him. "I have to talk to her. I have to straighten some things out. Can I phone you later?" Finally she looked up.

His eyes, troubled and questioning, lingered on her face.

"Alice, you will call me?"

"I swear I will."

"If I can help you, you know—"

"Not now, you can't," she said, interrupting him.

"Will you honestly tell me just one thing?"

"Of course."

"Is there another man in your life?"

She looked into his eyes. "No, there is not."

He nodded. "That's all I need to know."

Another car was driving into the parking area. *Get away from me,* her mind screamed. "Tom, I have to call home."

"At least let me walk you to the door," he responded, taking her arm. After they had gone a few steps, he stopped. "You're limping."

"It's nothing. I stumbled over my own feet." Lacey prayed her face wasn't showing the pain she felt when she walked.

Tom opened the door to the lobby for her. "When will I hear from you?"

"In an hour or so." She looked at him again, forcing a smile.

His lips touched her cheek. "I'm worried about you. I'm worried *for* you." He clasped her hands and looked intently into her eyes. "But I'll be waiting for your call. You've given me some great news. And a whole new hope."

Lacey waited in the lobby until she saw his dark blue BMW drive away. Then she rushed to the elevator.

She did not wait to take off her coat before she called the health club. The gratingly cheerful voice of the manager answered. "Edina Health Club. Hold on, please."

A minute, then a second minute went by. Damn her, Lacey thought, slamming her hand down to break the connection.

It was Saturday. There was a chance her mother was home. For the first time in months Lacey dialed the familiar number directly.

Her mother picked up on the first ring.

Lacey knew she could not waste time. "Mom, who did you tell I was here?"

"Lacey? I didn't tell a soul. Why?" Her mother's voice went up in alarm.

Didn't *deliberately* tell a soul, Lacey thought. "Mom, that dinner last night. Who all was there?"

"Alex and Kit and Jay and Jimmy Landi and his partner, Steve Abbott, and I. Why?"

"Did you say *anything* about me?"

"Nothing significant. Only that you'd joined a new health club with a squash court. That was all right, wasn't it?"

My God, Lacey thought.

"Lacey, Mr. Landi wants very much to talk to you. He asked me to find out if you knew whether the last few pages of his daughter's journal were written on unlined paper."

"Why does he want to know that? I gave him a complete copy."

"Because he said that if they were, somebody stole those pages from the copy while it was at the police station, and they stole the *whole* original copy. Lacey, are you telling me that whoever tried to kill you knows you're in Minneapolis?"

"Mom, I can't talk. I'll call you later."

Lacey hung up. Once again she tried the health club. She did not give the manager a chance to put her on hold this time. "This is Alice Carroll," she interrupted. "Don't—"

"Oh, Alice." The manager's voice became solicitous. "Your dad came in looking for you. I took him to the squash court. I thought you were still there. I didn't see you leave. Someone told us you gave your ankle a nasty wrench. Your dad was so worried. I gave him your address. That was all right, wasn't it? He left just a couple of minutes ago."

Lacey stopped only long enough to jam the copy of Heather Landi's journal into her tote bag

before she half ran, half hopped to the car and
headed for the airport. A sharp wind slapped
snow against the windshield. Hopefully he won't
figure out right away that I've left, she told herself. I'll have a little time.

There was a plane leaving for Chicago twelve
minutes after she reached the ticket counter. She
managed to get on it just before the gates closed.

Then she sat in the plane for three hours on
the runway, while they waited for clearance to
take off.

46

Sandy Savarano sat in his rental car, the street map of the city unfolded in front of him, the thrill of the chase warming him.

He could feel his pulse quicken. He would have her taken care of soon.

He had found 520 Hennepin Avenue on the map. It was just ten minutes from the Radisson Plaza, where he had been staying. He took the car out of PARK and stepped on the accelerator.

He shook his head, still irritated that he had come so close to catching her at the health club. If she hadn't fallen on the squash court, she would still have been inside while he was there, cornered, an easy target.

He felt adrenaline pumping through his body,

accelerating his heartbeat, quickening his breath. He was close. This was the part he liked most.

The attendant said he had noticed that Farrell was limping when she left the club. If she had hurt herself badly enough to limp, chances were she went directly home.

Alice Carroll was the name she had taken—he knew that now. Shouldn't be too difficult to find out the number of her apartment—probably would be on her mailbox in the lobby.

Last time she had slammed the door before he could get to her, he reminded himself grimly. This time she wouldn't get the chance.

The snow was getting heavier. Savarano frowned. He didn't want to have to deal with any weather problems. His suitcase was open in the hotel room. When he finished with Farrell, he planned to pack and be checked out in ten minutes. A guest who didn't check out and left his luggage behind invited questions. But if the airport closed down and the roads got bad, he would be trapped, which was of concern only if anything went wrong.

Nothing *would* go wrong, he told himself.

He glanced at the street sign. He was on Hennepin Avenue in the 400 block.

The other end of Hennepin was near Nicollet Mall with all its fancy stores. The hotels and new office building were there too. This end wasn't much of a neighborhood, he noted.

He found 520. It was a nondescript corner building, seven stories high, not large, which was better for him. Savarano was sure the building would have little in the way of security.

He drove around the side and through the parking lot. It had numbered spaces for residents, with only a few off to the side marked for visitors. They were all occupied. Since he had no intention of drawing notice by taking a resident's spot, he drove back out, parked across the street, and walked to the building entrance. The door to the small vestibule was unlocked. The names and apartment numbers of the residents were on the wall above the mailboxes. Alice Carroll was in apartment 4F. Typical of such buildings, in order to gain admittance to the lobby, it was necessary to either have a key or to use the intercom to get a resident to buzz down and release the lock.

Savarano waited impatiently until he saw someone coming up the walk, an elderly woman. As she opened the outer door, he dropped a key ring on the floor and bent down to retrieve it.

When the woman unlocked the door that opened to the lobby, he straightened up and held it for her, then followed her in.

She gave him a grateful smile. He followed her to the elevator, then waited until she had pushed the button for the seventh floor before he pushed four. A necessary precaution, the kind of attention to detail that made Sandy Savarano so good— and so successful. He didn't want to find himself getting off the elevator with Farrell's next-door neighbor. The less he was seen, the better.

Once on the fourth floor, he turned down the corridor, which was quiet and poorly lighted. All to the good, he thought. Four F was the last apartment on the left. Sandy's right hand was in his pocket, holding his pistol, as he rang the bell with his left hand. He had his story ready if Farrell wanted to know who was there before she opened the door. "Emergency Services, checking a gas leak," he would say. It always had worked for him.

There was no answer.

He rang the bell.

The lock was new, but he had never seen a lock he couldn't take apart. The necessary tools were in a kit he kept around his waist. It looked just like a money belt. It had always amused him that the night when he went to the Waring apartment, he had been able to let himself in with the key she had kept on a table in the foyer.

In less than four minutes of working with the lock on the door to 4F, he was inside, the lock securely back in place. He would wait for her here. It was better that way. Somehow he didn't think that she would stay out long. And wouldn't she be surprised!

Maybe she's gone to have her ankle x-rayed, he thought.

He flexed his fingers; they were encased in surgical gloves. He had been uncharacteristically careless that night he had been in Farrell's apartment in New York, and he had left a fingerprint on the door. That night he hadn't noticed that the index finger of the right glove had split. That was a mistake he wouldn't make a second time.

He had been told to search Farrell's apartment to be sure she hadn't made a copy of Heather Landi's journal for herself. He started toward the desk to begin the search.

Just then the phone rang. With swift, catlike steps he crossed the room to stand beside it, glad to see that the answering machine was turned on.

Farrell's voice on the tape was low and reserved. "You have reached 555-1247. Please leave a message," was all it said.

The caller was a man. His voice was urgent and authoritative. "Alice, this is George Svenson," he said. "We're on the way. Your mother just phoned the emergency number in New York to report you were in trouble. Stay inside. Bolt your door. Don't let anyone in until I get there."

Savarano froze. *They were on the way!* If he didn't get out of there immediately, he was the one who would be trapped. In seconds he was out of the apartment, down the corridor, and onto the fire stairs.

Safely back in his car, he had just joined the light traffic on Hennepin Avenue when police cars, lights flashing, roared past him.

That had been as near a miss as any he had ever had. For a few moments he drove aimlessly, forcing himself to calm down, to think carefully.

Where would Farrell go? he asked himself. Would she be hiding at a friend's place? Would she hole up in a motel somewhere?

Wherever she was, he figured she wasn't more than thirty minutes ahead of him.

He had to try to figure out how she would be

thinking. What would *he* do if he were in the witness protection program and had been tracked down?

I wouldn't trust the marshals anymore, Sandy told himself. I wouldn't move to another city for them and wonder how long it would take to be found again.

Usually people who left the witness protection program voluntarily did so because they missed their families and friends. They usually went back home.

Farrell hadn't called the Feds out here when she realized she had been traced. No, she had called her mother.

That's where she was headed, he decided. She was on her way to the airport and New York. Sandy was sure of it.

He was going there too.

The woman had to be scared. She wouldn't trust the cops to protect her. She still had a New York apartment. Her mother and sister lived in New Jersey. She would be easy enough to find.

Others had evaded him for a while, but no one had ever really gotten away. In the end he always found his prey. The hunt was always fun, but the actual kill was the best.

He went to the Northwest Airlines counter first. From the number of agents there, it was obviously the busiest carrier in Minneapolis. He was told that at present all flights were grounded by the snow. "Then maybe I'll be able to join my wife," he said. "She left about forty minutes ago. Her mother was in an accident in New York, and I imagine she took whatever flight she could get. The name is Alice Carroll."

The ticket agent was warmly helpful. "No direct flight to the New York airports left in the last hour, Mr. Carroll. She might have made a connection through Chicago, though. Let's check the computer."

Her fingers tapped the keys. "Here we are. Your wife is on Flight 62 to Chicago, which departed at 11:48." She sighed. "Actually, it only pulled away from the gate. Her plane is sitting right out there on the runway. I'm afraid I can't put you on it, but would you want to meet her in Chicago? There's a plane boarding right now. Chances are, they'll end up arriving only minutes apart."

47

Detective Ed Sloane and Priscilla Parker sat together as they waited for her son, Rick, to appear. The Harding Manor sitting room was exceptionally comfortable. The estate was a private home that had been donated as a rehabilitation center by a couple whose only son died of a drug overdose.

The cheerful blue-and-white-chintz sofa and matching chairs, complemented by the Wedgwood blue walls and carpet, were clear evidence to Sloane that these were the original furnishings and that those who could afford to pay to come here to kick their habits were being charged a fortune.

On the drive from Greenwich, however, Mrs.

Parker had told him that at least half the clients paid nothing.

Now, as they waited for Rick Parker, she nervously explained, "I know what you must think of my son. But you don't realize how much goodness and promise there is in him. Rick could still do so much with his life. I *know* he could. His father has always spoiled him, taught him to think of himself as above any discipline, or even any sense of decency. When he got into trouble over drugs in prep school, I *pleaded* with my husband to make him face the consequences. But instead he bought people off. Rick ought to have done well in college. He's smart, but he just never took time to apply himself. Tell me what seventeen-year-old kid needs a Mercedes convertible? What kid that age needs unlimited spending money? What young man learns about a sense of decency when his father puts a maid's uniform on his mistress of the month and brings her into his own home?"

Sloane looked at the Italian-marble fireplace, admiring the delicate carving. "It seems to me that you have put up with a lot for a long time, Mrs. Parker. More than you should have, maybe."

"I didn't have much choice. If I had left, I

would have lost Rick altogether. By staying, I think I accomplished something. The fact that he's here and willing to talk to you bears me out."

"Why did your husband change his mind about Rick?" Sloane asked. "We know that about five years ago he cut off his income from his trust fund. What brought that on?"

"Let Rick tell you," Priscilla Parker replied. She tilted her head, listening. "That's his voice. He's coming. Mr. Sloane, he's in a lot of trouble, isn't he?"

"Not if he's innocent, Mrs. Parker. And not if he cooperates. . . . It's up to him."

Sloane repeated those words to Rick Parker as he waited for him to sign a Miranda warning. The younger Parker's appearance shocked him. In the ten days or so since he had last seen him, Rick's appearance had changed dramatically. His face was thin and pale, and there were dark circles under his eyes. Kicking a drug habit isn't fun, Sloane reminded himself, but I suspect there's more to the change than the rehabilitation program.

Parker handed him the signed release. "All

right, Detective," he said. "What do you want to know?" He was seated next to his mother on the sofa. Sloane watched as her hand reached for and covered his.

"Why did you send Curtis Caldwell—and I'll call him that since it's the name he was using—to Isabelle Waring's apartment?"

Beads of perspiration appeared on Parker's forehead as he spoke. "At our agency . . ." He stopped and looked at his mother. "Or as I should say, at my father's agency, there's a policy of not showing an apartment unless we check out potential buyers. Even then you still get window-shoppers, but at least they'll be qualified."

"Meaning they can afford to buy a place you show them?"

Rick Parker nodded. "You know the reason I'm here. I have a drug habit. In fact I've got an *expensive* habit. And I simply haven't been able to cover it. I've been buying more and more on credit. In early October I got a call from my dealer, the one I owe the money to, saying that he knew someone who wanted to see the apartment. He also said he knew this guy might not meet our standards, but if he liked it, things could be straightened out."

"Were you threatened in case you didn't go along with that?" Sloane asked.

Parker rubbed his forehead. "Look, all I can tell you is I *knew* what I had to do. It was clear to me that I wasn't being asked for a favor; I was being told what to do. So I made up a story. In the office, we'd just finished selling several co-ops to some lawyers the firm of Keller, Roland, and Smythe had transferred to Manhattan, so I made up the name Curtis Caldwell and said he was from that firm. No one questioned it. That's all I did," he burst out. *"Nothing* more. I figured the guy could be a little shady, but I had no idea he was that bad. When Lacey Farrell told me that guy was the one who killed Heather's mother, I didn't know what to do."

Sloane noted immediately the familiar way in which Rick Parker referred to Heather Landi.

"Okay. Now, what had been going on between you and Heather Landi?"

Sloane saw Priscilla Parker squeeze her son's hand. "You've got to tell him, Rick," she said softly.

Parker looked directly at Ed Sloane. The misery in his eyes seemed genuine to the detective. "I met Heather nearly five years ago, when she came to our office looking for a West Side apartment," he said. "I started taking her around. She was . . . she was beautiful, she was vivacious, she was fun."

"You knew Jimmy Landi was her father?" Sloane asked, interrupting him.

"Yes, and that was part of what made me enjoy the situation so much. Jimmy had barred me from going into his place one night because I was drunk. It made me angry. I wasn't used to being denied anything. So when Heather wanted to get out of her contract for a co-op on West Seventy-seventh Street, I saw my chance to have some fun, at least indirectly, at Jimmy Landi's expense."

"She signed a contract?"

"An airtight one. Then she came back to me in a panic. She found out her father had already bought her a place on East Seventieth. She begged me to tear up the contract."

"What happened?"

Rick paused and looked down at his hands. "I told her I would tear it up, if I could take it out in trade."

You bastard, Sloane thought, she was a kid, new to New York, and you pulled that.

"You see," Rick Parker said, and now it

seemed to Sloane that he was almost talking to himself, "I didn't have the brains to realize what I really felt for Heather. I had been able to crook my finger, and any number of girls would come running. Heather had ignored my attempts to seduce her. So in the deal we made over the co-op contract, I saw a chance to get what I wanted and to even the score with her father. But the night she came to my apartment, she was clearly terrified, so I decided to back off. She really was a sweet kid, the kind I could actually fall in love with. In fact, maybe I *did.* I do know that I found *myself* suddenly very uncomfortable having her there. I teased her a little bit, and she started crying. So then I just told her to grow up, and to leave, that I was too old for babies. I guess I succeeded in humiliating her enough to scare her away from me for good. I tried to call her, to see her after that, but she wouldn't have any part of it."

Rick got up and walked to the fireplace as if he needed the warmth of the flames there. "That night, after she had been to my apartment, I went out drinking. When I left a bar on Tenth Street in the Village, I was suddenly hustled into a car. Two guys worked me over good. They said if I didn't tear up that contract and stay away from

Heather, I wouldn't live to see my next birthday. I had three broken ribs."

"Did you tear up the contract?"

"Oh, *yes,* Mr. Sloane, I had torn it up. But not before my father got wind of it and forced me to tell him what had happened. Our main office had sold the East Side apartment to Jimmy Landi, for Heather, but that deal was peanuts compared to another deal that I found out was in the works. At that same time, my father was brokering the sale of the Atlantic City property to him. If Landi had found out what I pulled on Heather, it could have cost my father millions. That's when Daddy told me to make all this go away, or get out. Don't forget, for my father, if there's a business deal involved, it doesn't matter that I'm his son. If I interfere, I will be punished."

"We have an eyewitness who claims that Heather ran from the après-ski lounge in Stowe the afternoon before she died because she saw you there," Sloane told him.

"I never saw her that day," Rick Parker said, shaking his head. He seemed sincere. "The few times I had run into her, that was the reaction I got: She couldn't get away from me fast enough. Unfortunately nothing would have changed that."

"Heather obviously confided in someone, who ordered you roughed up. Was it her father?"

"Never!" Rick almost laughed. "And tell him she had signed that contract! Are you kidding? She wouldn't have dared."

"Then who?"

Rick Parker exchanged glances with his mother. "It's all right, Rick," she said, patting his hand.

"My father has been a regular at Landi's for thirty years," Rick said. "He always made a fuss over Heather. I think Dad was the one who set the goons on me."

48

When her plane finally took off at 3:00 P.M., Lacey did not join in the spontaneous cheering and applause that erupted from the other passengers. Instead she leaned back and closed her eyes, sensing that the choke collar of terror she had felt tightening around her neck was easing. She was in a middle seat, trapped between an elderly man who had napped—and snored—for most of the wait, and a restless young executive-type who spent the time working on his laptop computer, but had tried several times to start a conversation with her.

For three hours she had been terrified that the flight would be canceled, that the plane would taxi from the runway back to the gate, that she would find Curtis Caldwell waiting for her.

Finally they were in the air. For the next hour or so—at least until they reached Chicago—she was safe.

She was still wearing the same sweat suit and sneakers she had worn to the Edina Health Club earlier that morning. She had loosened the sneaker on her right foot as much as she could, but had not taken it off for fear she would not be able to get it back on again. Her ankle was now swollen to twice its normal size, and the throbbing pains from her injury were shooting up as far as her knee.

Forget it, she told herself. You can't let it stop you. You're lucky you're alive to *feel* pain. You've got to *plan*.

In Chicago she would get on the first available flight to New York. *But what do I do when I get there?* she asked herself. *Where do I go? Certainly not to my apartment. And I could never go to Mom's place or Kit's house—I would only be putting them in danger.*

Then where?

She already had put one full-fare coach flight on her Alice Carroll credit card. Now she would have to book a second full-fare flight to New York. Her card had a three-thousand-dollar limit, and there might not be enough left to cover a hotel room in Manhattan. Besides, she was sure that when the U.S. Attorney's office became aware she was missing, a trace would be put on that card. If she registered in a hotel, Gary Baldwin would have his agents there before mid-morning. And then she would be trapped again. He had the power to hold her as a material witness in flight.

No, she had to find a place to stay, one where she wouldn't be putting anyone in danger, and where no one would think to look for her.

As the plane flew over the snow-covered Midwest, Lacey considered her options. She could call Gary Baldwin and agree to go back into the witness protection program. The marshals would whisk her away again, she would stay in a safe house for a few weeks before being sent to another unfamiliar city, where she would emerge as a newly created entity.

No way, she vowed silently. *I'd rather be dead.*

Lacey thought back to the chain of circumstances that had led her to this point. If only she had never received the call from Isabelle Waring, leading to the exclusive listing on Heather Landi's apartment. If only she had picked up the phone and talked to Isabelle when she had called the night before she was murdered.

If I had talked to Isabelle that night, she might have given me a name, Lacey thought. She might have told me what she'd discovered in Heather's journal. Man . . . that was her last word. What man? But I'm getting closer to whoever is behind all this. That's obvious. One of two things had happened. Either Mom somehow gave me away, or someone is getting inside information from the police about me. Svenson may have had to get an okay from New York for me to get another fifteen hundred dollars to register at the Edina Health Club. If there was a leak in the U.S. Attorney's office, that information might have been passed on. That scenario seemed unlikely, though. There were many people in the program; surely those who were in charge were carefully selected and closely monitored.

What about her mother? Mom had dinner last night at Alex Carbine's restaurant, Lacey thought. I like Alex a lot. He was especially wonderful the night Bonnie was injured. But what do we really know about him? The first time I met him, when he came to dinner at Jay and Kit's, he told us that he'd met Heather.

Jay may have known Heather too, a voice whispered to her. *He denied it. But for some reason when her name came up he was upset and tried to change the subject.*

Don't even think that Kit's husband might be involved in this, Lacey told herself. Jay may have his quirks, but he's basically a very good and solid person.

What about Jimmy Landi? No, it couldn't be him. She had seen the grief in his eyes when he took the copy of Heather's journal from her.

What about the cops? Heather's handwritten journal disappeared after I gave it to them, Lacey thought. Now Jimmy Landi wants to know if there were entries written on unlined paper at the end of the journal. I remember those three pages. They had spatters of blood on them. If the copies of those three pages disappeared while they were in police custody, then there had to be something important on them.

Her copy of the journal was in her tote bag, pushed under the seat in front of her. Lacey was tempted to take it out and look at it but decided to wait until she could study the unlined pages undisturbed. The guy on her right, with the computer, seemed to her the kind who would comment on them, and she had no intention of talking to anyone about all this. Not even complete strangers. *Especially* not complete strangers!

"We are beginning our descent . . ."

Chicago, she thought. Then New York. *Home!*

The flight attendant finished the speech about seats upright in a locked position and buckling up, then added, "Northwest apologizes for the weather-related delay you encountered. You may be interested to learn that the visibility lowered immediately after we took off. We were the last plane to leave the airport until flights were resumed only a few minutes ago."

Then I'm at least an hour or so ahead of anyone who may be following me, Lacey told herself.

Whatever comfort that thought provided, however, was driven away by another possibility. If someone was following her and thought she was planning to go to New York, wouldn't it be smart for him to have taken a direct flight and be waiting for her there?

49

Every nerve in Tom Lynch's body had shouted at him not to leave Alice alone. He drove five miles in the direction of his apartment in St. Paul before he made a fast U-turn and headed back. He would make it clear to her that he had no intention of getting in her way while she spoke to her mother and whatever other family members might be involved in their rift. But, he reasoned, surely she could have no objection to his waiting in the lobby of her building, or even in his car, until she was ready for him to come up. Clearly she's in trouble, and I want to be there for her, he thought.

Having made the decision to go back, Tom became wildly impatient with the overly cautious drivers who, because of the blowing snow, were moving at a snail's pace.

His first indication of trouble came at the sight of police cars parked to the front and side of Alice's building, their lights flashing. A cop was there directing traffic, firmly prodding rubber-necking drivers to keep moving.

A sickening sense of inevitability warned Tom that the police presence had to do with Alice. He managed to find a parking spot a block away from her building and jogged back. A policeman stopped him at the entrance to the building.

"I'm going up," he told the cop. "My girl-friend lives here, and I want to see if she's all right."

"Who's your girlfriend?"

"Alice Carroll, in 4F."

The change in the police officer's attitude con-firmed Tom's suspicion that something had hap-pened to Alice. "Come with me. I'll take you upstairs," the officer told him.

In the elevator, Tom forced himself to ask the question he dreaded to put in words. "Is she all right?"

"Why don't you wait till you talk to the guy in charge, sir?"

The door to Alice's apartment was open. Inside

he saw three uniformed cops taking instructions from an older man whom he recognized as the one who had driven Alice home the other evening.

Tom interrupted him. "What's happened to Alice?" he demanded. "Where is she?"

He could see from the surprise on the other man's face that he had been recognized, but there was no time wasted in greeting him. "How do you know Alice, Mr. Lynch?" George Svenson asked.

"Look," Tom said, "I'm not going to answer your questions until you answer mine. Where is Alice? Why are you here? Who are you?"

Svenson responded succinctly. "I'm a deputy federal marshal. We don't know where Ms. Carroll is. We do know that she had been getting threats."

"Then that guy at the gym yesterday who claimed to be her father was a phony," Tom said heatedly. "I thought so, but when I told Alice about him she didn't say anything except that she had to go and call her mother."

"What guy?" Svenson demanded. "Tell me everything you know about him, Mr. Lynch. It may save Alice Carroll's life."

When Tom finally got home, it was after four-thirty. The flashing light on the answering machine indicated he had received four messages. As he had expected, none of them was from Alice.

Not bothering to take off his jacket, he sat at the table by the phone, his head in his hands. All Svenson had told him was that Ms. Carroll had been receiving threatening phone calls and had contacted his office. She had apparently had a bad fright this morning, which was why they were there. "She may have gone out to visit a friend," Svenson told him, his tone unconvincing.

Or she may have been abducted, Tom thought. A child could see that they were avoiding telling him what was *really* going on. The police were trying to find Ruth Wilcox from Twin Cities Gym, but she was off duty over the weekend. They said they hoped to get a fuller description of the man claiming to be Alice's father.

Tom had told Svenson that Alice had promised to call. "If you hear from her, tell her to call me —immediately," Svenson ordered sternly.

In his mind, Tom could see Alice, quiet and lovely, standing at the window of the banker's home in Wayzata only a week ago. *Why didn't you trust me?* he raged at that image. *You couldn't wait to get rid of me this morning!*

There was one possible lead that the police had shared with him. A neighbor reported that she thought she had seen Alice getting in her car around eleven o'clock. I only left her at quarter of eleven, Tom thought. If that neighbor was right, then she left only ten minutes after I did.

Where would she go? he wondered.

Who was she, really? he asked himself.

Tom stared at the old-fashioned black rotary-dial phone. *Call* me, Alice, he half demanded, half prayed. But as the hours ticked by, as the morning light made its dim appearance, and the snow continued its steady fall, the phone did not ring.

50

Lacey arrived in Chicago at four-thirty. From there she took a five-fifteen plane to Boston. Once again she used her credit card, but she planned to pay cash for the Delta shuttle from Boston to New York. That plane landed at Marine Terminal, a mile from the main terminals at La Guardia Airport. She was sure anyone who followed her to New York wouldn't look for her there, and by not using her credit card for the shuttle, she might lead Baldwin's office to think she had stayed in the Boston area.

Before she boarded the plane from Chicago she bought a copy of *The New York Times*. Midway through the flight she glanced through the first section of the paper. Realizing that she was absorbing nothing of what she was reading, she began to fold the remaining sections. Suddenly she gasped. Rick Parker's face was looking up at her from the first page of Section B.

She read and reread the account, trying to make sense of it. It was an update on an earlier story about Rick. Last seen on Wednesday afternoon, when he brought a prospective buyer to see the apartment of the late Isabelle Waring, Richard J. Parker Jr., police now confirmed, was a suspect in Waring's death.

Was he in hiding? Lacey wondered. Was he dead? Had the information she passed on to Gary Baldwin Tuesday night played a part in this? She remembered that when she had told him about Rick being in Stowe hours before Heather Landi's death, Baldwin had offered no reaction. And now the police were naming Rick as a suspect in Isabelle's murder. There *must* be a connection, she decided.

It was only as the plane was landing in Boston that Lacey realized she had finally figured out the one place she could stay in New York where no one would ever think of looking for her.

It was 8:05 local time when she got off the plane at Logan Airport. With a silent prayer that he would be home, Lacey made a phone call to

Tim Powers, the superintendent of Isabelle Waring's building.

Four years ago, when she was leaving 3 East Seventieth after showing an apartment, Lacey had been instrumental in preventing what surely would have been a terrible accident, and one for which Tim Powers would have been blamed. It had all happened so quickly. A child broke free from his nanny and raced into the street, thanks to the fact that Tim had left the building's front door open while he worked on it. Lacey's quick action had kept the child from being hit by a passing delivery truck.

Tim, trembling from the shock of the near disaster, had vowed, "Lacey, it would have been my fault. If you ever need *anything*—anything at all—you can count on me."

I need it now, Tim, she thought as she waited for him to answer.

Tim was astonished to hear from her. "Lacey Farrell," he said. "I thought you'd disappeared off the face of the earth."

That's almost exactly what I've done, Lacey thought. "Tim," she said, "I need help. You once promised—"

He interrupted her. "Anything, Lacey."

"I need a place to stay," she said, her voice

barely above a whisper. She was the only one at the bank of phones. Even so she looked around, fearful of being overheard.

"Tim," she said hurriedly, "I'm being followed. I think it's the man who killed Isabelle Waring. I don't want to put you in danger, but I can't go to either my apartment or my family. He'd never look for me in your building. I want to stay, at least for tonight, in Isabelle Waring's apartment. And please, Tim—this is *very* important—don't tell anyone about this. Pretend we never spoke."

51

The day clearly was not over for Detective Ed Sloane. After leaving Rick Parker at the rehabilitation center in Hartford, he rode with Priscilla Parker to her Greenwich estate, where he picked up his own car.

On the drive to Manhattan, he phoned the precinct to check in. Nick Mars was there. "Baldwin's been calling for you, practically every few minutes," he told Sloane. "He wants to see you ASAP. He couldn't reach you on your car phone."

"No," said Sloane, "I'm sure he couldn't." Wonder what he would say if he knew I'd been riding around in a chauffeured limousine, he thought. "What does he want now?"

"All hell is breaking loose," Mars told him. "Lacey Farrell almost got nailed in Minneapolis, where the Feds had her stashed. She's disappeared, and Baldwin thinks she's headed for New York. He wants to coordinate with us to find her before she gets nailed here. He wants to take her into custody as a material witness." Then he added, "How did you make out, Ed? Any luck finding Parker?"

"I found him," Sloane said. "Call Baldwin and arrange a meeting. I'll join you at his office. I could be there by seven."

"Better than that. He's in midtown. He'll talk to us here at the precinct."

When Detective Sloane arrived at the 19th Precinct, he stopped at his desk and took off his jacket. Then, with Nick Mars in tow, he went in to see U.S. Attorney Gary Baldwin, who was waiting in the interrogation room.

Baldwin was still angry that Lacey Farrell had disappeared but took time from his anger to congratulate Sloane on finding Rick Parker. "What did he tell you?" he asked.

Glancing only once or twice at his notes, Sloane gave a full report.

"Do you believe him?" Baldwin asked.

"Yeah, I think he's telling the truth," Sloane said. "I know the guy who sells Parker drugs. If he was the one who told Parker to set up that appointment that got Savarano into Isabelle Waring's apartment, it was nothing he actually planned himself. He was just a messenger. Somebody passed the word to him."

"Meaning we won't get the big boys through Parker," Baldwin said.

"Exactly. Parker's a jerk, but he's not a criminal."

"Do you believe that his father ordered him roughed up when he tried to hit on Heather Landi?"

"I think it's possible," Sloane said. "If Heather Landi went to Parker Sr. to complain about Rick, it's even *probable*. On the other hand, that doesn't seem likely, because I'm not sure she would trust Parker Sr. I think she'd be afraid he might say something to her father."

"All right. We'll pick up Rick Parker's supplier and lean on him, but I suspect you're right. Chances are he's only a link, not a player. And we'll make damn sure that Rick Parker doesn't set foot outside that rehabilitation center without one of us alongside him. Now to Lacey Farrell."

Sloane reached for a cigarette, then frowned. "They're in my jacket. Nick, would you?"

"Sure, Ed."

The round trip took Mars about a minute. He plunked the half-empty cigarette pack and a grimy ashtray on the table in front of Sloane.

"Has it ever occurred to you to give up smoking?" Baldwin asked, eyeing both cigarettes and ashtray with disdain.

"Many times," Sloane responded. "What's the latest on Farrell?"

As soon as Baldwin opened his mouth it was obvious to Ed Sloane that he was furious with Lacey. "Her mother admits she knew Farrell was in Minneapolis, but she swears she didn't tell anyone. Although I don't believe *that* for a minute."

"Maybe there was a leak somewhere else," Sloane suggested.

"There was no leak from my office or from the federal marshal's office," Baldwin said, his tone icy. "We maintain security. Unlike this precinct," he added.

I let myself in for that one, Sloane acknowledged silently. "What's your game plan, sir?" he asked. It gave him a fleeting sense of satisfaction to know that Baldwin would not be sure if his addressing him as "sir" was meant as sarcasm or a sign of respect.

"We've flagged the credit card we gave Farrell. We know she used it to fly to Chicago, then to Boston. She's got to be on her way to New York.

"We have a tap on the phone in her apartment, not that I think she'd be stupid enough to go there," Baldwin continued. "We've got that building under surveillance. We have taps on her mother's phone, her sister's phone, and Monday there'll be taps on the phones in her brother-in-law's office. We've got a tail assigned to each family member, in case they try to meet her somewhere."

Baldwin paused and looked at Sloane appraisingly. "It also occurred to me that Lacey Farrell just might try to call you directly," he said. "What do you think?"

"I seriously doubt it. I didn't exactly treat her with kid gloves."

"She doesn't deserve kid gloves," Baldwin said flatly. "She concealed evidence in a murder case. She gave away her location when we had her protected. And now she's putting herself in an extremely risky position. We've invested a hell of a lot of time and money in keeping Ms. Farrell alive, and we've gotten nothing much back for it except complaints and lack of cooperation on her part. Even if she doesn't have any common sense, you'd think she'd at least be grateful!"

"I'm sure she's eternally grateful," Sloane said as he got up. "I'm also sure that even if you *hadn't* spent all that time and money, she'd probably like to stay alive."

52

As they had agreed, Lacey called Tim Powers from the Marine Terminal. "I'm getting in a cab," she told him. "Traffic should be light, so at this hour, I should be there in twenty minutes, a half hour at the most. Be watching for me, please, Tim. It is very important that nobody else sees me come in."

"I'll give the doorman a coffee break," Tim promised, "and I'll have the key ready to hand you."

It feels so strange to be back in New York, Lacey thought, as the cab sped over the Triborough Bridge into Manhattan. When the plane had made its final approach before landing, she had pressed her face against the window, drinking in the New York skyline, realizing how much she had missed it.

If only I could just go home to my own apartment, she thought. I'd fill the Jacuzzi, send out for something to eat, phone my mother and Kit. And Tom.

What was Tom thinking? she wondered.

As she had hoped, the traffic was light, and in minutes they were headed south on the FDR Drive. Lacey felt her body growing tense. Let Tim *be* there, she thought. I don't want Patrick to see me. But then she realized that in all likelihood Patrick wouldn't be around. When she had last seen the doorman, it was his plan to retire on January 1st.

The driver got off the FDR Drive at Seventy-third Street and headed west to Fifth Avenue. He turned left on Fifth, then left again on Seventieth and stopped. Tim Powers was standing outside the building, waiting for her. He opened the door and greeted her with a smile and a pleasant, "Good evening, miss," but he showed no sign of recognition. Lacey paid the driver and hobbled out of the cab, thankful that finally she would be able to stop moving around. It was just in time, because she could no longer deny the pain of her wrenched ankle.

Tim opened the door to the lobby for her, then

slipped her the key to the Waring apartment. He assisted her to the elevator, put his master key in the control, and pushed 10.

"I fixed it so you'll go straight up," he said. "That way there'll be no risk of running into anyone who knows you."

"And I certainly don't want to, Tim. I can't tell you how much—"

He interrupted her. "Lacey, get upstairs fast and lock the door. There's food in the fridge."

Her first impression was that the apartment had been kept in pristine order. Then Lacey's eyes went to the closet in the foyer where she had hidden the night Isabelle Waring died. She had the feeling that if she opened the door, she would see her briefcase still sitting there, with the blood-stained pages from the journal stuffed inside.

She double-locked the door, and then remembered that Curtis Caldwell had stolen the key Isabelle kept on the foyer table. Had the lock been changed? she wondered. She even fastened the safety chain, although she knew how ineffective a safety chain was when someone really wanted to get in.

Tim had drawn all the drapes and turned on lights for her, a potential mistake, she thought, if the draperies weren't usually kept closed. Someone watching the apartment, either from Fifth Avenue or Seventieth Street, might realize someone was there.

On the other hand, if the drapes *have* been kept closed, it would be sending a signal to open them. Oh God, she thought, there's no sure way to be safe.

The framed pictures of Heather that had been scattered through the living room were still there. In fact everything seemed to be much as Isabelle had left it. Lacey shivered. She almost expected to see Isabelle walk down the stairs.

She realized that she had not yet taken off her down jacket. The casualness of the jacket and her sweats was so far removed from the way she had dressed the other times she had been in this apartment that they added to her feeling of displacement. As she unfastened the jacket, Lacey shivered again. She suddenly felt as if she were an intruder, moving in with ghosts.

Sooner or later she had to force herself to walk upstairs and to look in the bedroom. She didn't want to go near it, but she knew that she had to see it just to be rid of the feeling that Isabelle's body was still there.

There was a leather sofa in the library that converted into a bed, and adjacent to the library was the powder room. Those were the rooms she would use. There was no way that she could ever sleep in the bed in which Isabelle had been shot.

Tim had said something about there being food in the fridge. As Lacey hung her jacket in the foyer closet, she remembered hiding there and watching as Caldwell rushed past.

Get something to eat, she told herself. You're hungry, and the irritation from that is just making everything else worse.

Tim had done a good job of putting together a meal for her. There was a small roast chicken, salad greens, rolls, and a wedge of cheddar cheese and some fruit. A half-empty jar of instant coffee was sitting on a shelf. She remembered that she and Isabelle had shared coffee from that same jar.

"Upstairs," Lacey said aloud. "Get it out of the way." She half hopped her way to the staircase, then held onto the wrought-iron railing for support as she climbed the steps to the bedroom suite.

She went through the sitting room to the bedroom and looked in. The draperies were drawn here as well, and the room was dark. She turned on the light.

The place looked exactly the same as it had the last time she had stood there with Curtis Caldwell. She could still picture him as he looked around, his expression thoughtful. She had waited in silence, believing he was debating about whether or not to make an offer on the apartment.

What he had been doing, she now realized, was making sure there was no way Isabelle could escape him when he attacked her.

Where was Caldwell now? she wondered suddenly, a feeling of panic and resignation washing over her. Had he followed her to New York?

Lacey looked at the bed and visualized Isabelle's bloodied hand, trying to pull the journal pages from under the pillow. She could almost hear the echo of Isabelle's dying plea:

Lacey . . . give Heather's . . . journal . . . to her father . . . Only to him . . . Swear . . .

With sickening clarity, Lacey remembered the gasps and harsh choking breaths between each painfully uttered word.

You . . . read it . . . show him where . . . Then Isabelle had made one last effort to breathe and speak. She'd died as she exhaled, whispering, *man . . .*

Lacey turned and hobbled through the sitting room and eased her way down the stairs. Get something to eat, take a shower, go to bed, she told herself. Get over your jumpiness. Like it or not, you know you've got to stay here. There's no place else to go.

Forty minutes later she was sitting wrapped in blankets on the couch in the library. The copy she had made of Heather Landi's journal was lying on the desk, the three unlined pages spread out side by side. In the dim light from the foyer, the bloodstains that had smeared Heather's handwriting on the original pages resembled a Rorschach test blot. What does this mean to you? it seemed to ask.

What do you see in it? Lacey asked herself. As exhausted as she was, she knew she was not going to fall asleep anytime soon. She turned on the light and reached for the three unlined pages. They were the hardest to read because of the bloodstains.

A thought came to her. Was it possible that Isabelle had been making a special effort to touch these particular pages in her last moments of life?

Once again Lacey began to read these pages, searching for some clue as to why they were so important that someone had stolen the only other copies that existed. She had no doubt that these were the pages that Caldwell had found it worth killing for, but *why?* What was the hidden secret in them?

It was on these pages that Heather had written about being caught between a rock and a hard place, about not knowing what to do.

The last entry that seemed upbeat was the one at the top of the first unlined page, where Heather wrote that she was going to have lunch with Mr. or Max or Mac Hufner, it was impossible to tell. She had added, "It should be fun. He says he's grown old and I've grown up."

It sounds like she was going to meet an old friend, Lacey thought. I wonder if the police have talked to him to see if Heather dropped any hint to him? Or did she have their reunion lunch *before* things went so drastically wrong for her?

The original journal had been stolen from the police. Had they made a list of the people mentioned in it before it was taken? Lacey wondered.

She looked around the room, then shook her head. If only I had someone I could talk to about this, she thought, someone to bounce ideas off of.

But, of course, there is not, she told herself. You are completely alone, so just get on with it.

She looked at the pages again. Neither Jimmy Landi nor the police have these three pages now, she reminded herself. Mine is the only copy.

Is there any way I can find out who this man is? Lacey wondered. I could look in the phone book, she thought, make some calls. Or maybe I could simply phone Jimmy Landi himself.

Again she paused. She knew she had to get to work on trying to solve the mystery hidden in those pages. If anyone was going to unravel the secret, clearly it would have to be her. But could she do it in time to save her own life?

53

When flights from the Minneapolis airport were resumed, Sandy Savarano took the first available direct flight to New York. He reasoned that Lacey Farrell must have grabbed the first plane she could get on, which was the only reason she had gone to Chicago. He was sure that from there she would connect to New York. Where else would she go?

While he waited for his flight, he got a list of scheduled departures of major airlines from Chicago to New York. His bet was that Lacey Farrell would stick with Northwest. It would make sense that when she deplaned she would go directly to the nearest Northwest agent and make inquiries.

Even though his instinct told him she would be on that airline, Sandy managed to cover most of the areas through which passengers deplaning from Chicago would have to pass.

Finding and gunning down Lacey Farrell had become more than a mere job for him. At this point, it was consuming him. The stakes had become higher than he wanted to play for. He liked his new life in Costa Rica; he liked his new face; his young wife intrigued him. The money he was being paid to get rid of Lacey Farrell was impressive but not necessary to his lifestyle.

What *was* necessary to him was not having to live with the knowledge that he had botched his final job—that, and eliminating someone who could send him to prison for life.

After checking all the New York flights for a stretch of five hours, Sandy decided to call it quits. He was afraid that he would only draw attention to himself if he hung around any longer. He took a cab to the brownstone apartment on West Tenth Street that had been rented for him. He would wait there for further information on Lacey Farrell.

He did not have the slightest doubt that by midafternoon tomorrow he would once again be closing in on his quarry.

54

Jimmy Landi had intended to go to Atlantic City for the weekend to see for himself that everything was in readiness for the opening of the casino. It was an exciting time for him, and he found it difficult to stay away. There were millions to be made, plus there was the genuine thrill of glad-handing the movers and shakers, the excitement, and the noise of the slot machines ringing as a hundred bucks' worth of quarters gushed out from them, making the players feel like big-time winners.

Jimmy knew that real gamblers were contemptuous of people who played the one-armed bandits. He was not. He was only contemptuous of people who played with other people's money.

Like people who gambled away salaries that were supposed to pay the mortgage or keep a kid in college.

But the people who could afford to gamble— let them spend as much as they wanted in his place. That was the way he saw it. His boast was quoted and requoted in articles about the new casino: "I'll give you better rooms, better service, better food, better entertainment than you'll find anywhere else, whether in Atlantic City, Vegas, or even Monaco." The opening weeks were booked solid. He knew that some people were coming just to pounce on anything they could find not to like, to complain about anything they could. Well, they would change their tune. He had vowed that.

He felt it was always important for a person to have a challenge, but it was never more important to him than now, Jimmy acknowledged. Steve Abbott was taking care of the day-to-day routine of running the operation, which freed him for the big picture. Jimmy didn't want to know who printed the menus or ironed the napkins. He wanted to know what they cost and how they looked.

But he didn't seem to be able to keep his mind on the casino, no matter how hard he tried. The problem was that since he had gotten back the copy of Heather's journal last Monday, he had become obsessed with it and was spending too much time reading and rereading it. It was like a gateway to memories he wasn't sure he wanted to revisit. To him, the crazy thing about it was that Heather only started the journal when she moved to New York to try for a show business career, but throughout it she referred to times in the past when she had done something with either him or her mother. It was like an ongoing diary and a memory book.

One thing in the journal that had bothered him was a suggestion that Heather had been afraid of him. What did she think she had to be afraid of? Oh sure, he had bitten her head off a couple of times, just like he always had with anyone who stepped out of line, but surely that wasn't enough for her to be *afraid* of him. He hated to think that.

What had happened five years ago that she was so anxious to keep from him? he wondered. He couldn't help dwelling on that part of her journal. The thought that somebody had pulled something on Heather and gotten away with it was driving him crazy. Even after all this time, he still needed to get to the bottom of it.

The question of those unlined pages from the journal was also gnawing at him. He could *swear* he had seen them. Admittedly he had only glanced at the journal the night Lacey Farrell brought it over, and the next night when he had actually tried to read it, he had gotten drunk for the first time in years. Still, he retained a hazy impression of seeing them.

The cops claimed they never got any unlined pages. Maybe they didn't, he told himself, but assuming that I'm not wrong, and that the pages were there originally, then chances are they wouldn't have disappeared unless someone thought they were important. There was only one person who might be able to tell me the truth, he thought: Lacey Farrell. When she made the copy of the journal for me, surely she would have noticed if some of the last pages were different from the others.

There were stains on them—he vaguely recalled that. Jimmy decided to go ahead and call Lacey Farrell's mother and again ask her to pass on to Lacey the question he needed to have answered: *Did those pages exist?*

55

Lacey glanced at the clock when she woke up. She must have been asleep for about three hours. When she opened her eyes, she felt as she always had when she was in the dentist's chair and under light sedation. She experienced a sensation of something hurting, although now it was her ankle rather than her teeth. She also felt out of it, but not so much so that she was unaware of what was going on. She could remember hearing faint street sounds, an ambulance, a police car or fire engine.

They were the familiar Manhattan sounds that always had elicited mixed emotions from her—she felt concerned for the injured but was aware of a sense of being protected. *Someone is out there ready to come if I need help,* she had always told herself.

I don't feel that way now, she thought as she pushed back the blankets and sat up. Detective Sloane had been furious because she had taken Heather's diary; U.S. Attorney Baldwin must have gone ballistic when he learned that she had told her mother where she was staying and then had run away.

In fact, he had threatened to take her into custody and hold her as a material witness if she didn't abide by the rules of the witness protection program, and she was sure that was exactly what he *would* do—*if* he were able to locate her. She stood up, automatically putting most of her weight on her left foot, biting her lip at the throbbing discomfort of the swollen right ankle.

She put her hands on the desk to steady herself. The three unlined pages still lay there, commanding her immediate attention. Once again she read the first line of the first page. "Lunch with Mr." —or was it Max or Mac?—"Hufner. It should be fun. He says he's grown old and I've grown up."

That sounds like Heather was referring to someone she had known for a long time, Lacey thought. Who could I ask? There was only one obvious answer: Heather's father.

He's the key to all this, Lacey decided.

She had to get dressed, get something to eat. She also had to remove any trace of her presence here. It was Sunday. Tim Powers said that he would warn her if a real estate agent intended to bring a potential buyer to see the apartment, but still she worried that someone might show up unannounced. She looked around, making a mental inventory. The food in the refrigerator would be a dead giveaway that the apartment was being used. So would the damp towel and washcloth.

She decided that a quick shower now would help to wake her up. She wanted to get dressed, to get out of the nightshirt that had belonged to Heather Landi. But what do I wear? she asked herself, hating the fact that she was once again going to have to find something in Heather's clothes closet.

Shortly after she had arrived there she had showered, then she had wrapped the big bath towel around her and made herself go upstairs again, to find something to sleep in. She had felt ghoulish opening the doors of the walk-in closet off the bedroom. Even though she only wanted to grab something to wear to bed, she couldn't help but notice that there were two different styles of clothes on the hangers. Isabelle had dressed conservatively, in flawless taste. It was easy to tell which were her suits and dresses. The rest of the rack and open shelves contained a collection of mini and long skirts, funky shirts, grandmother dresses, cocktail dresses that probably didn't consist of more than a yard of material, baggy over-sized sweaters, and at least a dozen pairs of jeans, all of it obviously Heather's.

Lacey had grabbed an oversized nightshirt with red-and-white stripes that must have belonged to Heather.

If I go out, I can't wear my sweat suit and jacket, she thought. I was wearing them yesterday. I might be too easy to spot.

She fixed herself coffee and a toasted roll, and then showered. The underwear she had rinsed out earlier was dry, but her heavy socks were still wet. Once again she had to go through the personal belongings of two dead women in order to get dressed.

At eight o'clock, Tim Powers called on the apartment intercom. "I didn't want to use the telephone in the apartment," he said. "Better that the kids and even Carrie don't know that you're here. Can I come up?"

They had coffee together in the library. "How can I help you, Lacey?" Tim asked.

"Obviously, you already have," she replied with an appreciative smile. "Is Parker and Parker still handling the sale of the apartment?"

"As far as I know. You've heard that Junior is missing?"

"I read that. Has anyone else from their office brought somebody in to look at the place?"

"No, and Jimmy Landi phoned the other day and asked about that. He's getting pretty disgusted with Parker. Wants the apartment sold, and soon. I told him straight that I thought it would have a better chance if we cleared everything out."

"Do you have his personal number, Tim?"

"His personal office number, I guess. I was out when he called and had to call him back. He picked up the phone himself."

"Tim, give me that number, please."

"Sure. You know this phone is still on. They never bothered to disconnect it. I spoke to Parker a couple of times when I saw the bill come in, but I think he liked having it in case he wanted to make a call. He came in and out of here on his own sometimes."

"Which means he might still do it," she said. She knew it would cost Tim his job if she were discovered using this place, so she couldn't risk staying much longer. Still, there was one other thing she had to ask him to do. "Tim, I've got to get word to my mother that I'm all right. I'm sure her phone is tapped so they can trace any call I might make to her. Would you go to a public phone and call her? Don't identify yourself, and don't stay on for more than a few seconds, or they'll be able to trace the call, although even if they do, at least it won't be coming from here. Just tell her I'm fine and safe and will call her as soon as I can."

"Sure," Tim Powers said as he stood. He glanced at the pages on the desk, then looked startled. "Is that a copy of Heather Landi's journal?"

Lacey stared at him. "Yes it is. How do you know that, Tim?"

"The day before Mrs. Waring died, I was up here changing the filters in the radiators. You know how we change them around October 1st, when we go from air-conditioning to heat. She was reading the journal. I guess she'd just found it that day, because she was very emotional and clearly upset, especially when she read the last couple of pages."

Lacey had the feeling that she might be on the brink of learning something important. "Did she talk to you about it, Tim?" she asked.

"Not really. She got right on the phone, but whoever she tried to call has an unlisted number."

"You don't know who it was?"

"No, but I think I saw her circle the name with her pen when she came across it. I remember it was right near the end. Lacey, I've gotta get going. Give me your mother's phone number. I'll call on the intercom and give you Landi's."

When Tim left, Lacey went back to the desk, picked up the first of the unlined pages, and brought it to the window. Blotched as the page was, she could detect a faint line around the name Hufner.

Who *was* he? How could she find out?

Talk to Jimmy Landi, she decided. That was the only way.

On the intercom from the lobby, Tim Powers gave Landi's phone number to Lacey, then went out for a walk, looking for a public phone. He had a supply of quarters with him.

Five blocks away, on Madison Avenue, he found a phone that worked.

Twenty-seven miles away in Wyckoff, New Jersey, Mona Farrell jumped at the sound of the telephone. *Let it be Lacey,* she prayed.

A hearty, reassuring man's voice said, "Mrs. Farrell, I'm calling for Lacey. She can't talk to you but she wants you to know that she's okay and will get in touch with you herself as soon as she can."

"Where is she?" Mona demanded. "Why can't she talk to me herself?"

Tim knew that he should break the connection, but Lacey's mother sounded so distraught he couldn't just hang up on her. Helplessly, he let her pour out her anxiety as he kept interjecting, "She's okay, Mrs. Farrell, trust me, she's okay."

Lacey had warned him not to stay on the phone too long. Regretfully, he replaced the receiver, Mona Farrell's voice still pleading for him to tell her more. He started home, deciding to walk back on Fifth Avenue. That decision made him unaware of the unmarked police car that raced to the phone booth he had just used. Nor did he know that the phone was immediately dusted for his fingerprints.

Every hour that I'm here doing nothing means that I'm an hour closer to being tracked down by Caldwell or taken into custody by Baldwin, Lacey thought. It was like being caught in a spider's web.

If only she could talk to Kit. Kit had a good head on her shoulders. Lacey walked over to the window and pulled the curtains back just enough to peer into the street.

Central Park was crowded with joggers, in-line skaters, people strolling, or pushing carriages.

Of course, she thought. It was Sunday. Almost ten o'clock on Sunday morning. Kit and Jay would be in church now. They always went to the ten-o'clock Mass.

They always went to the ten-o'clock Mass.

"I *can* talk to her!" Lacey said aloud. Kit and Jay had been parishioners at St. Elizabeth's for years. Everyone knew them. Her spirits suddenly buoyed, she dialed New Jersey Information and received the number of the rectory.

Somebody be there, she prayed, but then she heard an answering machine click on. The only thing she could do was to leave a message and hope that Kit would get it before they left the church. Leaving her phone number, even at a rec-tory, would be too great a risk.

She spoke clearly and slowly. "It is urgent that I speak with Kit Taylor. I believe she is at the ten-o'clock Mass. I'll call this number again at eleven-fifteen. Please try to locate her."

Lacey hung up, feeling helpless and trapped. There was another hour to kill.

She dialed the number for Jimmy Landi she'd gotten from Tim. There was no answer, and when the machine picked up, she decided not to leave a message.

What Lacey did not know was that she already had left a message. Jimmy Landi's Caller ID showed the phone number from which a call to him had been placed, as well as the name and address of the person to whom the phone was registered.

The message on the ID indicated that his caller had dialed from 555-8093, a number registered to Heather Landi, at 3 East Seventieth Street.

56

Detective Sloane had not planned to go to work on Sunday. He was off duty, and his wife, Betty, wanted the garage cleaned. But when the desk sergeant at the precinct phoned to say that a friend of Lacey Farrell's had called her mother from a pay phone on Seventy-fourth and Madison, nothing could have kept him home.

When he reached the precinct, the sergeant nodded toward the captain's office. "The boss wants to talk to you," he said.

Captain Frank Deleo's cheeks were flushed, usually a warning sign that something or someone had incurred his wrath. Today, however, Sloane saw immediately that Deleo's eyes were troubled and sad.

He knew what that combination meant. The sting had worked. They had pinned down the identity of the rogue cop.

"The guys in the lab sent over the tape late last night," Deleo told him. "You're not going to like it."

Who? Ed wondered, as faces of longtime fellow officers became a picture gallery in his mind. Tony . . . Leo . . . Adam . . . Jack . . . Jim W. . . . Jim M. . . .

He looked at the TV screen. Deleo pressed the POWER button, then PLAY.

Ed Sloane leaned forward. He was looking at his own desk with its scarred and cluttered surface. His jacket was on the back of the chair where he had left it, the keys deliberately left dangling from the pocket, in an effort to tempt the thief who was removing evidence from his cubby.

On the upper left section of the screen he could see the back of his own head as he sat in the interrogation room. "This was filmed last night!" he exclaimed.

"I know it was. Watch what happens now."

Sloane stared intently at the screen as Nick Mars scurried out of the interrogation room and looked around. There were only two other detectives in the squad room. One was on the phone with his back to Nick, the other was dozing.

As they watched, Mars reached into Sloane's coat pocket and slid out his key ring, cupping it in his palm to conceal it. He turned toward the cabinet containing the locked private cubbies, then spun swiftly around, quickly replacing the keys. He then pulled a pack of cigarettes out of the breast pocket of Sloane's jacket.

"This is where I made my untimely entrance," Deleo said dryly. "He went back to interrogation."

Ed Sloane was numb. "His father's a cop; his grandfather was a cop; he's been given every break. Why?"

"Why *any* bad cop?" Deleo asked. "Ed, this has to remain between you and me for now. That piece of film alone isn't enough to convict him. He's your partner. He could argue convincingly that he was just checking your pocket because you were getting careless and he was worried that you'd be blamed if anything else disappeared. With those baby-blue eyes of his, he'd probably be believed."

"We have to do something. I don't want to have to sit across the table from him and work a case together," Sloane said flatly.

"Oh yes you do. Baldwin's on his way here again. He thinks Lacey Farrell is in the neighborhood. There's nothing I'd like better than for us to be able to crack this case and rub Baldwin's face in it. Your job, as you well know, is to be damn sure Nick doesn't get the chance to lift or destroy any more evidence."

"If you promise me ten minutes alone with the jerk once we nail him."

The captain stood up. "Come on, Ed. Baldwin will be here any minute."

It's a day for show-and-tell, Ed Sloane thought bitterly as an assistant U.S. Attorney prepared to replay the conversation they had taped between Lacey Farrell's mother and her unknown caller.

When the recording began to play, Sloane's raised eyebrows were the only sign of the shock he was experiencing. He knew that voice from the countless times he had been in and out of 3 East Seventieth. It was Tim Powers, the superintendent there. He was the caller.

And he's hiding Farrell in that building! Sloane thought.

The others sat silently, listening intently to the

conversation. Baldwin had a cat-who-ate-the-canary expression. He thinks he's showing us what good police work is all about, Sloane thought angrily. Nick Mars was sitting with his hands folded in his lap, frowning—Dick Tracy incarnate, Sloane said to himself. Who would that rat tip off if he got wind that Powers was Lacey Farrell's guardian angel? he wondered.

Ed Sloane decided that for now, at least, only one person beside Tim Powers was going to know where Lacey Farrell was staying.

Himself.

57

Tim Powers tapped on the apartment door at ten-thirty, then let himself in with his master key. "Mission accomplished," he told Lacey, with a smile, but she could see that something was wrong.

"What is it, Tim?"

"I just got a call from a real estate agent with Douglaston and Minor. Jimmy's listed the apartment with them, and the agent told me he wants her to dispose of all the furniture and personal items in it as soon as possible. She's coming at eleven-thirty with someone to look the place over."

"That's only an *hour* from now!"

"Lacey, I hate to—"

"You can't keep me here. We both know that. Get a box and clean out the refrigerator. I'll put the towels I used in a pillowcase, and you take them to your place. Should the draperies be open or closed?"

"Open."

"I'll take care of it. Tim, how did my mother sound?"

"Pretty shook up. I tried to tell her you're okay."

Lacey experienced the same sinking feeling she had had when she revealed to her mother that she was living in Minneapolis. "You didn't stay on the phone too long?" she asked.

Despite his reassurances, she was sure that by now the police were scouring this neighborhood, searching for her.

After Tim left, carrying the telltale evidence that the apartment had been used, Lacey stacked the pages of Heather's journal together and put them in her tote bag. She would make one more attempt to reach Kit at St. Elizabeth's rectory, but then she had to get out of there. She looked at her watch. She had just enough time to try Jimmy Landi's number once more.

This time he answered on the fourth ring. Lacey knew she could not waste time. "Mr.

Landi, this is Lacey Farrell. I'm so glad I reached you. I tried a little while ago."

"I was downstairs," Jimmy said.

"I know there's a lot to explain, Mr. Landi, but I don't have time, so just let me talk. I know why you wanted to talk to me. The answer is yes, there were three unlined pages at the end of Heather's journal. Those pages were filled with her worries about hurting you. Heather referred repeatedly to being trapped 'between a rock and a hard place.' The only happy reference was right at the beginning, where she wrote about having lunch with some man who sounds like he must have been an old friend. Heather wrote that he said something to her about her growing up and his growing old."

"What's his name?" Jimmy demanded.

"It looks like Mac or Max Hufner."

"I don't know the guy. Maybe he's someone her mother knew. Isabelle's second husband was quite a bit older." He paused. "You're in a lot of trouble, aren't you, Miss Farrell?"

"Yes, I am."

"What are you going to do?"

"I don't know."

"Where are you now?"

"I can't tell you."

"And you are certain that there were unlined pages at the end of the journal? I was pretty sure I'd seen them in the copy you gave me, but I couldn't be absolutely positive."

"Yes, they were in that copy, I'm sure. I made a copy for myself as well, and those pages are in it. Mr. Landi, I'm convinced Isabelle was onto something and that's why she was killed. I'm sorry; I've got to go."

Jimmy Landi heard the click as Lacey hung up. He laid down the receiver as Steve Abbott came into his office. "What's up? Did they close down Atlantic City? You got back early."

"Just got back," Abbott said. "It was quiet down there. Who was that?"

"Lacey Farrell. I guess her mother got my message to her."

"Lacey Farrell! I thought she was in the witness protection plan."

"She was, but not anymore, I guess."

"Where is she now?"

Jimmy looked at his Caller ID. "She didn't say, and I guess I didn't have this on. Steve, did we ever have a guy with a name like Hufner work for us?"

Abbott considered for a moment, then shook his

head. "I don't think so, Jimmy, unless it was a kitchen helper. You know how they come and go."

"Yeah, I know how they come and go." He glanced toward the open door that led to the small waiting room. Someone was pacing outside. "Who's that guy out there?" he asked.

"Carlos. He wants to come back. He says working for Alex is too quiet for him."

"Get that bum out of here. I don't like sneaks around me."

Jimmy stood up and walked to the window, his eyes focused on the distance, as if Abbott weren't there. "A rock and a hard place, huh? And you couldn't turn to your baba, could you?"

Abbott knew Jimmy was talking to himself.

58

At ten past eleven, Lacey phoned the rectory of St. Elizabeth's in Wyckoff, New Jersey. This time the phone was answered on the first ring. "Father Edwards," a voice said.

"Good morning, Father," Lacey said. "I called earlier and left a message asking that Kit Taylor be—"

She was interrupted. "She's right here. Just a moment."

It had been two weeks since Lacey had spoken to Kit, going on five months since she had seen her. "Kit," she said, then stopped, her throat tight with emotion.

"Lacey, we miss you. We're so scared for you. Where are you?"

Lacey managed a tremulous laugh. "Trust me. It's better you don't know. But I *can* tell you that I have to be out of here in five minutes. Kit, is Jay with you?"

"Yes, of course."

"Put him on, please."

Jay's greeting was a firm pronouncement. "Lacey, this can't go on. I'll hire an around-the-clock bodyguard for you, but you've got to stop running and let us help you."

Another time she probably would have thought Jay sounded testy, but this morning she could hear clearly the concern in his voice. It was the way Tom Lynch had spoken to her in the parking lot. Was that only yesterday? Lacey thought fleetingly. It seemed so long ago.

"Jay, I have to get out of here, and I can't call you at home. I'm sure your line is tapped. I just can't go on living like I have been. I won't stay in the witness protection program, and I know the U.S. Attorney wants to take me into custody and hold me as a material witness. I'm sure now that the key to this whole terrible mess is to find out who was responsible for Heather Landi's death. Like her mother, I'm convinced she was murdered, and the clues to who did it have got to be in her journal. Thank God I kept a copy, and I've been studying it. I've got to find out exactly what caused Heather Landi to be so troubled during the last few days of her life. The clues are there in the pages of the journal, if I can just figure them out. I think Isabelle Waring tried to find out what happened, and that's why she died."

"Lacey—"

"Let me finish, Jay. There's one name I think is important. About a week before she died, Heather had lunch with an older man whom she'd apparently known for a long time. My hope is that he was somehow connected to the restaurant business and that you may know him, or could ask around about him."

"What's his name?"

"It's so blurred that it's hard to make it out. It looks like Mr. or Mac or Max Hufner."

As she said the name "Hufner," she could hear the rectory door chimes ringing loudly.

"Did you hear me, Jay? Mr. or Mac or Max Huf—"

"Max Hoffman?" Jay asked. "Sure I knew him. He worked for Jimmy Landi for years."

"I didn't say Hoffman," Lacey said. "But oh, dear God, that's it . . ."

Isabelle's last words . . . "read it . . . show

him . . ." *then that long shuddering gasp,* "*. . . man.*"

Isabelle died trying to tell me his name, Lacey realized suddenly. She was trying to separate those pages from the others. She wanted Jimmy Landi to see them.

Then Lacey realized what Jay had just said, and it sent a sudden chill through her. "Jay, why did you say you *knew* him?"

"Lacey, Max died over a year ago in a hit-and-run accident near his home in Great Neck. I went to his funeral."

"How *much* over a year ago?" Lacey asked. "This could be very important."

"Well, let me think," Jay said. "It was just about the time I bid on the job at the Red Roof Inn in Southampton, so that would have made it about fourteen months ago. It was the first week in December."

"The first week in December—fourteen months ago! That's when Heather Landi was killed," Lacey exclaimed. "Two car accidents within days of each other . . ." Her voice trailed off.

"Lacey, do you think that—" Jay began.

The apartment intercom was buzzing, a series

of soft quick jabs. Tim Powers was signaling her to get out. "Jay, I've got to leave. Stay there. I'll call you back. Just one thing, was Max Hoffman married?"

"For forty-five years."

"Jay, get her address for me. I *have* to have it."

Lacey grabbed her tote bag and the black hooded coat she had taken from Isabelle's closet. Hobbling, she left the apartment and went down the corridor to the elevator. The indicator showed that the elevator was at the ninth floor and ascending. She managed to reach the safety of the fire stairs just in time to avoid being seen.

Tim Powers met her inside the staircase at the lobby level. He pressed folded bills into her hand and dropped a cellular phone in her pocket. "It will take them awhile to trace any calls you make on this."

"Tim, I can't thank you enough." Lacey's heart was pounding. The net was closing. She knew it.

"There's a cab waiting out in front with the door open," Tim said. "Keep that hood up." He squeezed her hand. "Six G is having one of their family brunches. There are a lot of people coming in at once. You may not be noticed. Get going."

The cabdriver was obviously annoyed at hav-

ing to wait. The cab leaped forward into the traffic, slamming Lacey backward. "Where to,
miss?" he demanded.

"Great Neck, Long Island," Lacey said.

59

"I hope Mom gets here before Lacey calls back," Kit said nervously.

They were having coffee with the pastor in the rectory study. The phone was at Kit's elbow.

"She should only be ten minutes or so," Jay said reassuringly. "She was going to meet Alex in New York for brunch and was just ready to walk out the door."

"Mom is a basket case over all this," Kit explained to the priest. "She knows the U.S. Attorney's office blames her for the leak, which is ridiculous. She didn't even tell *me* where Lacey was living. She'd have a fit if we didn't give her a chance to talk to Lacey now."

"*If* she calls back," Jay cautioned. "She may not get the chance, Kit."

Had she been followed? Lacey wondered. She couldn't be sure. There was a black Toyota sedan that seemed to be maintaining a constant distance behind the cab.

Maybe not, she thought, breathing a slight sigh of relief. The car had turned off the expressway at the first exit after they came out of the Midtown Tunnel.

Tim had taped the unlock code to the back of the cellular phone he had lent her. Lacey knew Kit and Jay were waiting in the rectory for her call, but if she could get the information she needed another way, she would rather do it. She had to get the street address where Max Hoffman had lived, and where, please God, his wife still lived. She had to go there and talk to her and get from her anything she might know about her husband's conversation with Heather Landi.

Lacey decided first to try to get Mrs. Hoffman's address from the telephone information operator. She dialed and was asked what listing she required.

"Max Hoffman, Great Neck. I don't have his address."

There was a pause. "At the request of the customer, that number cannot be given out."

The traffic was fairly light, and Lacey realized that they were getting close to Little Neck. Great Neck was the next town. What would she do if they arrived there and she didn't have an address to give this driver? She knew he hadn't wanted to make the drive so far out of Manhattan in the first place. If she *did* get to where Mrs. Hoffman lived and the woman wasn't home or wouldn't open the door, what would she do then?

And what if she was being followed?

She called the rectory again. Kit answered immediately. "Mom just got here, Lacey. She's dying to talk to you."

"Kit, please . . ."

Her mother was on the phone. "Lacey, I didn't tell a soul where you live!"

She's so upset, Lacey thought. It's so hard for her, but I just can't talk to her about all this now.

Then mercifully her mother said, "Jay has to speak to you."

They were entering Great Neck. "What's the address?" the driver asked.

"Pull over for a minute," Lacey told him.

"Lady, I don't want to spend my Sunday out here."

Lacey felt her nerves tingle. A black Toyota sedan had slowed down and driven into a parking lot. She *was* being followed. She felt her body go clammy. Then she allowed herself a sigh of relief as she saw a young man with a child get out of that car.

"Lacey?" Jay was saying, his tone questioning.

"Jay, did you get the Hoffmans' street address in Great Neck for me?"

"Lacey, I haven't a clue where to get it. I'd have to go into the office and make phone calls to see if anyone knows. I did call Alex. He knew Max very well. He says he has the address in a Christmas-card file somewhere. He's looking for it."

For the first time in her horrible months-long ordeal, Lacey felt *total* despair. She had gotten *this* close to what she was sure was the information she needed, and now she was stuck. Then she heard Jay ask, "What can you do, Father? No, I don't know which funeral home."

Father Edwards took over. While Lacey talked again with her mother, the pastor called two funeral homes in Great Neck. Using only a slight ruse, he introduced himself and said that one of his parishioners wanted to send a Mass card for Mr. Max Hoffman who had died a year ago December.

The second funeral home acknowledged having made the arrangements for Mr. Hoffman. They willingly furnished Mrs. Hoffman's address to Father Edwards.

Jay passed it to Lacey. "I'll talk to all of you later," she said. "For God's sake, don't tell anyone where I'm going."

At least I *hope* I'll talk to you later, she thought as the cab pulled out from the curb on its way to a gas station for directions to 10 Adams Place.

60

It made Detective Ed Sloane's flesh crawl to be sitting next to Nick Mars, having to act as if everything were fine—"brothers all are we," as the hymn went, he thought bitterly.

Sloane knew he had to be on guard against sending out some hostile signals that Nick might pick up, but he promised himself that he would have his full say when everything was finally out in the open.

They began their vigil of watching the apartment building at 3 East Seventieth Street at about eleven-fifteen, immediately after the meeting with Baldwin broke up.

Nick, of course, didn't understand. As he parked halfway down the block, he complained,

"Ed, we're wasting our time. You don't really think Lacey Farrell got her old job back selling co-ops here, do you?"

Very funny, Junior, Sloane thought. "Just call it an old dog's hunch, okay, Nick?" He hoped he sounded genial.

They were there only a few minutes when a woman in a long hooded coat walked out of the building and got into a waiting cab. Sloane couldn't see the woman's face. The coat was one of those bulky wraparounds, with a lot of loose material, so he also couldn't see her shape, but as he watched her move he sensed something familiar about her that raised the hairs on the back of his neck.

And she was favoring her right leg, he realized. The report from Minnesota mentioned that Farrell had apparently injured her ankle at a gym yesterday.

"Let's go," Sloane told Mars. "She's in that cab."

"You're kidding! Are you psychic, Ed, or just holding back on me?"

"Just a hunch. The phone call to her mother was made five blocks from here. Maybe she picked up a boyfriend in that building. She was there often enough."

"I'll call it in," Nick said.

"Not yet, you won't."

They followed the cab through the Midtown Tunnel onto the L.I.E. It was one of Nick Mars's little witticisms that the initials for the Long Island Expressway told it all: LIE. He laughed as he repeated his observation.

Sloane wanted to tell Nick that those initials described him perfectly. Instead he said, "Nick, you're the best tail in the business."

It was true. Nick could manipulate a car in any kind of traffic; he was never obvious, never too close, sometimes passing and then getting in a slower lane and letting the other guy pass him. It was a talent, and a terrific asset for a good cop. And for a crook, Sloane thought grimly.

"Where do you think she's going?" Nick asked him.

"I don't know any more than you do," Sloane replied. Then he decided to lay it on: "You know, I've always thought that Lacey Farrell might have made a copy of Heather Landi's journal for herself. If so, she may be the only one with the complete journal, the whole thing. Maybe there's something important in those three pages that Jimmy Landi says we're missing. What do you think, Nick?"

He saw Nick's eyes shift toward him suspiciously. Knock it off, Sloane warned himself. Don't make him nervous.

It was Nick's turn to respond. "I don't know any more than you do."

In Great Neck the cab pulled over to the curb. Was Farrell getting out? Sloane wondered. He got ready to follow her on foot, if necessary.

Instead she stayed in the cab. After a few minutes, it pulled out and two blocks later stopped at a gas station, where the cabby asked for directions.

They followed her through town, past some obviously expensive houses. "Which one do you want?" Nick asked.

Is that what you're about? Sloane wondered. A cop's salary not good enough for you? All you had to do was to get out, kid, he thought. You could have changed jobs. You didn't need to change sides.

Gradually the neighborhood they were driving through changed. The houses were much smaller, closer together, but well kept, the kind of neighborhood Ed Sloane felt comfortable in. "Take it easy," he cautioned Nick. "He's looking for a house number."

They were on Adams Place. The cab stopped in front of number 10. There was a parking spot across the street, about five car lengths down, behind an RV. Perfect, Sloane thought.

He watched as Lacey Farrell got out of the cab. She seemed to be pleading with the driver, reaching back through the window, offering money. He kept shaking his head. Then he rolled up the window and drove away.

Farrell watched the cab until it was out of sight. For the first time he could fully see her face. Sloane thought she looked young and vulnerable and very scared. She turned and limped up the walk. Then she rang the bell.

It didn't look as if the woman who had answered the door, opening it only a crack, was going to let her in. Lacey Farrell kept pointing to her ankle.

"My foot hurts. Please let me in, nice lady. Then I'll mug you," Nick simpered.

Sloane looked at his partner, wondering why he had ever found him amusing. It was time to call in a report. He found it very satisfying that he would be the one to bring Lacey Farrell in, even though it meant turning her over to Baldwin's custody.

He did not know that an amused and equally satisfied Sandy Savarano was watching him from a second-story bedroom in 10 Adams Place, where he had been patiently awaiting Lacey Farrell's arrival.

61

Mona Farrell went back home with Kit and Jay. "I can't go into New York and have brunch while I'm worrying like this," she said. "I'll call Alex and ask him to come out here."

Kit's two boys, Todd and Andy, had gone skiing at Hunter Mountain with friends for the day. A baby-sitter was minding Bonnie, who was starting with another cold.

Bonnie rushed to the door when she heard them arriving.

"She told me all about how she's going to Disney World for her birthday with her Aunt Lacey," the sitter said.

"My birthday is coming *very* soon," Bonnie said firmly. "It's next month."

"And I told her February is the shortest month of the year," the sitter said as she put on her coat and got ready to leave. "That *really* made her feel good."

"Come with me while I make a phone call," Mona said to Bonnie. "You can say hello to Uncle Alex."

She picked up her granddaughter and hugged her. "Did you know that you look just like your Aunt Lacey did when she was *almost* five years old?"

"I like Uncle Alex very much," Bonnie said. "You like him too, don't you, Nana?"

"I don't know what I'd have done without him these past months," Mona said. "Come on, sweetheart, let's go upstairs."

Jay and Kit looked at each other. "You're thinking the same thing I am," Jay said after a moment of silence. "Mona admits that Alex encouraged her to make Lacey tell her where she was living. She may not have told him where Lacey actually was, but there are other ways to give it away. Like the way Mona announced at dinner the other night that Lacey had joined a new health club with a great squash court. Less than twelve hours later somebody followed Lacey from that health club, probably intending to kill her. It's hard to believe this was just coincidence."

"But Jay, it's also hard to believe that Alex would be involved with all this," Kit said.

"I hope he isn't, but I told him where Lacey was going, and now I'm calling the U.S. Attorney at the emergency number and telling him too. She may hate me for it, but I'd much rather see her held in custody as a material witness than dead."

62

"Why did you come here?" Lottie Hoffman demanded, after reluctantly admitting Lacey into her home. "You can't stay here. I'll call another cab for you. Where do you want to go?"

Now that she was face to face with the one person who might be able to help her, Lacey felt as though she were bordering on hysteria. She still wasn't sure whether or not she had been followed. At this point it didn't matter. All Lacey was certain of was that she couldn't keep running.

"Mrs. Hoffman, I haven't *got* any place to go," she declared passionately. "Someone is trying to kill me, and I think he's been sent by the same person who ordered your husband, Isabelle Waring, and Heather Landi killed. It has to stop, and

I think you're the one who can *make* it stop, Mrs. Hoffman. *Please help me!"*

Lottie Hoffman's eyes softened. She noticed Lacey's awkward stance, how she clearly favored one foot. "You're in pain. Come in. Sit down."

The living room was small but exquisitely neat. Lacey sat on the couch and slipped off the heavy coat. "This isn't mine," she said. "I can't go to my own home or reach into my own closet. I can't go near my family. My little niece was shot and almost killed because of me. I'm going to live like this for the rest of my life if whoever is behind all this isn't identified and arrested. Please, Mrs. Hoffman, tell me—did your husband know who was behind it?"

"I'm afraid. I can't talk about it." Lottie Hoffman kept her head down, her eyes on the floor, as she spoke in a near whisper. "If Max had kept his mouth shut, he'd still be alive. So would Heather. So would her mother." She finally raised her head and looked directly at Lacey. "Is the truth worth all those deaths? I don't think so."

"You wake up scared every morning, don't you?" Lacey asked. She reached over and took the elderly woman's thin, heavily veined hand. "Tell me what you know, please, Mrs. Hoffman. Who is behind all this?"

"The truth is I don't know. I don't even know his name. Max did. Max was the one who worked for Jimmy Landi. He was the one who knew Heather. If only I hadn't seen her that day at Mohonk. I told Max about it and described the man she was with. He got so upset. He said that the man was a drug dealer and a racketeer but that no one knew it, that everyone thought he was respectable, even a good guy. So Max made the lunch date with Heather to warn her—and two days later, he was dead."

Tears welled in Lottie Hoffman's eyes. "I miss Max so much, and I'm so scared."

"You're right to be," Lacey told her gently. "But keeping your door locked isn't the solution. Someday, whoever this person is, he'll decide that you're a potential threat too."

Sandy Savarano attached the silencer to his pistol. It had been child's play to get into this house. He could leave the same way he had come in—through the back window of this bedroom. The tree outside was like a staircase. His car was on the next street, directly accessible through the neighbor's yard. He would be miles away before the cops sitting outside even suspected something was wrong. He looked at his watch. It was time.

The old woman would be first. She was only a nuisance. What he wanted most was to see the expression in Lacey Farrell's eyes when he pointed the pistol at her. He wouldn't give her time to scream. No, there would be just long enough for her to make that whimpering little sound of recognition that was so thrilling to hear, as she realized that she was about to die.

Now.

Sandy put his right foot on the first step of the staircase, then with infinite caution, began his descent.

63

Alex Carbine called Landi's restaurant and asked to speak to Jimmy. He waited, then heard Steve Abbott's voice. "Alex, is there anything I can do for you? I hate to bother Jimmy. He's feeling awfully down today."

"I'm sorry about that but I need to talk to him," Carbine said. "By the way, Steve, has Carlos come to you guys looking for a job?"

"As a matter of fact, he has. Why?"

"Because if he's still there you can tell him he doesn't have one here anymore. Now put me through to Jimmy."

Again he waited. When Jimmy Landi picked up his phone it was clear from his voice that he was under immense strain.

"Jimmy, I can tell something's wrong. Can I help?"

"No, but thanks."

"Well, look, I'm sorry to bother you, but I've figured out something and wanted to pass it on to you. I understand Carlos is sniffing around for a job from you. Well, listen to me: don't take him back!"

"I don't intend to, but why not?" Jimmy responded.

"Because I think he's on the take somehow. It's been driving me nuts that Lacey Farrell was tracked down by this killer to where they had her hiding in Minneapolis."

"Oh, is that where she was?" Jimmy Landi remarked. "I hadn't heard."

"Yes, but only her mother knew it. She got Lacey to tell her. And since I was the one who told her to make Lacey tell her where she was living, I feel responsible."

"That wasn't too smart of you," Jimmy Landi said.

"I never pretended to be smart. All I could see was that Mona's guts were being torn out. Anyway, the night she learned that Lacey was in Minneapolis she bought a copy of the *Minneapolis Star Tribune* and had it with her at dinner. I saw her slip it back in the bag when I came to the table, but I never asked her about it, and I never saw it again. But here's what I'm getting at: I noticed that at one point, when Mona was off to the powder room and I was glad-handing a customer, Carlos was over at our table, supposedly straightening our napkins. I saw him move the bag, and it's entirely possible that he looked inside."

"It's just the sort of thing Carlos would do," Landi replied. "I never liked the guy in the first place."

"And then he was our waiter again on Friday night when Mona talked about Lacey joining a new health club. One with a squash court. It seems to me more than a coincidence that somebody showed up at that club looking for her a few hours later. You just have to put two and two together, right?"

"Hmmm," Jimmy murmured, "it sounds like maybe Carlos was working to earn more than a tip Friday night. I gotta go, Alex. Talk to you soon."

64

Ed Sloane could tell that something was spooking his partner. Even though it was cold in the car, Nick Mars was giving off an acrid odor of perspiration. Shiny droplets of sweat covered the forehead of his babyish face.

The instinct that had never failed him told Sloane that something was going terribly wrong. "I think it's time we go in and collect Ms. Farrell," he said.

"Why do that, Ed?" Mars asked, surprised. "We'll pick her up when she comes out."

Sloane opened the door of the car and drew his pistol. "Let's go."

Lacey wasn't sure if she actually heard a sound on the staircase. Old houses seem sometimes to have a life of their own. She was aware, however, that the atmosphere in the room had changed, like a thermometer suddenly plummeting. Lottie Hoffman felt it too; Lacey could see it in her eyes.

Later she realized that it was the presence of evil, creeping, insidious, enveloping her, so real it was almost tangible.

She had felt this same chill when she hid in the closet as Curtis Caldwell came down the stairs after killing Isabelle.

Then she heard it again. The faintest of sounds, but still very real. It wasn't her imagination! She knew that for certain now, and her heartbeat accelerated at the realization. There was someone on the staircase! I'm going to die, she thought.

She saw terror creep into Mrs. Hoffman's eyes, so she put a warning finger to her own lips, urging her to remain quiet. He was coming down the stairs so slowly, playing cat and mouse with them. Lacey looked around the room—there was only one door, and it opened just next to the stairs. There was no way out. They were trapped!

Her eyes fastened on a glass paperweight on

the coffee table. It was about the size of a base-
ball, and it appeared to be heavy. She couldn't
reach it without getting up, something she was
afraid to risk. Instead, she touched Mrs. Hoffman's hand and pointed to the paperweight.

The staircase became exposed to Lacey's view
halfway down. That's where he was now.
Through the wooden spindles, she could see his
one well-polished shoe.

A frail and trembling hand grasped the paperweight and slid it into Lacey's hand. Lacey stood
up, swung her arm back, and, as the assassin she
knew as Caldwell came into full view, threw the
paperweight with all the strength she could muster, at his chest.

The heavy piece of glass struck him right above
the stomach, just as he prepared to move quickly
down the remaining steps. The impact caused him
to stumble and drop the pistol. Lacey immediately lunged to try to kick it away from his reach,
just as Mrs. Hoffman, with faltering steps, made
her way to the front door and flung it open. She
screamed.

Detective Sloane rushed past her into the entry
hall. Just as Savarano's fingers were closing on
the pistol, Sloane lifted his foot and smashed it
down on Savarano's wrist. Behind him, Nick

Mars aimed his pistol at Savarano's head and started to pull the trigger.

"Don't!" Lacey screamed.

Sloane whirled and slapped his partner's hand, causing the bullet intended for Savarano's head to go through his leg instead. He let out a howl of pain.

Dazed, Lacey watched as Sloane handcuffed Isabelle Waring's murderer, the sound of approaching sirens shrilling outside. Finally she looked down into the eyes that had haunted her these past few months. Ice blue irises, dead black pupils—the eyes of a killer. But suddenly she realized she was seeing something new in them.

Fear.

U.S. Attorney Gary Baldwin appeared suddenly, surrounded by his agents. He looked at Sloane, at Lacey, then at Savarano.

"So you beat us to him," he said, grudging respect evident in his voice. "I was hoping to beat you to him, but no matter—it's a job well done. Congratulations."

He leaned over Savarano. "Hi, Sandy," he said softly. "I've been looking for you. I'm preparing a cage that's got your name on it—the darkest, smallest cell at Marion, the roughest federal prison in the country. Locked down twenty-three hours a day. Solitary, of course. Chances are you won't like it, but you never know. Some people don't stay sane long enough in solitary for it even to matter. Anyway, you think about it, Sandy. A cage. Just for you. A tiny, little cage. All your own, for the rest of your life."

He straightened up and turned to Lacey. "You all right, Miss Farrell?"

She nodded.

"Someone isn't." Sloane went over to Nick Mars, whose face was chalk white. He took his pistol, then opened his partner's jacket and took out his handcuffs. "Stealing evidence is bad enough. Attempted murder is a lot worse. You know what to do, Nick."

Nick put his hands behind his back and turned. Sloane snapped Nick's own cuffs on him. "Now they're really yours, Nick," he said with a grim smile.

65

Jimmy Landi did not emerge from his office all afternoon. Steve Abbott looked in on him several times. "Jimmy, you okay?" he asked.

"Never better, Steve," he said shortly.

"You don't look it. I wish you'd stop reading Heather's journal. It's just getting you down."

"I wish you'd stop telling me to stop reading it."

"*Touché.* I promise I won't bother you again, but remember this, Jimmy—I'm always here for you."

"Yes, you are, Steve. I know."

At five o'clock, Landi received a phone call from Detective Sloane. "Mr. Landi," he said, "I'm at headquarters. I felt we owed it to you to fill you in. Your ex-wife's murderer is in custody. Ms. Farrell has positively identified him. He's also being charged with the death of Max Hoffman. And we may be able to prove that he was the one who ran your daughter's car off the road, too."

"Who is he?" Jimmy Landi had the fleeting thought that he wasn't feeling anything—not surprise, not anger, not even grief.

"Sandy Savarano is his name. He's a paid hit man. We expect him to cooperate fully in the investigation. He doesn't want to go to prison."

"None of them do," Jimmy said. "Who hired him?"

"We expect to know that very soon. We're just waiting for Sandy to come to Jesus. Of much less magnitude, by the way, we have a suspect in the theft of your daughter's journal."

"Suspect?"

"Yes, in the legal sense, even though he admitted it. But he swears he didn't take the three unlined pages you thought we lost. I guess your partner was right. We never had them."

"You never had them," Jimmy agreed. "I realize that now. My partner seems to have a lot of the answers."

"Miss Farrell is here making a statement, sir. She'd like to talk to you."

"Put her on."

"Mr. Landi," Lacey said, "I'm awfully glad this is over. It's been an ordeal for me, and I know it's been terrible for you as well. Mrs. Max Hoffman is with me. She has something to tell you."

"Put her on."

"I saw Heather at Mohonk," Lottie Hoffman began. "She was with a man, and when I described him to Max, he was so upset. He said the guy was a racketeer, a drug dealer, and that no one suspected him, least of all Heather. She had no idea that . . ."

Even though she had heard it all before, it was chilling to Lacey to consider the appalling crimes committed after Max Hoffman warned Heather away from the man she was dating.

She listened as Mrs. Hoffman described the man she had seen that day. Clearly it was no one *she* knew, Lacey thought with relief.

Sloane took the phone from Mrs. Hoffman. "Does the man she described sound like anyone you know, sir?"

He listened for a moment, then turned to Lacey and Mrs. Hoffman. "Mr. Landi would be very appreciative if you'd stop by his office now."

All Lacey wanted to do was to get home to her own apartment, get in her own Jacuzzi, dress in her own clothes, and go to Kit's house to see everyone. They were having a late dinner, and Bonnie was staying up for it. "As long as it's just a few minutes there," she said.

"That's all," Sloane promised. "Then I'll drive Mrs. Hoffman home." Sloane was called to the phone as they were leaving the station house. When he returned, he said, "We're going to have company at Landi's. Baldwin is on his way."

The receptionist took them upstairs to where Jimmy was waiting. When Lottie Hoffman admired the handsome furnishings, Jimmy said, "The restaurant used to be half this size. When Heather was a baby this was her room."

Lacey thought that there was something in Landi's even, almost indifferent, tone that made her think of an unnaturally calm ocean—one in which an underwater current was threatening to turn into a tidal wave.

"Describe again exactly the man you saw with my daughter, please, Mrs. Hoffman."

"He was very handsome; he . . ."

"Wait. I'd like my partner to hear this." He turned on the intercom. "Steve, got a minute?"

Steve Abbott came into the office smiling. "So, you're out of your cocoon at last, Jimmy. Oh. Sorry, I didn't realize you had company."

"*Interesting* company, Steve. Mrs. Hoffman, what's wrong?"

Lottie Hoffman was pointing at Abbott. Her face was ghastly white. "You're the one I saw with Heather. You're the one Max said was a drug dealer and a racketeer and a thief. You're the reason I'm alone . . ."

"What are you talking about?" Abbott said, his brows knitting fiercely, the mask of geniality momentarily fallen from his face. All of a sudden, Lacey thought it was possible to imagine this handsome, debonair man as a killer.

Accompanied by a half dozen agents, U.S. Attorney Gary Baldwin came into the room.

"What she is saying, Mr. Abbott, is that you are a murderer, that you ordered her husband killed because he knew too much. He quit working here because he had seen what you were doing and knew his life wouldn't be worth a plug nickel if you knew. You've been dropping the old suppliers like Jay Taylor and buying from mob-owned businesses, most of the stuff stolen. You've done it in the casino, too. And that's only one of your activities.

"Max had to tell Heather what you are. And she had to decide whether to let you keep cheating her father or tell him how she found out about you.

"You didn't take the chance. Savarano told us you called Heather and said Jimmy had had a heart attack and she should get right home. Savarano was waiting for her. When Isabelle Waring wouldn't stop looking for reasons to prove Heather's death wasn't an accident, she became too dangerous."

"That's a lie," Abbott shouted. "Jimmy, I never . . ."

"Yes, you did," Jimmy said calmly, "you killed Max Hoffman and you did the same to my daughter's mother. And to Heather. You killed her. Why did you need to mess with her? You could have had any woman you wanted." Jimmy's eyes blazed with anger; his hands formed into giant fists; his cry of agony exploded through the room. "You let my baby burn to death," he howled. "You . . . you . . . ."

He lunged across the desk and wrapped his powerful hands around Abbott's throat. It took

Sloane and the team of agents to pry his fingers loose.

Jimmy's racking sobs echoed throughout the building as Baldwin took Steve Abbott into custody.

Sandy Savarano had completed his bargaining from his hospital bed.

At eight o'clock, the driver Jay had sent to pick up Lacey at her apartment called to say he was downstairs. Lacey was frantic to see her family, but there was a phone call she still had to make. There was so much to tell Tom, so much to explain. Baldwin, now suddenly her friend and ally, had told her, "You're out of the loop now. We've plea-bargained with Savarano, so we won't need your testimony to get Abbott. So you'll be okay. But keep a low profile for a while. Why not take a vacation until things settle down?"

She had replied only half jokingly, "You know I *do* have an apartment and a job in Minnesota. Maybe I should just go back there."

She dialed Tom's number. The now familiar